BURN IN BELL

A Samantha Bell Mystery Thriller

JEREMY WALDRON

ALSO BY JEREMY WALDRON

Dead and Gone to Bell

Bell Hath No Fury

Bloody Bell

Bell to Pay

Burn in Bell

Never miss a new release. Sign up for Jeremy Waldron's New
Releases Newsletter at JeremyWaldron.com

CHAPTER ONE

THE INSECTS BUZZED LOUDLY IN THE NEARBY TREES outside his car. A warm breeze traveled through the cracked window. The man listened for any unexpected noises; sounds that might persuade his natural instinct to cancel his plans for tonight. Besides the insects, there were no other warning bells to be heard.

Tonight was like any other. A beautiful summer evening in the beginning of July, parked somewhere along the quiet suburban streets of Denver, Colorado. Except, to the Shadow Stalker, it was the beginning of a self-righteous prophecy set to take effect tonight. It was his time to make a stand and show the world he was the master of his own destiny.

Ahead, a dark colored pickup truck turned onto the same street where he was parked and headed straight for him. The Shadow Stalker stared but didn't react to the headlights illuminating his cabin. No longer would he allow his past to dictate his future. It was a new beginning. A time to reclaim what was once his.

The vehicle passed without notice and the Shadow Stalker lifted his wrist to check the time on his digital sports watch.

It was ten minutes until nine p.m. The motions of tonight were right on schedule. Nothing could stop him now.

He closed his eyes and felt his lips pull at the corners. Confidence filled his chest with swelling pride and he couldn't wait to get started.

Placing one hand on the steering wheel, he rolled his neck and stared into the small ranch style house through an illuminated window. Inside was the victim that would bring his name into the spotlight. And though he wasn't interested in becoming famous, he did want the recognition he felt he deserved from a very select few individuals. If tonight went as planned, he'd get just what he was after in due time.

Flicking his gaze to the house next door, the television flickered through the window. Like everywhere, people were going about their dull and unimaginative lives waiting to die, working nine-to-fives and wishing they had more. The Shadow Stalker had once been like them, but not anymore. He was reawakened.

Inhaling a deep breath of warm summer air, the Shadow Stalker turned his gaze to his dash and plucked the photograph he'd kept near the speedometer. It was of him and his mother—the first and only woman he ever loved.

Brushing his thumb over the blank space where a father figure should have stood, the picture was taken when he was twelve years old. He was an only child and his mother said his father had died before he turned one. The story left a hole in his heart—an ache he still felt today. Though his mother did her best to raise him into the man he was today, he often wondered how things would have been different if only his mother would have told him the truth.

Out of the corner of his eye, the Shadow Stalker turned his head back to the house when the last of the home's lights flicked off.

"Nine p.m." He once again glanced to his wrist watch. "Right on schedule."

He waited another twenty minutes before exiting his car. Weaving through the shadows, he edged to the back of the house and lifted the doormat that hid the key beneath. It was an obvious secret that all but eliminated the toughest of obstacles—entering the house without having to resort to forcible entry.

"Time to shine," he whispered as he slid the key into the lock. Suddenly, a dog's bark was close enough to be nipping at his heels.

The Shadow Stalker turned to the neighbor's backyard and could hear the dog growling through the wooden privacy fence. A man yelled for the dog to stop from inside the neighbor's house where he'd seen the television on, but the dog didn't listen. The beast kept barking as the Shadow Stalker's heartrate spiked. Needing to keep his visit a secret, he faced the door and completed the turn of the key, listening to the lock click over. Without hesitation, he pushed the door open, ducked inside, and quickly shut it behind him.

With his back glued to the door, the Shadow Stalker took a moment to study his new environment. It felt oddly familiar, something he should have expected but didn't. He listened to the soft hum of a refrigerator and the clacks from an overhead fan, as even the scent in the air was familiar to him. It reminded him of something very close to his heart. It reminded him of home.

On tender feet he walked through the kitchen, stopping only momentarily to peek down the hall where he knew the homeowner was now sleeping. The bedroom door was cracked, but there were no signs of life. He was at liberty to move about as he pleased.

By way of moonlight shining through the thinly veiled curtains, he moved effortlessly past a gray cat scampering off.

Making himself at home, he stopped at the dining room hutch and began picking through each photograph proudly displayed on top as if studying his victim's family history.

It was a beautiful collection of both new and old. Anniversaries, coming of age events, and celebrations that made life worth living. And as the Shadow Stalker moved from one photograph to the next, his eyes welled with water.

"Damn you, Nana," he muttered beneath his breath.

His chin trembled as the old woman's matriarch eyes pierced his soul. There was so much love pouring out of her ocean blue eyes, it hurt to know that tonight would be her last. But he was called upon to make the ultimate sacrifice and together they would both pay the price.

"It's the only way," he said, placing the picture back where he found it. "We all must make sacrifices for the greater good. And I'll be forever grateful for yours."

Continuing his search, the Shadow Stalker opened all of the drawers in the hutch. He wasn't sure what it was he was hoping to find but the moment he found it, he knew that the universe had a way of showing him the signs.

He dove his hands into the drawer slowly and held the card gently as he moved it into the soft glow of streetlight.

"Perfect," he said as he brushed the pad of his thumb over the names imprinted on the card. "Unbelievably perfect."

As soon as he opened up the engagement announcement a diamond ring fell out and clattered against the floor. In a rush to silence the noise, he flattened the spinning ring with his foot and snapped his attention to where he knew the old woman was sleeping.

His blood sloshed in his ears but the house remained silent.

Bending over, he picked up the ring with only a brief inspection before dropping it into his front pants pocket. Excitement grew and there was a buzz of energy that lifted his spirits. He knew tonight would be his night, but never did he expect to hit a home run like this.

Erasing all evidence of his presence, he closed the drawer to the hutch and moved back to the kitchen. It was here he wanted to raise his flag and wave it in a place where Inspector Alex King was sure to see it. He opened the engagement card and perched it directly on the center of the table. Then he stood back and evaluated his work.

Something was missing but he didn't know what. After some thought, he knew just what it was. Pulling out a twenty-dollar bill, he placed it inside the card and said, "There. If this doesn't open your eyes, I don't know what will."

"Angel, is that you?" the old woman called from the back room.

The Shadow Stalker whipped his head toward the sound of her voice, stunned to hear she was awake.

"Hello?" the old woman called out again. "Angel?"

Knowing he had to do something, he turned toward the hallway and tucked his chin. A darkness filled his vision as he made his way to where the old woman's voice was still calling. This wasn't part of the plan but he'd have to make it work. He was ready.

Without turning on the lights, the Shadow Stalker could see the woman was sitting up in bed, squinting her wrinkled eyes into the dark hallway. "Who are you and what are you doing in my house?" she said.

"Easy, Nana."

"Billy, is that you?" The old woman clenched her bed sheets.

The Shadow Stalker walked toward the bed, watching the whites in the woman's eyes grow. "Angel sent me."

"She did?" The old woman sounded confused. "Why would she do that?"

He sat on the edge of the bed, reaching across the old

woman's lap for a bed pillow. She watched his every move, lines of confusion deepening with each second that passed. Her memory was fading and she had good days and bad. It was a gift given to the Shadow Stalker and one advantage he was sure to use tonight.

Placing the pillow on his lap, the Shadow Stalker ironed his palms over the top when saying, "There is something she wanted me to tell you." The woman looked directly into his eyes when he said, "You don't choose your family. They are God's gift to you, as you are to them."

"I know that saying," the old woman said, knitting her brows. "That doesn't sound like something Angel would say. Who are you?"

The Shadow Stalker tilted his head to one shoulder and scooted closer to the woman. "In a world of lambs and lions, we all must make sacrifices in order to get what we want."

"Lambs and lions?"

Without warning, the Shadow Stalker jammed the pillow directly into the old woman's face and used his weight to press her head deep into the mattress. The old woman's croaked screams were muffled by the thickness of the pillow and he held her there until finally her candle was blown out for eternity.

CHAPTER TWO

KING WAS PLANNING TO WINE AND DINE ME, BUT I countered and asked to have dessert first.

He didn't need me to explain. King could see the fire of desire burning in my eyes. By the time we skidded to a stop outside his house and kicked the front door open, all thoughts about what happened at Erin's vanished. King swooped me up behind the knees and carried me across the threshold like we'd just made our vows.

Hanging off his neck, I giggled like a school girl in love. "My knight in shining armor."

"Here to protect and serve."

I pulled his head down and closed my mouth over his. He kissed me hard and had me panting for more. But as soon as King let go of my legs and released his grip from around my waist, I knew he was thinking about the note we'd found with the burning bag addressed to him.

"Wait here," he said in his firm voice.

"Did housekeeping forget the champagne and rose petals?" I teased, hoping to ease the tension I could see stretching his shirt.

King pointed his finger at me but didn't look. "I'll be right back. Don't move."

Without moving my feet, I dipped my head and swept my hair up off my shoulders tying it off into a ponytail. King opened and closed doors, sweeping the house for possible intruders. I didn't see any signs of a break-in but the note left for King at Erin's had clearly gotten to him, too. Even over King's heavy footsteps, the note's words were all I could hear.

"You haven't forgotten about me, have you? Of course you have. Burn in hell, pig."

Someone wanted King to know they were watching him, and now I was second guessing our decision to come here in the first place. But when King's eyes locked on mine, he took me back into his arms and made me feel safe.

Taking my face between his hands, he kissed me softly. Flutters moved across my belly as I hooked my leg around his thigh. We picked up where we'd left off and all our worries disappeared in a flash.

"I forgot the champagne and rose petals." King made a face. "I hope you can forgive me?"

As I stared into his gorgeous eyes, I worried he was hiding the severity of what the note really entailed. Was his life in danger? Was someone he'd locked away now out to get revenge? Anything was possible. King put away some really bad people over the years. He must have had a name in mind of who'd written the note—someone he could point to when naming a suspect—but instead he deflected and kept focused on only making me feel sexy and safe.

"I don't need all that fancy stuff," I said, thrilled to have King all to myself.

King cocked his head to the side. "No?"

I shook my head. "All I need is your best performance."

He arched a brow and surprised me once again by

swooping me up into his arms and marching me straight into his bedroom.

CHAPTER THREE

W$_E$ LAY IN BED, WRAPPED IN EACH OTHER'S ARMS, listening to the other breathe. Our jobs were so demanding, it was hard to have time just to ourselves. In this rare moment of downtime, we stared into the ceiling without talking. After what felt like an hour of silence, we discussed the vacation we both craved and how great it would be to get away for a week. It was a pipedream and we both knew it. With him at the peak of his career and mine teetering dangerously close to its grave, there was no time to get away. This *was* our vacation and I intended to cherish every single minute of it.

King's fingers raked up and down my side and I felt at peace.

Everything was better when I was with him. My world brighter, my thoughts clearer. He was even a role model to my teenage son, Mason. I felt like the luckiest woman in the world when suddenly my stomach rumbled.

With my eyelids popping wide open, I stopped stroking his chest. I felt King angle his eyes to the top of my head. I was too embarrassed to even look him in the eye, suddenly feeling as if my luck had run out.

"Was the dessert I fed you not enough?" King teased.

I slapped my hand flat on his chest and clucked my tongue. "It was the right amount, in case you're wondering."

King smiled. "Because there is more in the tank if you need me to take you on another ride."

"Another ride?" I crawled up his body and pressed my lips against his. "I'm not an amusement park."

The corners of his eyes crinkled. "But I am."

I shook my head and slipped out of bed. King kept his eye on me as I wrapped a bedsheet around my naked body. He asked where I was going and I told him I was thirsty. Then I padded my way down the hall and into the kitchen to retrieve a couple beers from the fridge.

My toes were still tingling from our activities and there was no denying how much I liked being at his place. It felt like home. A place to escape my work and the responsibilities of my teenage son. But as I popped the tops on both bottles, I found myself once again looking over my shoulder, asking myself if King really was being stalked.

"There might be some leftover fried chicken in the fridge," King called from the bed.

"You want it?" I called back, shaking off my thoughts.

"I just want you. C'mon back."

I laughed at King's playfulness—even if his needs weren't a little desperate sounding. As I made my way back to my man, I was thinking how well he was fitting into my life. Against all odds, somehow, we were making it work. Life really was amazing.

"I hope you brought the entire six pack," King called out again as I stopped outside the spare bedroom that once housed his mother.

"There is plenty to go around," I responded, feeling the emptiness of Carol King's absence.

King's mother had recently moved into an independent

living facility after some hard negotiating by King. The move was hard for them both, but Carol's demands for care were quickly outpacing what King could provide himself. The truth was, Carol's mind was fully intact but her body was failing and she needed help.

King snuck up behind and wrapped his arms around me. "Did you get lost? You're not drinking alone, are you?"

I swung my arm across my chest and handed King his beer. "How is she doing?"

"Better than she'll lead you to believe." King told me how Avery Morgan, a recent graduate from the academy and King's protégé, helped him with the move.

"I bet Carol liked that," I said.

"Mom always did give preferential treatment to cops."

I moved to the bed and reached my hand inside a box full of his father's awards. There was a Silver Star for bravery, a Merit Award for Excellent Arrest, and many others. King's father, Marshall, had an outstanding career as an inspector and I knew King worked hard every day to fill the legacy his father left behind.

"Mom hasn't been the same since his death." King took the Merit Award for Excellent Arrest into his hands, stared at it, and said the saddest thing I'd ever heard him say. "If only I could be half as good a detective as he was, then maybe my legacy wouldn't be completely overshadowed by his."

CHAPTER FOUR

KING'S CELLPHONE BUZZED FIRST. THEN MINE STARTED going off. We shared a knowing look that our date night was over.

It was the never-ending cycle of a crime reporter and homicide detective. We lived a life on call. The best I could hope for now was that we'd both be back in King's bed before the night was over. But just like the vacation we had talked about taking, I knew it was another pipedream.

King kissed me on the cheek before running to catch his call. I was one step behind as our phones were in the same room. He got to his first. I watched him move to the front window and I took mine in the hall.

"This better be good," I said to Erin when I answered. King brushed past me in a hurry and disappeared into his bedroom.

Erin Tate, my co-host and partner on our growing but still infantile crime blog and podcast, *Real Crime News*, apologized for interrupting my evening—time she knew was rarely given to King and me—and then said, "It's better than good, Sam. It's great."

In a surprisingly fast fashion, King stepped into the hall fully dressed and on his way out the door. He kissed me goodbye and promised to pick this up after work. There was a dull glare in his eye that told me that the call he was responding to was an ugly one. I squeezed his hand, didn't ask any questions, and said I couldn't wait, not bothering him with the hiccup of realizing I was now without a car the moment he left.

"Don't you want to know what it is?" Erin asked impatiently.

"Quit it with the hype and just tell me." The front door opened and shut.

Erin's mood told me we weren't being called to a crime scene and I was thankful if that was the case. But it had to be something big for her to interrupt my night and be calling me at such a late hour.

"I know it's last minute," she said, "but I need you to get ready."

I looked down at the bedsheet I was wearing, feeling the breeze of nakedness beneath. "Ready for what?"

"We're going out to dinner."

I didn't react. Instead, I thought about how I hadn't eaten a significant meal since lunch. And since King was already out of the house, maybe dinner wasn't such a bad idea, if a little late.

I asked, "Like, me and you?"

"Like you, me, *and* Walter Walker."

"The Million Dollar Man?" I was as skeptical as my tone sounded. "What's he want with us?"

"Sam," Erin purred into my ear. "He's a fan of our show and wants to turn us into *stars*."

CHAPTER FIVE

DETECTIVE ALEX KING PARKED BEHIND ANOTHER unmarked sedan, turned off the engine, and gazed through the windshield at the familiar house with his heart thumping hard inside his chest. As soon as he received the call from his partner, Homicide Detective John Alvarez, he knew exactly who lived here. Despite asking, Alvarez refused to give King details to what happened, only saying to get his ass down here as soon as possible.

That was what worried King the most—the untold feeling of urgency.

King stepped out and moved beneath the flood of crimson and blue lights illuminating a path to the front door. Passing in front of the coroner's van he stopped to stare, wondering if the victim was already zipped up and inside.

"King," Alvarez called out from the front stoop. "Right here."

King snapped his focus away from the van and followed the hedge up the sidewalk, unable to find the strength to climb the front steps and enter the house. Alvarez stared, but understood his partner's hesitation.

It had been years since the last time he stepped foot inside the Hill residence, but to King it felt like yesterday. He could still hear the laughs around the dinner table, the love emanating from those around him.

"How bad is it?" King asked.

Alvarez took a step and moved closer. "You don't need to come inside."

King blinked and stared at the familiar front door. He wanted to ask who had been murdered, but found his words catching in his throat each time he tried to speak. In his gut, he already knew the answer to his question.

Seeing it in his eyes, Alvarez said, "It's Angelina's mother."

The blood drained from King's face. "Where is she?"

Alvarez placed a hand on King's shoulder and shook his head no.

"I need to see her." Before Alvarez could protest, King demanded, "Take me to her, John."

Alvarez's hand slipped off King's shoulder as he nodded. Together, they marched up the stairs. Before King could enter the house, Alvarez caught him by his arm. Alvarez gave King a hard look, then released his arm without saying another word.

King knew it was bad with the way his partner was acting, but how bad was it *really*? A cold chill moved up his spine the moment he entered the house. Making his way to the back bedroom where he knew Peggy Hill slept, he followed the sounds of the lab techs collecting evidence.

Once a place he considered his second home, it now felt cold and empty. Mrs. Peggy Hill still had photos of King with her daughter Angelina hanging on the walls and perched on the hutch, as if clinging on to a happier time in her life. It was difficult to see, as it felt like a lifetime ago to King.

Chief Medical Examiner Leslie Griffin was inside the

bedroom when King entered. She hovered over Peggy's limp body, meticulously working.

"Died of asphyxiation," she said upon King's entrance.

King moved to Peggy, his eyes traveling down her arms. He remembered how devastated Peggy was when Angelina called off their engagement—the way she clung to him as if the breakup between him and her daughter hurt her as much as it hurt him. Now the ache was back, intensified by the fact that the life they once shared was truly over.

King looked for marks on Peggy's neck, and Leslie read his mind. "Pillow," she said, sweeping her gaze to the right of Peggy's head.

King flicked his gaze to the indented pillow next to Peggy's head, a circular stain from what King assumed to be from Peggy's mouth as she fought off her attacker.

"Anything else?" King asked Leslie.

The ME shook her head. "This story is written like one we've seen before."

With his hands buried in his pockets, King knew immediately what she was referring to. There was little evidence, hardly any clues, and King feared Peggy's murder was nearly identical to a case King couldn't solve nearly six years ago. A case that still haunted him today.

King locked eyes with Leslie and they shared a knowing look. The ME shrugged and said, "It's possible."

"Alex," Alvarez said from behind. "There is something in the kitchen you need to see."

Before leaving, King ordered the lab techs to not stop short of collecting any evidence that could assist them in finding the person responsible. Peggy Hill was a friend—had nearly become his mother-in-law—and this time, King wouldn't let the perp get away.

"If our guy is back in action," he said, "then let's make sure this is his last victim."

CHAPTER SIX

THE SHADOW STALKER WAS BACK IN HIS VEHICLE AND IN A new part of town hiding beneath a large tree whose deep shadow cut across the street. His plan had been set in motion and there was no turning back. He didn't regret what he'd done to Peggy Hill, nor did he feel any remorse after taking her life.

Spinning the expensive heirloom engagement ring he had taken from Peggy Hill's house between his fingers, his mind was stuck on the great inspector himself.

Only minutes ago, he had watched Inspector Alex King rush out of his house and speed away to what was surely the call that would bring them back into each other's lives. At least, that was his intention.

Staring with unblinking eyes, the Shadow Stalker calmed when a pair of headlights reflected in his rearview mirror. He wasn't afraid of being seen or being caught. It was easy to get away with murder as long as you remained unassuming and kept your disguise intact. Which he did, as he thought of himself as the absolute best to have ever tormented a cop.

The vehicle approached from the back and he turned his

head to catch sight of a tall blonde behind the wheel. Then, as if on cue, the red Bronco's brake lights lit up and pulled to the curb.

"This is interesting," he said to himself.

Turning his focus back to the inspector's house, the Shadow Stalker imagined his face when figuring out the message he had left for him. It nearly made him burst out laughing. There was no way in hell Alex would have seen this coming.

The Bronco idled and Alex King was all he could think about.

He knew more about the inspector than King knew about himself. But still, The Shadow Stalker had been surprised to learn of his relationship with crime reporter Samantha Bell who he knew was still inside the inspector's house.

Of course, the Shadow Stalker thought it a perfect fit; the two of them could control and manipulate the narrative with the powers and positions they held. It was brilliant, really. By design? Perhaps. But the real question was how the Shadow Stalker could use this surprise revelation to his benefit.

"A work in progress," he whispered to himself. "And something I would be delighted to explore."

But the answer to that, too, would reveal itself in due time as he worked to throw the inspector's life into a quick and chaotic spiral.

Suddenly, the lights in the house turned off. Opening his car door, the Shadow Stalker stepped out onto the grass needing to see her face himself. A second later, the front door opened and Samantha Bell revealed herself without ever noticing she was being watched from across the street.

"Burn in hell you two lovebirds. The games are just beginning."

CHAPTER SEVEN

SAMANTHA BELL JUMPED INTO THE PASSENGER SEAT OF THE red Bronco and, before the vehicle was gone, the Shadow Stalker slithered his way undetected toward the inspector's house.

He didn't bother going to the front door whose porch light had been left on. Besides, it was safe to assume Samantha was smart enough to have locked it on her way out. Instead, he edged around to the back, letting himself through the privacy fence gate to try his luck at the back door.

Reaching for the doorknob, he turned it but the door didn't budge. It was locked.

Not surprised, he worked under the cover of darkness. Pulling his multi-tool 7-in-1 pocket lock pick set he managed to get the door open in less than a minute. No alarms were tripped and he entered with surprising ease.

"Who needs to call the cops when you are one," he muttered to himself as he closed the door behind him, fascinated that King's house didn't have an alarm.

The Shadow Stalker supposed a department issued gun was all someone needed to feel safe, and he was sure the inspector had several of those nearby at all times. He'd bet this house was well armed—an arsenal beneath the floors—in case someone like him ever broke inside.

"Hands up, don't shoot," he laughed when lifting his wrist to set his watch's timer for three minutes.

It was all the time he allotted himself before having to leave. Next, he flipped the switch to a small Maglite and moved swiftly through the inspector's home.

The Shadow Stalker wiggled his nose at the sticky scent of sex lingering in the air and he sensed tonight was special for the two of them.

"A rare romantic evening that was sadly cut short because of me." He laughed. "So sorry to ruin it for you."

He cared nothing of their relationship, and certainly wasn't interested in Samantha Bell as much as he was Alex King. After all, it was him who he was after. He just needed Samantha to leave so he could have the inspector's house all to himself—a chance to really get to know the man who he thought he knew everything.

He stepped through doors and pulled drawers open, always having wondered what the inside of Alex's house was really like. He wanted to know how the man lived, what he ate, how he cared for his body. Everything. After all, the inspector was an enigmatic creature when not wearing his badge, and it was the little things that the Shadow Stalker didn't know that made him most curious to learn.

"Where shall I place the next ripple?" he asked himself when floating down the hallway, fingering the engagement ring inside his front pocket.

The house itself was bland without any sort of surprise. Perhaps he'd built up his expectations too high during the months he had spent planning for today. He had always pictured the house to be much more extravagant than what he was seeing now.

The Shadow Stalker stopped and turned his head. Peering into the hallway bathroom, it was there he decided to place the ring next to the sink.

"Welcome back home," he said, turning on a heel and stepping through the threshold of the guestroom. He shined his light across several cardboard boxes and tilted his head to one side. "Moving somewhere?"

His watch dinged. Sixty seconds to work.

Quickly, he rifled through the boxes and couldn't believe the treasure he had found. Framed pictures and life's memorabilia not only from Alex's life, but that of his father's as well. He picked up one award given to Marshall King, then another.

"Now I understand why you idolized the man," he said, tilting an award into the light. "But I know the truth and, soon, you will too."

CHAPTER EIGHT

An hour passed in the blink of an eye. After a quick stop at home thanks to Erin swinging by King's to pick me up, I was showered and dressed, feeling nervous for attracting the attention of someone with as much money, power, and clout as Walter Walker.

Walker wasn't just anybody. He'd magically taken both startup and failing businesses and grown them into empires. That had to be the reason he wanted to talk to us, and though I knew of his name from editorial meetings I'd sat in on at the *Times*, I never expected to be sitting down with him for dinner.

I moved to the bed and slipped my feet into a pair of heels I rarely wore. This was so out of character for me; it felt like I was dressing for prom. But I wanted it to go well—make a solid first impression. It was what Erin and I had been working so hard to achieve. Build our audience and tell stories that resonated with our fans. It was a simple mission but there was a lot at stake. Especially when I thought about the constant threat of closure at the *Colorado Times*.

I moved to my dresser and stood in front of the mirror,

carefully choosing what earrings to wear. It was a slim collection, but the jewelry I did own, I cherished.

Erin was more confident than I was when it came to the business side of things. She always had been. We began our journey on a whim nearly a year ago, and Erin had been working tirelessly marketing our talents bringing in whatever ad dollars we could generate. It wasn't much, but the numbers were steadily growing in an upward trajectory that kept me hopeful about possibly having a bright future for ourselves.

With one earring on, I turned my head for the other. Taking a step back, I stared at my reflection, marveling at the woman I had become.

"You deserve this," I said in a low volume. "And so does Mason."

I really believed this might be the lucky break we'd been waiting for.

I found Erin in the living room with her legs draped over the arm of my sofa chair, playing on her phone. My yellow lab, Cooper, was curled up on his bed at her swinging feet. I asked them both, "How do I look?"

Erin turned her head just as the front door opened behind me. Cooper jumped up and ran to the door with his tail wagging. He greeted my sister, Heather, and when she saw what I was wearing, her mouth opened and suddenly everyone was giving me the same look.

"What?" I asked, wondering if I'd sprouted wings.

"Nothing." Heather shook her head and continued to gape. "You look stunning."

I bit my cheek and made a face.

"Really." She closed the door and stepped inside. "I don't recognize you."

Laughing, I twirled and relished in the rare feeling of having soft silk fabric swish around my calves before finishing with a curtsey. I wished King could have seen this.

I asked, "It's not too much, is it?"

Erin was now on her feet. "You look like a star."

I raked her over and told her she looked gorgeous too in her equally long jet-black dress.

She leaned in to give me a hug and spoke softly into my ear, "We're going to kill it tonight."

My eyebrows pulled together. Erin pulled back and gave me a questioning glance. I asked, "Why now? Why does it feel so out of the blue?"

Erin lifted one side of her face and said, "I may have pitched him an offer and asked if he would like to meet with us."

"You did?"

"I think it's time. Don't you?"

Smiling, I said, "I do. Now, let's see what the Million Dollar Man wants to do with two crime junkies."

"What are you two talking about?" my sister asked. "And where are you going?"

Erin looped her arm through the crook of mine and we laughed our way out the door, saying, "Don't worry. We won't be out late."

CHAPTER NINE

As soon as we arrived to the restaurant, Erin reached over and grabbed my hand. "Remember. It's just a meeting. Nothing different than what we do every day."

I was still staring at the entrance to the restaurant when I turned to Erin and gave her a small, reassuring smile. I knew she could see my lack of confidence in my eyes, but I couldn't keep my nerves from getting the best of me every time I thought about how much this meeting could change my life.

"I'm fine." I turned my head and flashed Erin a stern look of false confidence. "Really."

"Just be yourself."

As soon as were inside, the hostess greeted us and immediately invited us to follow her to a private room in the back where Walter Walker was waiting. I worried how long he'd been waiting.

Walker stood as soon as he saw us coming. Dressed in a three-piece suit worth more than my car, I felt my steps shorten the moment we locked eyes. His dark eyes pierced me with a glimmering gaze that had me feeling like he hadn't noticed Erin at all.

"The courageous Samantha Bell," he said, rounding the table with extended arms.

"And my cohost," I rolled my wrist and introduced my friend and business partner, "the audacious Erin Tate."

Walter Walker clasped his hands together and bowed before leaning in to gently kiss my cheek. His scent—a musky spice—was the same as King's and instantly made me feel at home. He did the same for Erin but seemed to have his sights set on me.

"Thank you for meeting me on such short notice."

"You're lucky we didn't have anything better going on tonight," I said with a completely straight face.

Walker's eyes locked on mine and I wasn't sure if that pissed him off or not. Didn't really care. But I needed him to know who he wanted to work with and, like Erin said, I was just being myself.

Walker angled his head toward the woman standing behind him. "Meet my lovely assistant, Gemma Love."

With a smile stretched to my ears, I extended my hand to Ms. Love. "Pleased to meet you."

Gemma locked eyes as if assessing my worth and, though it was an awkward introduction, I kept my hand available. The room spun and I could feel Erin and Walker giving each other a look. Finally, Gemma stepped forward and took my hand inside her own. Everyone smiled.

Gemma had a firm grasp, surprisingly strong for someone an inch shorter than myself, and she was absolutely beautiful. It spoke volumes for who Walter Walker was and the type of people he hired.

"The pleasure is all mine," she said.

"Please sit." Walker turned to the table and directed traffic. "Let us drink wine and get to know each other."

"Sounds fabulous," Erin said, taking a seat next to Gemma.

I fell into the seat next to Walker, feeling like he'd planned it that way. We shared a smile before the wine was poured. I kept getting little scents of King and couldn't help but notice how small I felt when sitting next to him.

There were already several appetizers on the table— shrimp and oysters on ice, ahi sushi rolls and edamame. Naturally, I was impressed. Walker rolled out the red carpet for us and was treating us like we were the celebrities instead of him. I just hoped he wouldn't stick us with the bill by the time this was all over.

"Samantha, tell me," Gemma said from across the table, "why are you still working for a failing paper when there is so much money to be made in entertainment?"

Erin raised her eyebrows and hid her smirk inside her wine glass. It was clear she appreciated Gemma's approach of skipping small talk in favor of diving headfirst into why we were here in the first place.

"Well," I rolled my shoulders back, not wanting to pretend to be something I wasn't, "investigative journalism is about uncovering the truth. I'm not interested in chasing ratings and, quite frankly," I rolled my gaze to Walker, "I'm scared to know what a world without local reporting will look like."

Walker nodded and smiled as he raised his glass. Then Gemma surprised me with, "So when you say *truth*, you mean like what happened to Governor Philip Price when he got caught up in your story?"

It was a sucker punch to the gut, knocking the air out of me. How did she know about my personal failure—something as intimidate as that mistake? Did Governor Price tell her? Walker certainly had access to someone like Price. Walker had done his homework. What else did he know? And, more importantly, what else should I be prepared to defend?

I flicked my gaze to Erin, thinking about the bumpy ride I

experienced when working The Lady Killer story. It just so happened to be the same story I had first met Erin on and what began our journey working together. Was that what this was about? To prove that they already knew our story?

"Sometimes we get it wrong," I swept my gaze back to Gemma, "and when we do, we publicly correct our errors and admit our mistakes."

Gemma pursed her lips and I watched her reptilian eyes focus in on me again. It was clear she didn't like me from the moment she laid eyes on me, but I didn't appreciate her sour looks either. I could brush it off, assuming it was all by design so Walker could gauge how well I worked under such scrutiny.

Walker sipped his wine, enjoying the show before commenting on how great the food was. Then he turned to me and said, "Is it possible, Samantha, that the *Times* may be holding you back?"

"How so?"

"What I mean by that is, perhaps you're only meeting your true potential when telling your stories through the website and podcast you and Erin created."

Erin brought her elbows to the table. "The paper gives us clout. Including access to people and places we wouldn't otherwise receive if only referencing our website."

"And that is what I'm hoping to change." Walker winked and it suddenly became clear how manipulative this man could be.

I was curious to how he planned on making our small platform carry the same weight as the *Colorado Times*, so I asked. Over the next half hour, Walker laid out his plan for *Real Crime News*, our brand, and how after he was finished building off of the foundation we created, we'd be able meet with anyone we wanted.

"Sounds convincing." Erin nodded her head.

"Because it will work," Walker said.

I asked, "But why do you care? There are dozens of other people doing exactly what we're doing. What makes us special?"

Walker pulled his hand away from his wine glass and scooted closer to me. I felt my heartrate tick up a notch at the thought that he might be brazen enough to reach under the table and touch my thigh.

"Simple, Samantha. I'm a fan of true crime and I don't think *Real Crime News* has received the recognition it deserves."

"Amen to that." Erin raised her glass. Gemma followed, and I wanted to, but Walker was still holding his eyes on mine, keeping my hand from making its move toward my glass.

"Samantha," Walker smiled, "you don't know it yet, but you two are rock stars."

"We're barely known outside of Colorado," I countered.

Walker laughed and finally retreated back into his own air space. "Famous people have the quality that made them famous long before anyone knew who they were."

"I'm not sure I want to be famous," I said, much to Erin's disapproval.

"Don't worry," Walker lifted his glass into the air, "you'll do that yourself whether or not you ask for it."

"Then remind me why it is we're here again?"

Walker tilted his head and winked. "To make sure the truth gets told."

CHAPTER TEN

"This has his name written all over it." King exited the bedroom and followed his partner to the kitchen with forensics snapping photos behind him. "You know which case I'm referring to, don't you?"

Alvarez was marching down the hallway when he looked over his shoulder and said, "Just take a look at something else; then tell me if you still think it's him."

King barely glanced at the framed photographs—some of which he was in—hanging on the wall as he passed beneath them. His vision blurred from the similarities between Peggy Hill's alleged murder and that of a case six years ago that he couldn't solve. But why here? Was it a coincidence or was there a reason Peggy had been chosen?

Their heavy footsteps shook the floorboards, reverberating deep into King's bones. He masked his confusion with anger and reminded himself to not rule out the possibility of a copycat killer, either. At this point, anything was possible.

Alvarez snapped on his latex gloves and King followed suit.

"There." Alvarez pointed to the center of the dining room table. "Recognize that?"

King stood, towering over the wooden table, staring at a very familiar white card with fancy letting inscribed on the front. Suddenly, he was swept up in the past. Bright flashes lit up the backs of his eyes. "You found it just like that?"

It was the engagement announcement to King's wedding that never got sent out. It was opened and perched perfectly for all to see. Did the killer want King to find it? It certainly seemed so.

Alvarez stepped forward and plucked it off the wooden table, handing it to King. "Something tells me Peggy wasn't the one who put this out."

King pinched the card between his fingertips and felt a stone form in his throat. He thought about the night he asked Peggy's daughter Angelina to marry him. He could still hear her squeal the word *yes*. Before that day, he'd never been happier.

"Though I've never been invited to a wedding where the couple *paid* for guests to come." Alvarez was referring to the twenty-dollar bill attached to the inside.

King looked at the date of when the twenty-dollar bill was printed. *2014.* "This is new."

When King pointed to the print date, Alvarez asked, "Then did you plan to have Desmund Tutu officiate your wedding? Because I'm not making sense of any of this."

King stared at the words scribbled across Andrew Jackson's white cheeks. He shook his head and said, "It was my father's favorite quote."

Alvarez wrinkled his brow and looked at King like he was crazy. "Your father?"

King swept his gaze up and stared. "Marshall King."

"I know who your father was, but what's he got to do with any of this?"

King scrambled to make sense of it himself. He glanced over his shoulder, thinking about how and why Peggy might have been murdered. He tried to piece it all together but nothing was making sense. Was he too close to the victim to see the clues? He had his doubts, but what message was this person trying to send him? He didn't know, but there was something else on King's mind. Now he wondered if that was also connected to the crime committed here tonight.

"I don't know," he said, setting the card back on the table.

Heading for the exit, Alvarez called after him. "Where are you going?"

What King needed was to breathe fresh air and clear his head. But first he needed to let Angelina know her mother had been murdered.

CHAPTER ELEVEN

KING HATED THE SILENCE. HE WISHED HE COULD SEE HER face as he broke the news—hold her in his arms just to let her know that she wasn't alone. They were grieving together. Then Angelina's tiny voice cut through the line. "I'll be there as soon as I can."

King picked his head up. "I'll stay here until you arrive."

Ending his call, he thought about the woman who'd come so close to being his wife. Her heart was broken. He could hear it in her voice and he hoped he masked his own pain in order to be the rock he knew Angelina needed. An unexpected death was one thing, but to know your mother had been murdered was unthinkable.

With watering eyes, King curled his fingers into his palm and made a fist. He couldn't help but feel responsible for Peggy's untimely death. Someone had chosen this house, *and* Peggy, for a reason. King knew that reason was himself. What had he done to make someone want to kill Peggy? Who did he piss off? What were they trying to prove? Of course, he couldn't tell Angelina any of this. Even if he could, he wasn't sure he would want to.

"Go get some coffee," Alvarez suggested as he caught King rubbing his eyes.

King lifted his head and swung his gaze to his partner. "Angelina is on her way now."

Alvarez nodded. "There is no sign of a break-in."

"What are you saying? Peggy knew the person who murdered her?"

Alvarez let his eyes wander to the police line. He shrugged his shoulders. "At this point, anything is possible." Sweeping is gaze back to King, he said, "You know you'll have to ask her where she was tonight?"

King nodded, already mulling over how he'd approach the delicate subject with Angelina. It didn't make sense. She couldn't have been the one to do it. He was still stuck on the cold case from six years ago, the one the press called *The Pillow Strangler*.

Mrs. Hill lived a quiet life of community service, family, and church. A routine life whose pattern could be learned in as short as a week's time. There were no secrets when it came to Peggy. She was the type of woman who wore her emotions on her sleeve. The more King considered it, the more sense it made that the suspect he couldn't catch six years ago would taunt him by killing the woman he *thought* was his mother-in-law by smothering her with a pillow.

King turned and faced the house, trying to make sense of the message left for him.

"Why does this feel personal?" Alvarez asked.

King could still smell the many Wednesday night dinners he and Angelina had shared with Peggy when they were dating. It was here, at this house, he'd received the news he would make detective. He could feel his heart break again with the memory of Angelina walking away, unable to marry someone whose job was so dangerous, calling their relationship quits before vows were made.

King said, "Because it is."

Alvarez tipped his head back and gave King a questioning look.

King skirted around him and headed for the neighbor's front door. "Has anyone asked the neighbors if they saw anything?"

Alvarez followed, said he didn't think anyone had. But once in sight of the front door, King hit the brakes and stared with a blank expression falling over his face. A flashback to the note tacked to Erin Tate's door had him hearing Sam read what it said.

"You haven't forgotten about me, have you? Of course you have. Burn in hell, pig."

"Jesus, what is it now?" Alvarez asked.

King blinked. "I was followed earlier."

"Followed?"

King told him what happened.

"Probably some punk kids," Alvarez said.

King didn't think so.

"Wait, you still think it could be him?"

"Why not?" King met Alvarez's gaze. "It's got to be that bastard, Orville Boyd," King said.

Orville Boyd was the only suspect in the Pillow Strangler serial murder case six years ago. King was convinced it was him terrorizing the elderly. But the district attorney insisted they didn't have enough evidence to bring charges. Then one day, the murders stopped and Orville Boyd quietly slipped under the radar. The case was shelved without ever being solved.

"Someone like him just doesn't stop," King said, already planning how to track him down.

Alvarez lifted his gaze over King's left shoulder when King heard his name being called. He turned to find Angelina waving her arms above her head from behind the police line.

He held up his finger and told her to wait, then turned back to Alvarez. "Boyd would know about Peggy. Hell, he probably thinks she's my mother-in-law. He'd also know about my father."

Alvarez blew out a heavy breath. "Go talk to Angelina. I'll see if the neighbor saw anyone who fits Boyd's description— or at least what I remember of it."

Without another word, King ran to the police line. "It's all right, Officer Morgan."

Officer Avery Morgan turned to King. "She says she's the victim's daughter."

"It's because I am," Angelina's voice cracked, her eyes moist and heavy.

"She's with me," King said, taking Angelina by the hand. "I'm so sorry," he said, finding a quiet place to talk. "How are you holding up?"

Angelina stared into his eyes with tears welling in the corners. She fell into his arms without warning and King caught her fall, embracing her inside his strong arms. He felt her familiar hands press into his sides and he was surprised to find himself clenching deeper into the familiar body he once loved so much.

"Who would want my mother dead?" Angelina sobbed into his shoulder.

"I don't know—" Angelina tightened her squeeze. King could feel the confusion screaming through her temples. "But we'll find whoever did this. I promise."

Angelina lifted her head and locked her eyes on his. "Can I see her?"

King stared into her wistful eyes, debating how to phrase his next sentence without her losing his trust. "I'll take you to the morgue," he nodded, "but first I need to ask you where you were tonight."

CHAPTER TWELVE

I WAS UP EARLY THE NEXT DAY TAKING COOPER ON A RUN through the Regis University campus. The future of *Real Crime News* kept cycling through my mind. Erin and I had to pin down what we wanted to accomplish.

When I started blogging, it was a way to tell the rest of the story that didn't get put into print. As the newspaper started to decline and the seismic shift in the industry rattled across the country, I thought it could be my way to survive in a profession I loved. But now that Walker was flirting with an offer to take what we'd built to the next level, I was scared of having to choose one or the other.

Walker didn't present it like that, but with as much money as he suggested he was willing to throw at the project, I knew I wouldn't be able to do both.

It was fifteen minutes before eight by the time I got back to the house. Allison Doyle, one of my dearest friends, was already inside and at the table with Mason.

"Mom, Allison said she can help me make money online." Mason was bright-eyed like he'd just been given a secret to tonight's winning numbers.

Allison looked to me and smiled. "Affiliate income."

"As long as you don't quit your day job," I said to my son.

Mason bounced across the kitchen, talking about the car he would buy with the money he earned. I gave Allison a look and she just smiled.

"You do remember the reason I'm here?" Allison gave me the once over, noticing I'd just come back from a run.

"I do."

"And you're ready to do it again?"

I'd promised her I would join her on her walk through the park as a way to train for the marathon our friend Susan Young was organizing for little Katie Garcia who was battling leukemia. I didn't mind going back out.

A minute later we headed out the door, calling goodbye to Mason as we left. Allison immediately asked how my date with King was last night.

My cheeks burned with the thought of it. "It wasn't much of a date," I said, explaining how we just went back to his place before he was called to work.

"Sometimes that's all a girl needs." Allison rolled her eyes over to me. "To be held by her man."

As we crossed the street and entered the campus, I told her about our sudden dinner meeting with the Million Dollar Man and Walker's offer to supply us with seed money to propel our newscast to the next level.

Allison gave me a sideways glance. "You're finally going to leave the paper."

Allison picked up the pace, pumping her arms. She'd lost a lot of weight since sticking to the exercise regimen the doctors suggested she get on after her health scare a couple months ago. I was proud of her for what she'd accomplished, and now to think Allison was about to briskly walk a marathon? I would have never seen it happening six months ago.

"That's just it; I don't want to." I shared my concerns, explained my fears. Allison listened to it all without placing judgement before I turned the table over to her.

"Did I tell you my cousin Marty was released?"

"That's great news," I said.

Allison had told me the story of Marty Ray a time or two before, and I was surprised to hear he had been released from prison.

Marty had been locked up for five years for a crime Allison—and a great deal of others—insisted he didn't commit. I didn't know the exact details to the case, but Allison convinced me Marty was just another example of how the justice system failed so many.

Allison told me how she couldn't wait to see him and surprised me by saying, "I've offered him to come work with me."

When I didn't react, Allison asked me why. I turned to look her in the eye. "It's a noble gesture, hun, but does he know anything about your business?"

The rubber soles of Allison's shoes scuffed across the concrete path as she came to an abrupt stop. Planting her hands on her hips, the crease between her brows deepened. "Someone has to believe in him. Why not me?"

I hadn't meant to offend. "It should totally be you, but I know how hard it is to run a successful business."

"What are you saying, Sam; I shouldn't do it?"

"That's not what I'm saying at all."

"Then what are you saying?"

Allison was short but had the attitude of a lioness protecting her young. It was the reason I loved her so much, but never enjoyed having her roars directed toward me.

"What you do for a living requires a great deal of skill," I said. "Skills even I don't have."

Her dark eyebrows shot up her forehead. "You would if I trained you."

My cell started ringing. Screening the call, I saw that it was my editor with the *Times*, Ryan Dawson. "I've got to take this, it's Dawson."

Allison stepped off the path and faced the mountains, wiping the sweat off her brow. I moved to a nearby tree and stood in the shade.

"Dawson, what's up?"

"Rumor has it you're shopping your podcast around looking for sponsors."

"And who did you hear that from?"

"Is it true?"

"Erin and I had dinner with someone."

"Someone who?" Dawson asked. "Never mind." He was already making me feel guilty for even thinking about taking Walker's offer. But then he let it go and said, "I need you in the newsroom ASAP. I caught wind of a story only you can tell."

CHAPTER THIRTEEN

AVERY MORGAN WAS STARING OUT THE BUS WINDOW thinking about how it seemed like only yesterday she was graduating from the academy. The last six months had been a whirlwind introduction to her new life as a police officer and it was everything she imagined it would be.

The brakes hissed and the bus rolled to a stop. Avery removed her earbuds. Her music stopped long ago, and she'd since been lost in her thoughts as she stared out the window at the world outside.

Of course, a lot of the reason she liked her job so much was because of Alex King making sure she was assigned the best training officer in the department—Officer Lester Smith.

Smith was a veteran of twenty years and had served all of them inside the Denver Police Department. He loved working the streets, mingling with the citizens and people in his community. He was a wealth of information and Avery soaked up his wisdom like a sponge, determined to be the best policewoman on the force.

With the bus still stopped, Avery peeked over the seat in front of her to see what the holdup was. Anxiously bouncing her knee, she still had an hour before she needed to be in for work, but Avery had a couple stops to make before then and couldn't afford to waste another minute.

"C'mon," she mumbled as she watched a black man of about six-two discussing something with the driver. "Just get on or get off."

As if hearing her grumble, the man suddenly turned and made his way to the back of the bus. He approached Avery and she quickly made a profile, putting the skills she'd learned on the job to the test.

A second later, she looked away and the bus started rolling.

Staring out the window, she visualized the man inside her head. She noted the distinguishing features that caught her attention. How his bald head shined like a polished gymnasium floor. And how his muscles bulged beneath his bright white shirt that highlighted the dark ink of his jailhouse tattoos. When she thought she remembered it all, she turned and glanced at him once more. He dropped his duffle bag to the floor next to her.

He nodded and smiled.

She did the same as a text message came through on her phone. She read it.

Thanks for helping with Mom. She's coming for dinner tonight and we'd love for you to join. Let me know if you can make it.

Avery messaged Alex King back, saying of course she'd love to have dinner. *But only if you promise to run in Sunday's marathon...*

...Still thinking about it.

I can register for you...

No thanks.

Avery would do anything for King. He was like an uncle to her and someone she looked up to. But she still didn't fully understand what happened last night and why he looked so emotionally distressed. Was it the look of a veteran detective having seen one too many homicides in his career? Avery didn't know, but she hoped maybe tonight King could tell her why.

"Are you running the marathon?"

Avery turned to the stranger sitting across from, her wondering if he had spied on her text to King. She turned her screen face down on her thigh, deciding if this man deserved a response or not.

"I saw your shoes." The stranger pointed at her running shoes and Avery relaxed.

Avery glanced down at her sneakers dangling off her backpack. "On my way to register now. What about you, will you be running?"

He shook his head, a friendly glimmer lighting up his crinkled eyes. "I prefer the weight room to running. But my cousin, she'll be joining the race."

Avery smiled, stealing glances his way.

The man looked ahead. "God, it feels so good to be back."

Avery caught the man grinning before asking, "Are you from Denver?"

The man nodded, continuing to stare out the front window as if breathing fresh air for the first time in a long time. Then he turned to look Avery in the eye. "But it's been a while."

"This city has grown up, but it hasn't changed all that much."

The man extended his large hand toward Avery. "I'm Marty."

"Avery." Avery watched her hand get swallowed up by his.

"It's nice to meet you, Avery."

Their eyes locked.

"Nice to meet you, Marty."

They both smiled as the bus bumped along.

CHAPTER FOURTEEN

I STOOD ON MY FRONT PORCH WITH COOPER LEANING HIS weight against my right leg as we watched Allison drive off into the distance. Panting, Cooper gave me the look like he was ready to take a rest. I couldn't blame him. A run and a brisk walk were more than what we normally did on any given day. Plus, it was beginning to get hot.

The door abruptly opened behind me and Mason came barreling out.

"Where are you off to?" I asked.

"Jamaal's," he called out, stuffing a basketball into his backpack before jumping on his bike.

I said, "Keep me in the loop with your day."

Mason promised he would and was off to the races.

I smiled, proud of the man he was becoming. He was looking more like Gavin by the day. A thick head of hair, inching his way past six feet, and an incredible smile when he wanted to put on the charm. Mason was working just as hard as his father did, too.

Work hard, play harder, I could hear my deceased husband say as if his angel was watching over me now.

When I entered the house, Erin was sitting at the kitchen table with my sister who'd recently moved to Denver from the East Coast to be closer to Mason and me while she studied to become a nurse. It seemed like the revolving door to my house was in full swing today. I appreciated the company.

"Walter Walker?" My sister quirked a brow as soon as she caught sight of me. "That's who you two had a date with last night?"

"It wasn't a date," I said, opening the freezer and tossing several ice cubes into a glass before filling it with water.

"You're going to take his money, aren't you?" Heather pressed further.

I turned my attention to Erin, listening to Cooper make a mess at his water bowl. "You just had to tell her, didn't you?"

"How could I not?" Erin tucked her golden hair behind her ear. "This is a once in a lifetime opportunity."

Which was also the reason I was hesitating.

"Oh my god. You're actually thinking of declining it?" Heather's lips parted.

I hated how well she knew me sometimes. But she was right. I was.

I said, "There is a lot to sift through."

"Samantha Bell." Heather slapped her palm on her knee in an exact replica of what my mother would do when she didn't like my decision. "Blow it up. Go big. Make your show legit."

I reminded Heather my career was already legit and our platform had always been real. "I don't need Walter Walker's recognition to prove my career is a success."

Erin said, "But maybe that is exactly what he needs to see."

We both rolled our eyes to Erin. Erin stared into mine, looking coy.

"What did you do?" I asked.

Shifting her weight around in the chair, Erin tipped her shoulders forward and said, "Don't be mad, but I've invited Walker to shadow us today."

I cocked my jaw and felt the muscles strain in my head. I wasn't sure that was such a great idea. Once again, I began questioning Walker's true intentions. It felt to me like Walker was the rich kid playing superhero, and I wasn't sold.

"I don't know," I said, shaking my head.

We didn't need to complicate our lives and risk getting hurt—or worse, killed—because of his inexperience. I expressed all this to Erin and, though she had concerns herself, she thought it important for him to fully understand what we did before investing so much capital into our platform.

"It will be fine, Sam. Besides, it's not like we are in the middle of a big investigation."

Maybe Erin was right. Perhaps now was the best time to bring Walker along for a ride. But then I thought about what Dawson had waiting for me at the newsroom, and I reminded Erin I still had duties to the *Times*.

"What's Alex think about all this?" Heather asked.

"Haven't spoken to him about it."

"Maybe you should." Her face shined with hope. "If anyone can open your eyes to what you'd be missing out on, it would be him."

CHAPTER FIFTEEN

As soon as I was out of the shower, I tried King's cellphone again. After several rings it clicked over to voicemail. This time I left him a message.

"Alex, baby, it's me. I've got some news to share." I paused to swallow down the lump of concern I had growing inside of me. Where was he? Why wasn't he answering my calls? "Call me as soon as you get this."

King had completely disappeared on me. I could still see the dull look of pain glazing over his incredible blue eyes on his way to whatever call he got last night. It was that look that had me worried for what he wasn't sharing with me.

I was about willing to do anything to not think about where he might be, but nothing I did could keep my thoughts from straying back to King.

As I toweled my hair dry, I thought about how I'd only seen that look on him once before—when Gavin died. It was the shock-to-the-system kind of look that I would never forget. Something was up. I needed him to call me back before I went looking.

"You ready yet?" Erin called from the front of the house.

"Be out in a minute," I hollered back, moving to my closet, rifling through my clothes, deciding what image I wanted to portray for Walker.

I hadn't completely written Walker off yet, no matter what I told Erin. I still wanted to get to know him better. If Erin insisted he shadow us for the day, then I would use the time to interview him and see if he truly was a good fit for us.

"Careful what you wish for." I laughed as I stepped into a pair of blue jeans, then pushing my head through a dark purple tank top.

When I emerged on the other side, my phone was blinking and buzzing with incoming messages, but none were from the only person I wanted to hear from.

Sitting on the edge of my bed, I thumbed through my phone and put a call in to Lieutenant Kent Baker's desk. He picked up after the second ring and I told him who I was.

"Hold tight, Mrs. Bell, I'll send you over to media relations."

I smiled, sensing he was joking. Baker had been a friend of Gavin's and was someone I could trust. Despite our often-conflicting stances on police work and me getting the story out to the public, we still maintained a good relationship after all these years.

"But I called to speak with you," I said.

He sarcastically responded, "The department is doing the best we can with the resources we have available." A short pause had us both smiling. "Jokes aside, how are you, Sam?"

I told him I was fine, but was hoping he could tell me if he'd spoken to or seen Alex.

"Not since last night. I assume you've tried calling him?"

"I have. It's not like him to go quiet on me." I could hear Baker's jaw popping as if he was biting his tongue, holding back valuable information that could help me trace King's whereabouts.

He asked, "This is about last night?"

My brows knitted. "What happened last night?"

"I can't say without jeopardizing the investigation. But I can tell you this one hit home for King."

"Is he okay? Did something happen?" My mind raced with a speeding heart.

"Go to his house, Sam," Baker said sincerely. "I'm sure he's just trying to clear his head. There's a lot of work to do and not a whole lot of time."

As soon as I ended my call with the lieutenant, I sat there staring at the floor feeling my head spin. Why hadn't King called or come to my place if the scene was as bad as Baker made me think it was? Did it have to do with the note tacked to Erin's front door? Something told me it did.

There were so many questions and only one thing to do. I gathered my things and marched into the kitchen telling Erin it was time to go.

CHAPTER SIXTEEN

"WHOSE CAR IS THAT?" ERIN ASKED AS SOON AS I PULLED IN front of King's small house near Washington Park, south of downtown.

It was the first thing I noticed, too. Parked next to King's unmarked police sedan was a silver Ford Focus whose plates I didn't recognize.

Erin was still staring at the mystery vehicle when she asked, "Maybe King got a new car?"

I didn't bother responding. There was no need for me to waste my breath. He hadn't. Instead, I opened my door and told Erin to wait in the car.

"Sam, are you kidding me?" Erin bent her elbow and unbuckled her belt. "I'm coming with you."

"No you're not." I shut the door before I had to listen to more of her protests.

Walking toward the house, I knew something wasn't right. I didn't have a good feeling about this. I looked up and down the block and into neighboring houses. Everything seemed normal. As I dug out my key, I thought how King better have a good reason for not responding to my calls.

"Hello?" I entered the house without having to use my key. "Alex, are you home?"

I heard movement in the kitchen and found King at the table alone. His spine straightened when staring at me, his eyes blinking like emergency flashers. He didn't say anything, only flicked a quick glance to the hallway bathroom door. Suddenly, it opened and I couldn't believe who walked out.

My heart totally stopped. I recognized her immediately and now understood why Alex wasn't responding to my texts. *Are you serious?*

She stared and smiled through brightly painted lips. Her loose curls framed her heart-shaped face before cascading down the middle of her back. I tried to hide the look of shock turning my face red, but it proved to be impossible. Angelina Hill was stunningly beautiful and suddenly I felt like I had interrupted something that wasn't meant for me to see.

I snapped my neck back to King. He was still sitting stiff as a board in his chair with a look on his face that said he hadn't expected to have to explain his way out of this. But that was exactly what I was going to have him do.

I couldn't look him in the eye. Sweeping my watery gaze across the table, I noticed the picture album spread between the mugs of coffee as the two of them were apparently having a good time traveling down memory lane.

What the hell was he doing with his ex-fiancé? And why did I feel like I didn't belong?

The silence in the house was deafening. No one knew what to say or how to break the ice. King opened his mouth and shut it as he struggled to find the words to explain what exactly was going on. His throat burbled like a brook lacking life-giving oxygen and it was just awkward sounding.

I snapped my neck to Angelina and her eyes immediately flicked to the clock.

"I better get going," she said to Alex. "Thanks again for the coffee."

"No. Please stay," I said, realizing my tone was more jagged sounding than I intended.

Hot flashes of jealousy had pellets of sweat forming across my back as I reminded myself to remain confident in what King and I had. But the questionable circumstances of what I had walked in on overpowered every single rational thought.

King stood and stepped toward me.

"Excuse me," I said, brushing him off, "but I need to use the toilet."

Angelina got out of my way as I barreled toward her. It was a smart move. I had no intention of stopping. She said nothing to me and it was better that way. Closing the door behind me, I locked myself inside with my chest heaving.

Turning on the faucet, I stared into the mirror hearing my thoughts echo off my cranium walls. I splashed cold water on my face but it did little to cool me off. When I opened my eyes, I was hit by another shocking surprise.

There, next to the sink, was an expensive looking diamond ring that could have only been left by Angelina.

"No you didn't," I whispered a hot breath. "Who does this chick think she is?"

The ring glimmered beneath the light. I couldn't look away. My mind was now racing out of control, wondering when she'd arrived and if she'd stayed the night.

Turning off the water, I picked up the ring. It was heavy, beautiful, and held the weight of their failed engagement so many years prior. She wasn't trying to get back with him, was she?

No matter how much I refused to believe it, everything inside me told me she was.

CHAPTER SEVENTEEN

Susan Young was staring through the tent curtain, watching the line of marathon participants grow when she heard her name being called from behind.

She turned to find event organizer, Hazel Beck, moving swiftly toward her, anxious to give a proper introduction. The women shook hands and Beck said, "Great to finally meet you in person."

"Surprised it's taken us this long."

"I've heard many wonderful things about you. I'm so glad you called." Beck turned her attention toward the tables of staff working to organize the event. "As you can see, we're swamped with runners registering and could use all the extra hands we can get."

Susan held up both her hands. "I've got two, but they work like four."

Beck laughed. "I hope so."

Only a few short weeks ago, Susan had learned about three-year-old Katie Garcia's battle with leukemia and had wanted to organize a fundraiser to assist with the ballooning medical costs. When the idea of hosting a Denver City marathon crossed her desk, Susan put a call in to Hazel Beck. Beck was already months deep into hosting a similar event and once she learned Katie's story, she was happy to team up with Susan.

Beck continued, "The event is taking on a life of its own."

Beck moved at a hundred miles per hour, never missing a beat. Susan quickly caught up—loving the energy of hosting an event of this magnitude. Beck gave Susan the rundown, explaining the registration lines, who was who, and how there was a table for online applicants coming to pick up their bibs and swag bags separate from those registering in person today.

It was easy for Susan to understand; she had done this type of work hundreds of times before. When Beck asked if Susan had any questions, Susan said, "Piece of cake."

Beck grinned. "Sorry I couldn't get you here before the chaos."

"Not to worry."

They moved into the next tent. A man of about six-one with wavy dirty blond hair smiled when locking eyes with Susan. Susan smiled back, wondering who the man was. She was an attractive woman who had the miraculous ability to turn heads wherever she traveled, and apparently today was no different. She'd once again caught the attention of another man.

Beck saw friendly glances being stolen in Susan's direction and said with a smile, "His name is Tristan and he's our safety director."

"A doctor?" Susan asked, suddenly finding the man less attractive. Her last boyfriend had been a doctor, and their sudden breakup still hurt. She didn't want to even think about dating a doctor again—even one as good looking as this Tristan guy was.

"Homecare nurse," Beck assured her. "And a wonderful one at that, from what I hear."

One of Beck's assistants interrupted and whispered something into her ear. Beck nodded, then lifted her eyebrows when saying to Susan, "Police Chief Gordon Watts just arrived. If you'll please excuse me."

Beck rushed off and Susan moved to assist Tristan. "You look swamped, how about I help?"

Tristan quickly gave Susan the rundown on registration protocol. "It's easy as pie," he said after moving a couple registrants through the line. "You ready to open up a lane of your own?" Susan was. "I'm here for another hour if you have any questions, then I have to jet off to work."

Susan opened up her lane, and quickly settled into a rhythm all her own. A half-hour passed before she encountered her first problem. A beautiful young woman stepped up to the table. "What's your name, sweetheart?"

"Avery Morgan."

Susan entered Avery's name but couldn't find her name on the list. "Have you registered or are you doing so now?"

"Already registered."

Tristan swiveled toward Susan and flashed Avery a wide grin that made Avery smile. "Running with the department?" Tristan asked Avery.

Avery's eyes flashed with surprise. "How'd you know?"

Tristan pointed to her shirt. A logo of the Denver Police Foundation, a non-profit organization, was proudly displayed on her left shoulder. Avery was one of dozens of officers participating in the event.

Avery laughed.

"Let's find your name," Tristan smiled, "and get you set for Sunday's race."

CHAPTER EIGHTEEN

ALLISON DOYLE WATCHED THE THICK THUNDERHEAD approach from the west. The large battleship clouds piled high in the sky, threatening to release torrential curtains of rain within the hour. It was an indication of what was to come. Right now, she was forced to hide from the hot sun still blazing overhead.

Wrapping her lips around the straw of her iced coffee, Allison pulled back a refreshing sip that jolted her awake. Customers came and went to the coffee shop where she instructed Marty to meet her. It was a few blocks from her office, and an easy reference point to begin their reunion into what would hopefully be a productive future.

Allison couldn't stand still. She was feeling excited, a little nervous, and couldn't stop thinking about what Samantha said on their walk earlier today.

"He'll be fine." Allison kept reassuring herself. "Marty needs someone to believe in him. If not me, then who?"

Palming her cellphone, Allison checked the time and sighed. She didn't want to admit Marty was running late, but he was. She hoped it wasn't an early indication of what she could expect from him—and certainly didn't want Samantha to be right. If only he had a cellphone of his own, then she could call to make sure he wasn't lost.

Rocking on her heels, she decided to give him another five minutes before walking back to the office. Feeling tired from her walk with Samantha, her ankles were beginning to swell. Bending her knee, she rubbed the pain away questioning her decision to participate in Sunday's marathon.

It wasn't so much that she didn't think she could do it, but rather a matter of having too much on her plate to commit to something that big. The prospect of having to train Marty was only half of her current stress. She also had a big industry summit approaching, which she wasn't prepared for at all. She couldn't back out of either commitment.

Suddenly, a pair of broad shoulders brushed past her and Susan watched as the tall man opened the door to the coffee shop. Without him realizing it, a single bill of money floated from his pocket and Allison bent over to pick it up, calling out, "Hey, you dropped this."

The tall man didn't even stop so she called out a second time. This time a little bit louder.

"Excuse me, sir, you dropped your money." She thrust her arm out so that he could see what he had lost.

With his hand still on the door handle, he turned and said, "Keep it."

Allison's eyebrows squished. "But it's yours."

"Not anymore." He smiled and disappeared inside leaving Allison spinning in a whirlpool of confusion.

"What the hell was that about?" a deep voice said from behind.

Allison whipped around. Marty locked eyes with his cousin and smiled. Allison spread her arms to the sides and catapulted into his. They hugged and laughed. Allison had tears of joy. When their celebration ended, Marty asked, "That man giving you trouble?"

"Easy soldier." Allison squeezed his shoulders. "You're no longer in the jailhouse."

Marty pointed to the glass door. "'Cause I'll have a word with him if you want?"

The corners of Allison's eyes crinkled. "I'm flattered, really, but I was only telling him that he dropped his money." Allison opened up her palm and showed Marty the folded up twenty.

Marty looked to the money, then swept his gaze up to Allison. "You kept it?"

Allison said, "He wouldn't take it back."

Marty looked through the window, squinting his eyes to see through the glare. "Who does that?"

"I suppose it's his way of paying it forward." Allison's eyes traveled over Marty's single duffle slung over his shoulder, assuming it was all the possessions he owned. "But it doesn't matter because I'm not going to argue with him about it."

Marty laughed. "You haven't changed a bit."

"God, it's so good to see you."

"You too, cousin." Marty's gaze softened. "Thank you for doing this."

Allison pinched her lips. "Just don't make me regret it."

Marty slung his arm over Allison's shoulders. "I'll do my best."

"Now, c'mon." Allison wagged her head and started walking. "Let me show you to your new office."

CHAPTER NINETEEN

ANGELINA WAS GONE BY THE TIME I EXITED THE BATHROOM and the house was even quieter than before. I found King in the kitchen cleaning dirty dishes and loading them into the dishwasher. He'd since closed up the picture book he and Angelina were looking at, clearly not interested in making it a conversation piece, and I was glad.

Leaning against the counter's ledge, I folded my arms and asked in a low, non-confrontational voice, "What was that about?"

King was slow to respond. He turned off the water and looked me in the eye when he said, "Peggy Hill was murdered last night."

Slowly, my head floated back on my shoulders. I recognized the name, knew it to be Angelina's mother, and couldn't believe what I was hearing. How insensitive it was of me to assume it was only about me. King and his relationship with the Hill's went back to a time long before I was a part of his daily life. That wasn't something that was easy to erase.

With wide eyes, I thought about the conversation I had

with Lt. Baker and asked King, "Was that the call you were on last night?"

King nodded once—still looking me in the eye.

I turned and looked away. I felt awful for making assumptions as to why Angelina was here, clearly enjoying King's company.

"Is Angelina okay?" I asked.

King's voice was raspy like gritted sandpaper. "No."

I imagined as much. But Angelina fooled me. She hid her emotions well. Even I couldn't have done it as well as she did if standing in her shoes. Angelina held no visible signs of grief, nor gave off any indication of the emotional strike of lightning I imagined she had experienced. Was that because she was in the presence of King? Or was it because the truth hadn't sunk in yet?

"I know what it looks like." King dried his hands with a towel and took me at the waist, digging his fingertips into the soft part of my hips, pulling me against his hard abdomen. "It was a late night and she had no one else she could talk to."

So you brought her here? *Why not go to a coffee shop?* I argued with him inside my head.

I tipped my head back and allowed my eyes to sway back and forth with his. They were tired looking but not as dark as when I'd last seen them.

King tilted his mouth forward and kissed me.

My moist lips melted into his as our tongues gently touched. Pressing my palms deeper into his chest, I felt his heart beat against the balls of my hands. I regretted my resentment toward them both. I didn't know what had gotten into me, but I knew King was once madly in love with Angelina, and there was still the ring she'd left behind.

Did she do it on purpose? I was afraid to ask King. He didn't have to tell me we were okay. He reassured me with his actions and had me feeling like we were stronger than ever.

But I still mentioned the ring. "It's next to the sink in the bathroom," I said.

Mischief flashed in his eyes. "Would you like to be the one to return it?"

Maybe I would have under different circumstances, just to make sure there wasn't any question who King belonged to. But I didn't want there to be any further misunderstanding.

He said, "I'll call her."

"Thanks," I said as King reminded me about dinner with his mother and Avery tonight.

I was looking forward to it, was excited to get to know Avery better, thrilled to be pulled deeper into King's life. We moved to the table and King made me coffee. When our eyes met, there was a serious look in his that gave me pause.

He asked, "You remember the Pillow Strangler?"

I did. "Orville Boyd," I said, recalling who the police's primary suspect was. "Is that who killed Peggy?"

King's eyelids hooded over his irises and I was afraid of what he might say next.

Then my entire day's plans changed when he said, "We think he's back."

CHAPTER TWENTY

THE SHADOW STALKER IRONED HIS HAND DOWN THE FRONT of his cotton shirt—the touch suddenly transporting him back to last night. His shirt had a similar feel to the pillow he used to smother Mrs. Peggy Hill, and it was the same incredible sense of euphoria he longed to feel again.

Closing his eyes, he leaned back in his chair and spun around in a complete rotation. He smiled into the ceiling, expressing the feeling of joy he had when knowing he took someone else's life. Because of it, he felt empowered, reawakened—like he'd been given a second chance at life.

Suddenly, he slammed his feet to the ground and stopped his chair from spinning. Turning his head toward the softly playing radio, he paused to listen to the morning's newsflash.

He'd been waiting all night to hear his name being called, had ensured that he'd make the morning news cycle by making an anonymous call to send the inspector to Peggy Hill's house last night. He wanted to be recognized as the best, wanted the inspector's friends to know who he was. Yet as he listened to the news, he couldn't believe there wasn't one mention of his kill.

"How could this be?" His words fluttered softly over wet lips. "It was the perfect attack. What did I do wrong?" His call. His anonymous call wasn't urgent enough. It had kept the media away.

Grumbling, the Shadow Stalker felt more than inadequate. If he couldn't even get the attention of local media outlets, how could he ever expect to gain the attention of Inspector Alex King?

Tucking his chin, he lowered his brow reminding himself to be both patient and persistent.

It was important he remembered this was only the beginning of his journey. There was still time. If his first kill didn't produce the desired outcome, another certainly would.

"The world needs to see that I exist," he said.

As soon as the news was over and the radio switched back to playing music, the Shadow Stalker leaned back into his chair and forced his shoulders to relax. A minute later, the room darkened and he was oblivious to his surroundings.

Living in a constant state of daydream, his thoughts soon shifted to the old woman Peggy Hill. He thought how devastated her daughter must be to learn that she was dead.

A part of him wished it wasn't necessary to affect so many lives only to satisfy his own selfish need to get close to Alex King. But it was impossible to do anything without the ripples of consequence fanning across the waters of life.

His hands ironed down his thick thighs, his fingers curling over his kneecaps.

As the walls surrounding him grew quieter, it was impossible for his thoughts not to scramble their way back to the inspector. The Shadow Stalker wondered how long it would take for Alex King to learn he was behind the murder. He thought his clues were obvious, but perhaps not.

Then he thought about Angelina Hill and smiled. "If only

I could have seen both your faces during your time of reunion."

Spinning in his chair, he laughed when imagining the old feelings Alex and Angelina once shared resurface again. Memories like what they shared were impossible to erase. The Shadow Stalker planned to use that to his advantage.

He closed his eyes and imagined fireworks lighting up the night's sky. The vivid image of Alex and Angelina being together once again was powerful enough to elicit a joyous celebration. The foolish part of him expected to receive a thank you card in the mail—perhaps even an invitation to their future wedding.

"You're getting ahead of yourself." He laughed, as he often did.

But he was having a great deal of fun imagining the future he wanted to share with the inspector. "Oh, the wave it will cause in your current relationship with Samantha." He smirked.

A knock on his door. He swiveled around to see who it was.

"I thought you'd be interested in this," the face at the door said.

The Shadow Stalker rolled his chair across the floor and took the flier to Sunday's marathon into his hands. His face was bright with possibility. "Thank you."

If it wasn't obvious enough he was coming after King, then perhaps his next kill would be more precise. After all, patience was the key to a successful reunion and friendships took time to build as he slowly worked his way into King's inner circle.

There was still so much work to do. He could hardly wait to get started.

CHAPTER TWENTY-ONE

ONCE BACK AT THE CAR, I DROPPED INTO THE DRIVER'S seat with Erin staring at me like I had a hole in my head. Her painted fingernails tapped on the center console in an even rhythm of annoyance.

"Sorry it took so long," I said.

I knew we were on a deadline—hadn't forgotten about our arrangement to have Walker shadow us for the day—but my relationship with King *always* came first. No matter what.

"You want to talk about it?" she asked, turning her attention to her cellphone.

Sliding the key into the ignition, I just wanted to get going. I hadn't meant to stay so long; just wanted to know King was alive and well. Angelina had changed everything.

"He's working a new case we might be interested in looking into."

"That's not what I'm talking about." Erin rolled her eyes to me and quirked a brow.

I stared into her shimmering irises with question marks practically flashing across her gaze.

"I'm talking about the gorgeous woman I saw leave the house."

My lungs squeezed out a wheezy breath that immediately gave away my insecurities. I held her gaze and listened to the local morning talk show play in the background as the host discussed mayor Noah Goldberg's police body cam measures, arguing if it was actually making the city safer or doing the opposite.

Finally, I gave in. "Her name is Angelina Hill."

Erin gave me a look that suggested she thought my man was wandering off the reservation. There was no way I could mention King's past engagement now—didn't want to inflate the potential for added drama—so instead, I glanced to Erin's phone and said, "Mrs. Peggy Hill, Angelina's mother, was murdered last night."

Erin's face tightened—I could see her already getting to work. "Any suspects?"

"King has a theory the killer might be someone they couldn't convict six years ago." I shared the name Orville Boyd and continued, "Same MO—targeting older women in their sleep, suffocating them with their own pillows."

Thinking six years back, struggling through my own depression with the loss of Gavin, I remembered how this particular case destroyed King's confidence in his ability to do good police work. The press, including the *Times*, had called the police incompetent with how they were handling the investigation, unable to make an arrest. Then Erin asked something I wished she didn't.

"So why bring a material witness to his house? Shouldn't he have conducted the interview at the station?"

I put my foot on the brake and the car into gear. "It's a long story."

"Is it one we can share with Walker? I'd like to show him just how good we are."

I was afraid of damaging King's case before it had a chance of getting off the ground—if there even was an investigation underway. But mostly I was terrified that if the Pillow Strangler was indeed back, we'd scare him into hiding before King had a chance to catch him, redeeming himself for past failures.

"Let's just keep this between us until King says otherwise." I eased my foot off the brake and set the wheels in motion.

Erin rubbed her forehead and reluctantly agreed. "But mark my words Sam, as soon as we find ourselves even just a little bit involved, we're diving in headfirst."

If only she knew how involved I already was.

CHAPTER TWENTY-TWO

WALTER WALKER'S OFFICE WAS IN THE DENVER TECH Center, a business and economic trading hub home to several major businesses and corporations in the southeastern corner of the city. This part of town was always busy and traffic was ruthless but we made it there with minutes to spare.

"You can at least pretend to want to be here," Erin said to me as we boarded the elevator on our way up to meet Walker.

I was staring at the floor, thinking how Walker was already a hindrance to our job. But maybe my distraction was really about Angelina. I couldn't stop seeing the ring or hearing King say he would call her to tell her what she had forgotten. I regretted the decision to not do it myself, but it was really none of my business.

I asked Erin, "Are you sure this is a good idea?"

Erin had a nice inheritance from the death of her father, and though I didn't know the details to that story, I assumed by Erin's willingness to accept outside investment was because what she had didn't come close to what Walker was willing to offer us.

"No."

Her answer surprised me. "Then why are we here?"

"Think of it like this—" She stepped closer, wanting me to look her straight in the eye. "We're dating. Feeling him out to see if we're a good fit. And if we are," she smiled, "why not allow him to help us fulfill our dreams?"

Keeping my eyes locked with hers, I knew Erin could see that I was scared of getting what I wanted. Maybe she was too, though she never said it in those terms.

The elevator ride up to Walker's office floor was quick. Once we slowed to a stop, Gemma Love was standing at the doors, greeting us by our first names.

She was welcoming and cordial but I couldn't help but notice that her smile never hit her eyes. Once again, I felt my walls of protection go up around me. Gemma had a knack for making me feel like I was the subject of her own private investigation. I couldn't explain it, or why Erin didn't seem to feel the same.

We moved down the hall and Erin chatted up Gemma as we were led deeper into the bowels of Walter Walker's head-quarters. She felt right at home—her business sense shining bright—where I naturally slinked back into my role as a journalist, looking for someone to interview in an attempt to uncover the dirt hidden inside these walls.

Keeping one ear on what they were saying, I made note of everything I saw.

Walker portrayed narcissism at every corner I turned. There were portraits of himself, him photographed shaking hands with other famous and prominent people. Glitter, glamour, and gold. Walker was everything that I was not.

I would never date this guy, I thought, thinking about Erin's dating analogy.

We couldn't be more opposite. This guy had more money than I could ever imagine and he wanted to work with us. Why? Did something happen to him that made him want to seek justice for others? Or did he inflict some kind of pain and suffering on others and now wanted to cancel out his wrongs? I didn't know, but maybe I'd just found my first clue.

Halfway down the hall, I stopped to stare at a Sherlock Holmes watercolor painting. It was marvelously done, but the meaning couldn't have been more glaringly obvious.

"It's just the two of us most of the time." Gemma turned back to look at me, as if to say it was just she and Holmes working together when Walker was jet-setting across the globe.

Erin followed Gemma as they both floated toward me. Erin asked, "Is Mr. Walker currently exploring other investments?"

Gemma smirked. "When it comes to business, Walter is a consulting detective who has a knack for sniffing out the winners."

Gemma stood beside me and gave me a knowing look.

I turned back to Holmes, who was also a consulting detective, though fictitious, and admittedly had trouble trusting women. Did Walker share the same trait? It would have been quite the contradiction if he did, considering his assistant was female and he was actively recruiting us. Nonetheless, I made a mental note of it and filed it away to reference for later.

"Mr. Walker has associates around the globe, but I'll let him tell you about his other ventures if he so desires." Gemma wagged her head, anxious to move the train forward. "Come. Walter will meet us in the fishbowl shortly."

I took one last glance at Holmes before turning upstream. Gemma's hips swayed like the waves of an ocean as she drifted confidently into the conference room where bottles of water and a platter of fruit and bagels were waiting.

There were two folders, one with each of our names on it. I asked about them as soon as I saw them.

"Those are meant for inspiration," Gemma said, gently pushing Erin's toward her.

Gemma's eyes lit up but her tone was patronizing and peppered with superiority. Again, more traits of Holmes I couldn't ignore.

Brushing Gemma's tone off, curiosity got the best of me and I decided to open my folder. Inside was a list of unsolved cases. I thumbed through them. Some were in Denver, others throughout the state of Colorado. There were also a few in other states, but there was enough evidence to highlight one glaring fact I couldn't ignore. All of the cases in Denver were one's I knew King had been assigned to work himself—and all of them were still considered open and unsolved.

Was that what this was about? Did Walker want to expose me to King's flaws? Or was I reading too much into his intention?

When Erin lowered herself into a chair, I swept my gaze across the room and found myself staring at a corkboard tacked with crime scene images. Then a headline I recognized caught my attention—*ARE DENVER DETECTIVES TO BLAME?*

My heartrate kicked up a notch when Gemma distracted my thoughts.

"Walter is beyond excited to be joining you two today."

"What we do," I turned to look Gemma in the eye, "it's really not that exciting."

Gemma smirked and sharpened her gaze. "Working with Walter, it's always exciting."

CHAPTER TWENTY-THREE

I WAS STANDING AT THE CORKBOARD, ATTEMPTING TO DULL my senses when glossing over the graphic images of a slaughtered woman who had been brutally murdered at the hands of her captor, when Walter Walker entered the room.

Between the graphic images was the headline to the article *I'd written*.

It was like entering the war room to an active investigation—reliving the horrible nightmare as if it happened yesterday.

I heard Walker greet Erin behind me as I was trying to wrap my brain around what exactly Walker was attempting to connect to a case that happened so many years ago.

My eyes traveled over the woman whose breasts had been cut off. I asked myself if this was an unsolved case or just something Walker found interesting. The victim's skin was scarred with cigarette burns and it had zero connection to my article Walker displayed with it.

I flicked my attention to a photograph of a beautiful young woman staring brightly into the camera, so full of life. Naturally, my heart ached for her loss. But I couldn't find any explanation to why my article was linked to her death.

I sidestepped and re-read what I had written four years prior. A woman was brutally sexually assaulted and left for dead in a ravine. There was an outcry from the public and, though there was plenty of evidence to suggest the police should have made an arrest in the case, they hadn't. Instead, I had uncovered how the investigators working the case drastically mishandled key evidence, all but ruining any chances of finding out who was responsible for the woman's death.

Remembering it as if it was yesterday, I blamed myself for not keeping the pressure on the police department to pursue the person responsible. It was my responsibility and I'd failed. The leads and evidence drying up and with the lack of interest by my senior editors. Not long after, she was all but forgotten...until now.

Walker eased his way closer and I heard his light footsteps approaching just before he filled the empty space to my right. We both stared at the board in silence for a solid minute before he said, "I keep thinking that one day the answer will just click."

I wondered how many hours he had worked on this case himself. Collectively, the case had thousands of hours already attached to it with nothing to show for the effort.

"You have an interesting infatuation for cold cases," I said, still feeling reserved about working with him.

I didn't like how he pushed his way into our world. He had Erin by the pigtails and she was already seeing us dancing on the national stage. But not me. I planned to pick Walker apart and do proper vetting without Erin swaying my opinion before I had time to decide myself whether or not I wanted to work with Walker.

Walker turned to me and said, "It's not much different than your own, wouldn't you say?"

"I wouldn't say. We're nothing alike."

Walker smirked and turned back to face the board.

Who was this guy? What did he truly hope to achieve by bringing us into his circle? It certainly wasn't about money. He had plenty of that. Fame? He had that, too. What then? The truth? The truth to what?

"Did you look at the folder I prepared for you?"

I nodded.

He gave an arched look. "And?"

I stepped one foot back and turned to face him. "Have you ever thought that maybe some cases are meant to be left unsolved?"

He barely reacted. "I don't believe you mean that."

I asked, "You want to know the truth?"

"I do."

I glanced to Erin who was busy discussing something with Gemma. "The truth is, Erin wants this more than I do."

"And what is holding you back?"

I wasn't about to admit my fears to a complete stranger. Instead, I said, "I have many reservations, but it wouldn't hurt to first know what it is you want from me."

He licked his lips and took his time when choosing his words carefully. Erin interrupted and called my name. "Sam, we can have the contract by the end of today."

Gemma stepped forward. "Assuming all goes well today."

Walker knew he had his out. When I was certain he wasn't going to answer my question, I swung my gaze over to Gemma.

Something in the way she said *"Assuming all goes well today"* didn't sit well with me. It made me think that whatever happened today would dictate how the contract would be written. Again, I was having my doubts—paranoid that we might be being taken advantage of in some regard I couldn't yet see.

"Let's not get too excited," I said.

Gemma masterfully changed the topic by stating to Erin, "We had the pleasure of watching your documentary work."

Erin perked up.

"It was marvelous." Walker smiled. "I do hope you'll be doing more in the future. Perhaps one of these cases in the folder?"

"Doubtful." Erin laughed. "But never say never. Podcasts are my new story form."

"Yes. Of course." Walker nodded just as my cellphone dinged.

I checked to see who it was. Dawson. *Shit.* "We got to go," I said as if realizing for the first time just how late I was to meet with my editor.

"Well, you're quite good at what you do." Walker turned to look at me. "The both of you."

"Thank you." Erin stepped to the door. "Shall we get started?"

"Yes." Walker held my gaze when he smiled. "I can't wait to put your skills to the test."

CHAPTER TWENTY-FOUR

CAROL KING WAS FIDGETING WITH THE REMOTE, UNABLE to get the TV to respond, when she grumbled to the nurse, "I pay for this service. The least you can do is make sure that it works."

The nurse, Tristan Knight, reached for the remote. "It's not the TV. It's the remote, Mrs. King."

"It's not the smelly remote." Carol whacked the plastic against the wooden armrest of her chair before pointing the remote back at the TV. "If it was, it would be doing what I'm telling it to do."

"Mrs. King, please just listen to me." Knight struggled to get Carol to stop banging the remote against her kneecap, afraid she might break it or, worse, cause injury to herself. "Use the input button and select the TV option."

"This thing worked fine before the move." Carol ignored the advice and kept repeating the same efforts that repeatedly failed her.

"Please, allow me to do it for you." Tristan reached for the remote but Carol quickly reeled it back, tucking it deep into her armpit, guarding it like a pit bull.

Carol snarled at the nurse when suddenly her son appeared at the door.

"Mom, he's only trying to help." Alex King entered his mother's room at the assisted living facility, rolling his eyes. His mother's behavior was a test of patience and he felt sorry for the nurse having to put up with her stubbornness.

"Now get away from me, you no-good nothing," Carol growled at Tristan.

"Mom, relax." King raised his voice getting her to listen. "He's only trying to help. If you would only listen."

Tristan retreated with both palms facing out. King's mother was as hard-headed as a hammerhead shark, but King also knew that he was one of the few people in the world she would truly open her ears for.

King nodded to Tristan, muttered a quick thanks for the effort, and gave the *sorry about my mother, she can be a handful* look that made Tristan accept his apology. A second later, Tristan exited the room and gently closed the door behind him.

Carol stared at King, still unsuccessfully clicking away at the remote. "I told them my son chose the cable TV package, but look at this blue screen."

"And you're right," King said. "I did."

He opened his palm and asked to have the remote. Carol reluctantly gave him what he asked for and, as soon as he had it in his hand, he hit the input button and selected the TV option—just as he heard the nurse say to do. The screen flicked to life and he surfed the channels to make sure his mother had access to the service they paid for. It was just as it should have been.

"Would you look at that," Carol said, bright-eyed and bushy tailed. Then she narrowed her eyes and said to Alex, "The breakfast today was awful. It tasted like cardboard."

King grinned, thinking how his mother could never be

satisfied no matter what anybody did. "I'm sure it was just fine," he said.

Carol spat, "It was awful. Trust me."

King's mother lived her life one problem to the next. If it wasn't the remote or how awful breakfast was, it would be something else entirely. King was prepared for it—knew the first month away from home would be the toughest. He just hoped his mother wasn't asked to leave before she settled into her new life at the facility.

"How did Dad ever survive living with you?" King teased.

"Your father and I saw the world the same way."

King knew that wasn't true. Dad was optimistic, saw the good in everything and everybody—even after witnessing the worst society threw at him.

Carol was still giving a deadpan look when she flicked her eyes back to her son and asked what he was doing here.

"The director called about your behavior, Mom." King kneeled beside her and looked his mother in her grayish blue eyes. "You haven't even been here a full week and I'm already getting a call from the principal."

"Really?" Carol frowned. "Because it feels like I've been here for years."

"It's not that bad, Mom. You agreed to come *here*." King bounced his gaze around her quaint and homey room. "We talked about this. Remember?"

Carol stared at the television, not making any indication she was listening to anything her son said.

"The good news is," King stood, "I'll be picking you up for dinner."

Without taking her eyes off the TV screen, Carol said, "I'm not interested in being a third wheel to your dinner date with Samantha."

King assured her she wouldn't be. "Avery has agreed to come, too."

His mother's eyes perked up. "Avery? Really?"

King nodded. "You wanted to congratulate her on her new position. I thought this might be a good way to get us all together."

Suddenly, the local news station stole both of their attentions. "Denver police are investigating the suspicious death of an elderly woman—"

Carol tipped forward and King turned to look. Then the news anchor gave the location of the crime and King could see on his mother's face she recognized the street address.

"Did you know about this?" she asked.

King bit his lip and sighed.

"Is it—?" Carol's voice cracked.

"It's Peggy Hill, Mom."

Carol's face froze as she stared at the TV—a look of shock drifting over her eyes.

King stood and found himself staring at his mother's bed pillows, thinking about how he needed to track down Orville Boyd before another innocent woman found herself dead.

Carol looked up at her son. "You weren't going to tell me, were you?"

"I'm sorry, Mom." King knew Peggy and his mother had been friends and he wasn't sure how best to break the news. He now realized she'd learn of it sooner or later and regretted not being the first to tell her what happened.

Carol's face hardened when she turned her eyes back to the screen. "At least now Dad has some familiar company with him. He always did like Peggy."

"Yeah." King swallowed the lump down in his throat. "Yeah, he did," he said on his way out the door, once again reminding his mom to be ready for dinner at five.

CHAPTER TWENTY-FIVE

WALTER WALKER WANTED ACTION BUT INSTEAD I GAVE him a glimpse into what it was really like doing the exhausting work of journalism. Stepping inside the newsroom, I turned to Walker and said, "This is where the real story lives."

Walker stood about a foot taller than me and I watched him slowly take it all in—the sights and sounds—a slow frown pulling his lips toward the floor.

I'd told him on our way from his office to mine how my editor had a story waiting for me and I needed to report for duty. He was insistent to learn the details, but I had nothing to reveal as I didn't know myself.

"The decline of the free press," he muttered out with a breath of disbelief.

A satisfying grin tugged at my lips as I kept moving toward my desk. As we walked, I kept my eye out for Dawson. It was one thing to hear the struggles of a newspaper, and something else entirely to see it for yourself.

The collective mood of my colleagues trying to salvage

whatever might be left could be felt—desperation was in the air at every step.

"These people are the real stars to the show," I said, pointing to the men and women with pencils tucked behind their ears, their fingers tap dancing across their keys.

Walker puckered his lips and made a sour look. "Pitiful place to work."

I smiled. Indeed it was, but it was my pitiful existence that I cherished with all my heart. I was happy to present it to him, because the more I got to know this man of power and influence, the more I believed it was my responsibility to pull his expensive designer shoes back down to earth so he could see what exactly was at stake.

"Money might be drying up for papers like the *Times* but the stories aren't." Erin made sure Walker knew our value. "There are more stories now than ever, and it's up to us to make sure we continue telling them."

"Exactly." Walker snapped his fingers and pointed at Erin. "The one constant in life is change, and you two are leading the next wave into the new frontier. It doesn't matter what happens here," his eyes lifted as he looked around, "because you've secured your future by taking control of your careers."

Stepping inside my cubicle, I ignored Walker's renewed pitch as to why now was the time to step out on my own. I set my car keys and phone on my messy desk and listened to my voicemails and checked my emails. There was nothing exciting to report—not even anything from Dawson.

"So, where is the story?" Erin asked.

I shook my head. "I'll have to find Dawson."

"But there is a story, right?" Walker planted his hands on his hips. "If not, we can start with any of the cold cases I laid out in your folders."

"Just hang on a second, cowboy." I stood and looked for signs of Dawson.

When I didn't see him, Walker asked me, "What are you going to do when these doors finally shut?"

"The same thing I've always done. Survive."

"If the doors closed today, would you be able to support yourself financially?"

I knew I couldn't. Not even if I took every penny for myself of the ad dollars our blog and podcast were making. Walker knew I was vulnerable, and a part of me thought that could be the reason he was so aggressive in his pitch. He wanted a piece of the pie before I had leverage to negotiate how much I was actually worth.

I said, "Let's not play hypothetical."

"Are you asking Sam to leave her job?" Erin asked Walker. "Because, if you are, you can consider your deal DOA. Dead on arrival."

I didn't react—couldn't afford to reveal my sudden appreciation. Erin was guarding what I held close to my heart and it made me happy to know she was actually internalizing my concerns.

Walker swept his gaze off Erin and grinned when he asked me, "How much would it take for you to leave your job and go fulltime today?"

I froze and blankly stared at his bold—yet tempting—question. "You can't be serious?"

Walker raised his eyebrows, a glint in his eye. We squared off and, just before I was going to tell Walker to go to hell, Dawson arrived, saying, "I told Samantha before we moved to this dump that there wasn't much of a future here, but now I'm curious to know what is being offered."

"Nothing worth discussing," I said, turning to my computer.

Out of the corner of my eye, I kept seeing Dawson glance at Walker like maybe he recognized him. Erin introduced the two of them without mentioning anything about the vision

Walker had for *Real Crime News*. Then Dawson launched into editor mode, not realizing which ears were listening.

"Sam, I was hoping you would have been here sooner."

My fingers tapped at the keys. "I'm moving as fast as I can."

Then Dawson said something he should have kept to himself. "I hope it's because you were working the murder that happened last night."

I spun around to see his face with my own eyes. Everyone seemed to have leaned forward at the same time. Six round eyeballs stared at me like I had grown a second head—all of them willing me to respond. I knew the exact murder Dawson was referring to, but now that Dawson had Walker's full attention as well, I wondered who Dawson's source was. He didn't stop there.

"An inside source is saying the victim was close to King." Dawson furrowed his brow. "Did he say anything to you?"

I thought about my brief encounter with Angelina, could feel myself softly whispering a quick prayer for her mother. "I'm aware."

The collective gasp I thought I heard was only the force of my imagination. But the eyeballs were still staring as a wave of heat moved up my collar.

"So you know how the victim died?" Dawson pressed further, his mouth inching its way closer to my ear.

Everyone was waiting to hear my answer. I did, but didn't want to share what I knew in front of Walker—the bloodhound with his nose to the air.

"I'd like to know." Walker coaxed Dawson into telling him.

Dawson took a step back and angled his body toward Walker as he explained everything he knew about Peggy Hill, still unaware who he was telling.

"The Pillow Strangler?" Walker asked with arms crossed.

We all turned our heads, surprised to hear Walker say the name. They were talking like old friends, finishing each other's thoughts. I couldn't believe what I was witnessing.

"You know?" I said with knitted brows.

Walker met my eye, his neck still craned forward with held interest. "It was in the folder I gave you as possible stories to investigate."

He went on to tell me what I already knew. How the police had a suspect they never brought charges against—how they let a murderer go free. I didn't recall seeing it in the folder from Walker, so how did he know?

Now Dawson was the one giving me the look of surprise.

He stared with his eyebrows forming the narrowest *V* I'd ever seen. I knew what it was he was thinking. I could see the sense of betrayal flashing over his eyes. This was a mistake. I should have never brought Walker here. My mistake snowballed when Walker launched into his pitch of how he was actively recruiting Erin and me to be the two stars of *Real Crime News* for his next big investment opportunity.

"Is that right?" Dawson said with barely moving lips—one eye on Walker, the other on me.

I kept my mouth shut as I eyed the exit.

"Maybe this is it?" Walker said excitedly as he turned to look at me.

I cast my gaze to the floor. My worlds were colliding—my loyalties being tested—and I wasn't ready for any of what was about to happen next.

From the very beginning I'd suspected Walker was a bad idea, but now I was sure of it.

When I turned my attention to Erin she mouthed a quick apology, taking the blame for what was happening. I could see she was excited to start working the story of the Pillow Strangler.

"Orville Boyd," Dawson said, pressing a folded piece of

paper into my hand. "If there is a story here, Sam, I'd like you to find it."

I closed my grasp and felt the paper crumble inside my hand. Dawson gave me a knowing look—a look that said he owned my time first before anyone else. And he was right. The *Times* came before anything Walker was currently offering me.

Dawson said, "Maybe Detective King can weigh in on the matter."

Walker folded his arms and smiled like he'd just declared victory. But was he smiling because we now had a story, or for his sleaze-ball move to make it look like I had already accepted his investment money? Probably both.

Dawson made for the exit but, before leaving the cubicle, he rolled his gaze off Walker's shoulder and looked me in the eye. "And, just so we're clear, you still work for me."

CHAPTER TWENTY-SIX

DETECTIVE ALEX KING WAS ON HIS WAY OUT OF THE assisted living facility when Tristan Knight caught his arm. "Detective—before you go, can I have a word?"

King quickly glanced to his vehicle where John Alvarez was staring through the glare of his windshield wondering what was taking so long. King had been worried about his mother's behavior but he still had police work to do. "You've got a minute," he said to Tristan.

"It won't take long. I've printed off an itemized list for services paid for." Tristan handed it over to King. "Just so there isn't any question what your mother has available to her."

King scrubbed a hand over his face and reviewed the invoice.

"Of course, we can add or subtract anything you'd like at any time."

King shook his head no and proceeded to fold up the printed invoice. He tucked it into his back pocket and inched closer. "I'm sorry about my mother. I know how difficult she can be."

"Don't worry about it," Tristan said sincerely. "I can only imagine how tough the transition can be."

King nodded and opened his wallet. He plucked out his business card and handed it to the nurse. "I want you to personally call me on my cell if she acts up again. Your job is difficult enough without her sour attitude."

"I appreciate it." Tristan took the card into his hand. "But I'm sure there'll be no need for me to call."

King was skeptical. Something caught his eye and he asked about it. "Will you be running in Sunday's race?"

Tristan cocked his head to the side and gave King funny look.

King pointed the bright green wristband Tristan was wearing. "I recognized the wristband."

"Ah, yes." Tristan looked at his arm. "No, I won't be running. But I am the safety director so I'll be there throughout." Tristan smiled. "What about you?"

King thought about how Avery was pushing him to compete. "Still undecided. But, if I do, I don't plan on setting any records."

The men shared a friendly laugh and King turned and headed for the exit. On his way out the door, Tristan called out, "Detective." King stopped and turned. "If you do decide to run, good luck."

"Thank you," King said, pushing the door lever open with his hip, feeling the dry heated air hit his back.

"It's supposed to be a hot one."

CHAPTER TWENTY-SEVEN

"PATROL JUST KNOCKED ON BOYD'S DOOR." ALVAREZ watched King get situated behind the steering wheel. "No one was home."

King closed his car door and fixed his gaze on the GPS perched on the car dash. "Then what address is that?"

Alvarez shifted his eyes to the screen. "Boyd's last known place of employment."

They shared a look. King started the car and began to back out. It wasn't far from where they were, and King knew the importance of getting ahead of this before something bad happened again.

Alvarez asked, "Everything good with your mother?"

"Cranky and pissed off as always." He stopped and put the car into gear. "So, yeah, she's doing great."

Alvarez chuckled. He knew Carol King about as well as he knew his own mother. "It will take some time, but she'll get used to her new quarters soon enough."

King knew as much, but with him being the target of some lunatic's games, this was the best place for his mother—even if she didn't recognize that yet.

Twelve minutes later they were pulling the frontend of their vehicle into the auto shop where they hoped Orville Boyd was still employed. The place was small, only having two garage bays available. A dozen cars were waiting to be serviced and another half-dozen ready to be picked up.

"American made models," Alvarez said at first observation. "My kind of guy."

Together they stepped out and entered the garage to the sounds of a radio playing classic rock. A pair oil stained legs was sticking out from beneath a Ford Bronco.

"I'll be with you just one moment," the man said from under the car.

"Take your time," King said, peeking his head into the office. He read the name Mike Kern on the business cards at the register and greeted the leashed golden retriever curled up in the corner, snoozing the day away.

"Can I help you?"

King introduced himself. "And that's my partner John Alvarez."

The man flicked his gaze between them. "What can I do for you, Officers?"

King asked, "Are you Mike Kern?"

Mike glanced at Alvarez, still wiping the grease and oil off his hands. "I am. What's this about?"

"Orville Boyd." King paused before asking, "Does he still work here?"

"Not for some time now," Mike said. "He stopped coming into work and I was forced to let him go. Last I heard, he picked himself up a shift at the trash recycling plant there in Arvada."

Alvarez looked to King.

"Why you ask?" Mike tossed the oil rag on top of a bucket behind him. "This isn't about those cases from years ago, is it?"

King stepped forward. "Have you talked to Mr. Boyd since you let him go?"

Mike shuffled his feet, openly staring without blinking. Then he nodded. "He showed his face just last week. Showed up out of the blue."

"What did he want?"

Mike shook his head, pulled at his collar. "I don't know if he was drunk or on drugs but he wouldn't shut up about how the cops ruined his life. Maybe he was looking for sympathy from me. Which he didn't get." Mike wagged his finger at King. "Did he do something?"

"What makes you think he did?" Alvarez asked.

Mike snapped his attention to Alvarez. "Jesus, oh God, he did, didn't he?"

King brought Mike's focus back around. "Tell us more about Boyd's visit last week."

Mike said, "I thought he was just talking out of his ass—"

"What did Boyd tell you he was going to do?"

"I can't say." Mike cast his gaze to the tips of his boots. "The guy is nuts-o. Heck, I'm afraid he might wake up and decide to kill me for having to let him go. You just never know with people like that."

"What did he say he was going to do?" King asked again.

Mike inhaled a deep breath and sighed. "He said he would make sure those cops that ruined his life would pay for what they did to him."

CHAPTER TWENTY-EIGHT

I COULD FEEL WALKER'S KNEE BOUNCE WITH EXCITEMENT from the backseat of my car. Though I didn't show it, I felt like I was quickly losing control of the entire situation.

Walker was proving to be the liability I'd feared, and Dawson was doing what he could to hang on to his best crime reporter. Unfortunately for me, I was stuck between a rock and a hard place and no one was giving me the chance to set the record straight.

I kept stealing glances at Walker's reflection in the rearview mirror thinking how I should have never brought him into the newsroom—let alone agreed to have him shadow us for the day. It was a mistake on my part, but he needed to understand that he'd crossed a line with what he said to Dawson and I couldn't allow it to happen again.

Flipping around in my seat, I turned to face Walker. "What you did in there could have cost me my job."

Walker's knees stopped bouncing. He rolled his gaze to me and said, "I apologize for my slip of the tongue. Sometimes I forget how the game of bureaucracy is played."

I ground my teeth. I couldn't believe how out of touch he

was. A part of me wondered if that was his intention. What did Erin see in him that I couldn't? We locked eyes and didn't let go. I didn't have it in me to scream at him like I was already doing inside my own head. Instead I said, "This ride-along today is a privilege. You understand? I can drop you off at any moment. And as far as turning us into stars, Erin and I can do that ourselves."

Walker arched a single brow as if mocking me for being so dramatic. "Is that what you want? To climb the mountain yourselves?"

Erin reached her hand over the console and gently touched my knee.

"What did Dawson give you?" she asked, attempting to change the subject.

My heart was knocking hard enough to form pellets of sweat along my hairline. My mood was wildly swinging and I wondered if seeing Angelina with King was a factor to my building anger. I couldn't seem to let that go, either.

Erin kept tapping at my knee, each tap getting harder.

I could practically hear her thinking, *Sam, don't ruin this for us,* but Walker needed to be dealt with.

"I saw him push something into your hand." Erin stopped tapping. "What was it?"

I'd glanced at the note Dawson gave me on our walk to the car. I didn't know how Dawson acquired it, but I knew what he wanted from me. He'd given me the map to find it.

Walker asked, "Who's Detective King?"

Ignoring Erin, I asked Walker, "What else do you know about the Pillow Strangler?"

Everyone was on their own agenda jockeying for position. We were going nowhere fast.

Walker's eyes crinkled. I was still surprised by him knowing so much about Orville Boyd. Though I'd looked in the folder he made for me back at his office, I hadn't seen anything about the case. So how did he know? I must have just missed it when flipping through the dozen or so cases. But now I needed to know why it was on *his* radar.

"It's laid out in the folder I gave you." Walker raised his chin. "But you should have known that."

Was King's name mentioned in the folder, too? Did he know that King worked the Pillow Strangler case? Did he know that *I* did?

"Homicide Detective Alex King is with the DPD," Erin said, answering Walker's question for me.

I gave her a look of disbelief and her eyes flickered with the same heated fire as my own.

Walker was still staring into my eyes when he asked, "You have a special relationship with him?"

"You can say that."

Walker caught on. "Isn't that a conflict of interest?"

"Not when our interests are shared."

Walker smiled. "You're more business savvy than you give yourself credit for, Mrs. Bell."

Was he suggesting the only reason I was with King was to get information from him? If he was, he couldn't be further from the truth. I bit my tongue when, suddenly, Walker launched into telling us everything he knew about the Pillow Strangler.

Erin and I listened with open ears, waiting for him to tell us something we didn't already know. But it never came. Walker finished by saying, "It wasn't about robbery or sexual assault. Just a simple pleasure found in killing victims who couldn't fight back."

I hated to admit it, but I was impressed.

"I need to see who this weak man is with my own eyes," Erin mumbled, her thoughts shifting to Orville Boyd.

Walker continued on with Boyd and told us his age, relationship status, where he went to high school, and the names of those who bullied him. Now he had my full attention, too. I wondered where he learned everything and how he knew it all without referencing any notes.

"When it comes to someone like Boyd," Walker said, "it's your classic case of a middle-aged loner looking toward something that will bring him the attention he believes he deserves."

Walker knew more about Boyd than I did. I saw the first glimmer of learning to work together. As if reading my mind, Walker said, "We're in this together, Mrs. Bell. Whether you want to admit it or not. We need each other."

Erin flashed me a knowing look. Walker was right; I didn't want to admit we needed each other, but it appeared we did.

"At least until you decide you don't."

Erin covered her mouth to stifle her laugh. I started the car and put the wheels in motion. "Dawson gave me Boyd's address," I said, finally telling her what was inside the note.

"I knew it!" Erin slapped her hands together. She twisted around and looked to Walker. "We've got ourselves a story, everyone."

CHAPTER TWENTY-NINE

TWENTY MINUTES LATER, WE PULLED UP TO A QUIET single-story house tucked securely at the end of a cul-de-sac. The grass was left unkempt and the yard had been taken over by weeds.

Erin asked, "Are you sure this is where he lives?"

From what I remembered of Boyd, this was the way he preferred to live. In squalor and deprivation, a direct result of his debilitating depression he'd suffered throughout his life.

"It's the address Dawson gave me," I said.

"Then we should check it out," Walker said from the backseat.

I asked Walker, "What does your research say?"

"Some said he moved to Oregon, others said he headed south and is now residing in Mexico." As Walker briefed us on the different theories about what might have happened to Boyd, I noticed that his house wasn't too far from where he lived when the world turned on him.

"I thought I heard he changed his name," I said.

"Though it would have been smart," Walker said, "it was only rumor."

Erin unbuckled her belt and said, "Sometimes the best hiding is in plain sight."

Indeed, she was right, I thought as everyone sank deep into their own thoughts as if preparing for what was to come. Despite how the house appeared to be empty, I prepared myself to face Boyd for the first time in six years. I didn't know what to expect. So much time had lapsed, he could be anybody now. But if I was right about anything, I knew Orville Boyd wouldn't be thrilled to see me.

As silence swirled around me and I stared at what we thought was Boyd's house, I remembered everything I'd written about him—everything backed by sources and information ethically obtained—and not once did he change his own story or admit guilt. He maintained his innocence throughout, even when everyone seemed to be blaming him for the murders that stacked up throughout the city. But now with Peggy Hill's murder resembling the crimes Boyd was being accused of committing, I had no choice but to confront him and see how he reacted to the accusations.

"Well," Erin turned to me, "should we see if he's home?"

I flicked my gaze to the rearview mirror. Walker was unusually quiet, his knee still. He was staring at the house and I couldn't help but notice his face had gone pale.

The corners of my lips pulled into a smirk as I sensed his fear. It was good he was afraid. Fear was what would keep us alive if something happened.

"Here's how it's going to go down," I said, setting the ground rules for Walker. I twisted around in my seat, needing to make sure he understood the risks. Then I saw what was in his lap and asked, "Are you on your phone?"

He turned the screen to me. "Gemma."

"You've got to be kidding me." I snapped my neck and looked at Erin. "Tell him, will you?"

Erin met Walker's gaze and explained, "Everything we do

needs to stay between us. We can't risk contaminating jury pools, driving our primary story underground, or spawning hoaxers which will only make finding the truth that much more difficult."

"Understood." Walker nodded.

"And that includes Gemma," I said.

Walker held his breath and flicked his eyes to Erin before finally agreeing. "Okay. Everything stays between us."

Inhaling a deep breath, I gripped the steering wheel feeling somewhat satisfied by his response. But I couldn't allow him to mess things up. Our job was about uncovering the truth, not chasing ratings. Today, it was my show and he'd do what I said. This case was personal for me and I wanted to do right by King.

I opened my car door first and gave Walker one more piece of instruction. "Now, don't say anything and certainly don't touch anything. Got it?"

Walker lifted his hand and mock saluted me.

With car doors closing, we looked up and down the block before turning our attention to the house. Erin checked the mailbox and, as soon as it opened, envelopes spilled out of it.

"Whose name is on the mail?" Walker asked.

I snapped my finger and pointed in his direction. His mouth clicked shut. "No matter what happens, don't move away from the car," I said.

Walker rooted his hands into his hips and sighed. As I moved toward Boyd's residence, I heard him whispering notes to himself.

After Erin confirmed Boyd's name was indeed on the mail, she asked, "What are we going to do if he is here?"

"Still enjoying our date with Walker?" I asked quietly as we approached the front door.

By the look in her eye, Erin still believed Walker's investment in our company was a good thing. "Just be easy on the guy," she said. "He's a hobbyist sleuth who has the resources to really turn our show into something bigger than we've ever imagined."

I whispered, "He has a strange obsession of wanting to get into the mind of the killer."

Erin shortened her gait and said, "We can do a lot of good with that money. Just give him a chance."

"I haven't dropped him at the curb yet, have I?"

Erin glanced back at Walker standing near the car, foot on the curb. "It appears you have."

Touché. I knocked on the front door and, when there was no answer, I tried spinning the knob. "It's locked."

Erin peeked through the window. "Curtains are drawn, too."

I turned and glanced over my shoulder. What had Boyd been doing all this time? Why did he stay in the Denver area? Was I partially responsible for ruining a perfectly innocent life, or was he really guilty?

"If I were him," Erin said, "I would have moved out of the city as soon as my name dropped out of the daily news cycle."

I would have done the same, and I thought about all those things as I stood on stiff legs anticipating the door opening at any second. Erin knocked again and a second later we heard the backdoor slam shut.

My eyes popped wide open. "Did you hear that?"

As soon as Erin looked at me, we took off running to see what caused the door to slam. I was scared for what was waiting for us, but it didn't slow me down. All I could see inside my head was an equally afraid Boyd running as fast as he could. Except, when we rounded the back, we found nothing.

"I know what I heard," Erin said, breathing hard.

"Me too."

There was no sight of Boyd anywhere, but then we heard the door slam again.

I reached for the top of the privacy fence, gripped the top, and pulled myself up. I peeked over the top when suddenly a black blur leapt six feet into the air. A Rottweiler barked and snapped its sharp fangs at the tips of my fingers just as I released and let go. I fell back to the ground, feeling my heart race.

"It's just a dog door," I said, hunched over and gripping both of my knees. "Boyd's not here."

"Then who is taking care of the dog?" Erin asked as the animal kept barking at us through the fence. Erin shoved her hand through her hair and kept spinning in circles, looking for any sign of Boyd. "What do you want to do, Sam?"

With my hands on my hips, I thought about our options —thought about Peggy Hill and my desire to cross Boyd off my list of suspects. Then I noticed Walker had disappeared. "Oh, shit," I said. "Where did he go?"

Erin's posture slumped just before we jogged to the front of the house looking for Walker. He wasn't by the car, or hiding from the sun beneath the tree spread out like an umbrella in the front yard. I spun in circles until I heard a window break on the other side of Boyd's house.

"You got to be kidding me?" Erin took off running toward the sound of shattering glass.

I followed and we were both shocked to find Walker staring down into a window well. I hit the brakes and noticed the glass was broken just as I suspected. I asked, "What did you do?"

"I didn't do anything," he said.

"Then how did that happen?"

"I was just walking by when suddenly the glass shattered."

Erin dropped on all fours and peered through the dark hole. "I don't see anything," she said.

None of this made any sense and the guilty look on Walker's face had me once again doubting his ability to be a contributing team member.

Erin pushed herself up and stood. "Boyd has to be inside."

I was staring through the broken glass with my head spinning. I couldn't believe what I heard next.

CHAPTER THIRTY

PATROL OFFICER LESTER SMITH HANDED OVER A PINK SLIP to the driver of the vehicle he'd stopped.

The driver pinched the citation between his fingers and slumped further into his seat as he barely looked at the ticket. With a frown tugging his lips toward the floor, the driver thought something seemed...off. After taking a closer look at the pink piece of paper, he snapped his neck toward the officer.

Officer Smith kept his smile in check at the perplexed look on the driver's face.

"I really hate to be the one to tell you this," the driver said, "but you must have given me the wrong slip." He pushed the paper through the window—the corners flapping as cars passed behind.

"It's the correct slip." Officer Smith grinned. "I'm letting you off with a warning."

The driver's eyes lit up. He couldn't believe his luck.

"Slow down and drive safe. You're approaching a school zone."

"Thank you, Officer. Yes, of course. I'll drive safe and not speed."

Smith turned to his vehicle, smiling as he walked away.

"Why did you fool him like that?" Officer Avery Morgan joined her training officer's side.

Together, they walked back to their police cruiser whose emergency lights were still flashing. Through the sounds of the occasional traffic zipping past, Smith's smile hit his eyes when he said, "An old trick I learned from one of the best."

Now Avery was as curious as ever to hear the rest of the story. "And what trick would that be?" she asked.

"The goal is the same no matter the call of duty," Smith said as they shut their doors, muffling the sounds of traffic. "As police officers, we need to have the public *voluntarily* comply with the law."

Avery was buckling her seatbelt when she said, "So you scared him into compliance?"

"You're on the right track." Smith nodded. "I used simple psychology to get him to think twice about speeding."

Avery sat back and thought the tactic was brilliant. "You make him believe he's getting a ticket, then you quickly swing the pendulum the other way with your surprise."

"Exactly." Smith smiled at his apprentice. "It only works if I have their full attention, and I gain it by manipulating their emotion."

Avery was impressed. "Who was the genius who taught you this trick?"

"My training officer, of course." Smith grinned.

"And does this genius have a name?"

Smith's eyes glimmered as he started the car and merged into traffic. "Marshall King."

Avery's lips parted—she didn't know that Marshall King had been the one to train Smith on field tactics. But now her position was starting to make more sense.

"It's no coincidence that you were assigned to me," Smith said with one hand on the wheel.

"No, it certainly wasn't."

Avery stared out into the baseball fields they passed. Once, not too long ago, she'd played softball on those same fields as a kid. Alex had coached her, and his father Marshall had coached him. Today, school children from her neighborhood played on the swings nearby.

Smith glanced in Avery's direction. "King wanted to make sure you were in good company."

She knew she was. Avery liked Smith, was learning a lot from him. He was confident, calm, patient, *and* courageous. Everything that made conducting police work easier.

"Well, I'll make sure to thank him later," Avery said. "I'll be joining him for a family dinner once our shift is over."

Suddenly, a report about a suspected robbery in progress in a nearby neighborhood crackled to life on the police band. Avery stared at the radio, making note of the address.

"That's just a few blocks away," she said to Smith.

"Respond to the call," he told her.

Avery picked up the receiver and responded to the call. Her heart knocked in her chest, both nerves and excitement flashing before her. Smith flipped on the lights and punched the gas as Avery prepared herself for the most intense encounter of her career thus far. She just hoped that all her training would prepare her for what came next.

CHAPTER THIRTY-ONE

Officer Smith killed the sirens just before they turned onto the dead-end street. Racing to the end of the cul-de-sac, Avery had her eyes peeled for anything fitting the description of their suspects.

They were first on scene, the intensity level high.

"South corner of the building." Smith gave the location of two suspects spotted.

Relaying the message to dispatch, Avery said, "White. Female. Mid-thirties. Early forties. Appear to be unarmed."

As soon as the car stopped, they flung their doors open and drew their guns from their holsters.

"Police. Don't move," Smith shouted to the two women who immediately tossed up their hands. "Step away from the house and approach my vehicle slowly with your hands behind your head." They did as they were told. "Stop. Turn around and slowly get on the ground."

Out of the corner of her eye, Avery caught movement of a third suspect. "Stop! Police!"

She took off running, chasing down the suspect. As soon as she rounded the side of the house, she came face-to-face with a man much bigger than she was. His hands were relaxed down at his side and his legs planted in a wide, confident stance.

"Hands on your head," she shouted.

"Do you know who I am?" the man protested.

"This is your last warning," Avery stated. "Get on the ground and keep your hands where I can see them."

His right hand lifted and Avery's heartrate spiked.

"Hands!" She feathered the trigger, praying to God that she wouldn't have to use it.

"Easy," the man said. "Don't shoot. My names is Walter Walker and I'm armed."

"You're what?" one of the women behind Avery shouted.

Nerves sent her entire body into an intense sweat. "Where is your weapon?"

The man curled his wrist and pointed to his left armpit.

"Keep your hands where I can see them." The man angled to the side and Avery was completely on edge. "Don't move!"

Walker raised his hands and slowly dipped to both knees as he stared Avery in the eye from over his shoulder. "I'm not the enemy here," Walker argued. "I have done nothing wrong."

As soon as his first knee planted into the ground, Avery rushed the suspect and placed the heel of her boot between both shoulders, shoving his face into the grass. She quickly disarmed the suspect before restraining his hands behind his back.

"You better have a good reason for this," Walker grumbled into the grass.

Her heart was beating so fast she didn't know what to say.

"In fact, why don't you just tell me your name and badge number so I can speed up the process when I do call my lawyer."

"Officer Avery Morgan—"

"Well, Officer Morgan, you just messed with the wrong person."

CHAPTER THIRTY-TWO

"I'm out of here," Patty O'Neil said quietly as she leaned inside Allison's office. "You need anything from me before I leave?"

Allison glanced at the time. She didn't know where the day went, but it was nearly six o'clock. "No. I should be leaving soon, too." She turned her tired eyes to her colleague and smiled. "Have a good night."

Without thinking, Allison turned back to her computer monitor and closed out the last of her client's ad accounts, making sure they were set for the night. All day she hustled to cross off her list of tasks between putting out the fires that arose with a handful of her clients. Thinking about the traffic and conversion conference, she noticed Patty was still standing at the door.

Allison swiveled around in her chair and asked, "What is it?"

Patty stepped inside the office and lowered her voice. "It's your cousin. He's been sitting in there doing nothing most of the day."

Allison knew Patty didn't mean anything other than to let

Allison know she'd forgotten about him. But, still, Allison didn't like the image it sent for company morale. "Shit," Allison muttered as she stood.

"I'd love to help with the transition." Patty caught Allison's eye. "All you need to do is ask."

Allison stopped and smiled. "I know, honey. I'm just not sure I know what to do with him yet."

"I'll give it some thought tonight. I'm sure we can come up with a list of things he can do." Patty wished Allison goodnight again and headed out the door.

As soon as Patty was gone, Allison walked down the hall to where she'd last left Marty. This morning. She found him still tucked behind his computer, live streaming the Colorado Rockies game. He glanced in her direction and she pulled up a chair to watch the game with him. When the inning ended, Allison said, "I'm sorry for leaving you here with nothing to do."

"Best job I've ever had," Marty teased.

"Well don't get used to it." Allison tipped forward, resting her elbows on her knees. "It's not as glamorous as it looks."

Marty looked uneasy when he said, "Truth is, this isn't my thing. I'm not a computer guy."

Allison flicked her eyes to the screen. "You've managed to stream the game."

"Anyone can do that."

"I know it's not easy, and I'm still trying to figure out how best I can use you."

"I can find another job."

Allison had her doubts, and certainly didn't want him to be turned down again and again because of his history. Looking him in the eye, she asked, "Are you hungry?"

Marty's eyes sparkled at the thought of food. He pressed his hands to his stomach and swiveled back and forth in his chair. "Starving."

"C'mon." Allison used his shoulder as a crutch as she stood. "Let's get some dinner."

As they locked up the office and headed out the door, Allison hoped food could get Marty talking about what kind of expectations he had for himself. She didn't want him to think she had all the answers when it came to living his life. She needed to hear it from him—make sure he had a voice.

"What are you in the mood for?" she asked, when a woman's voice caught her by surprise.

"Allison Doyle?"

Allison spun her head forward and gave the woman a quick once-over. "Yes. That's me."

"My name's Gemma Love." She took a hesitant step when seeing Marty. Turning her gaze back to Allison, she continued, "I would have called, but I was in the neighborhood and, well, thought it would be better to speak to you in person. Do you have a moment?"

Allison glanced to Marty, then flicked her eyes back to Gemma. "What's this about?"

Gemma kept stealing glances at Marty, raking over what Allison knew to be prison tattoos. Marty stood there looking like Allison's personal security detail and was apparently an intimidating sight to be seen.

Gemma said, "A private matter."

"Look," Marty said, "we can do dinner another time."

Allison volleyed her eyes back and forth between them, wanting to go with Marty but also curious to what this woman wanted. "Perhaps we can schedule a time to meet tomorrow," she said to Gemma. "We were just on our way to dinner."

"I'm sorry, but this can't wait." Gemma tightened her grip on her purse strap. "It's imperative I talk with you tonight."

Marty slid his thumb through the strap of his duffel bag and said, "Go on."

Allison looked up at her cousin. "What are you going to do?"

"Don't worry about me. There's always basketball at the park." Marty was backpedaling up the sidewalk when he said, "I'll see you back at the house."

"At least let me take your duffel."

"Go." Marty smiled and turned on a heel.

Allison glanced to Gemma—asked for one second with her eyes—and hurried to catch up with him before Marty got too far. "Here, take this." She handed Marty the twenty-dollar bill given by the stranger outside the coffee shop earlier. "Use it to buy yourself a burger or something."

"One day," Marty took the twenty, "I'll pay you back."

"Don't worry about it." She pushed herself up on her toes and hugged her cousin. "I'm just glad to have you home."

CHAPTER THIRTY-THREE

IT HAD BEEN AN UNBELIEVABLY CHALLENGING AFTERNOON and I was still thinking about Walker. I had to convince Erin to forget about him. King opening his door snapped me to the present and what mattered right now.

Scents of pasta drifted over his shoulders as I smiled into his soft gaze. Stepping forward, King clamped his hands into my soft hips and pressed his lips against the center of my forehead.

"It's so good to see you," he murmured, forgetting everything that happened this morning.

After a brief thought about Angelina, I leaned forward and slid my hand around his tight waistline. Pushing my opposite hand up the center of his chest, I stood on tip toes and pulled his mouth down over mine.

We kissed and it felt like home to be held inside his protective arms.

I still couldn't believe what transpired at Boyd's residence only a few hours ago. I was certain Walker was going to have his lawyers sue the department by how aggressive Avery had stuck her boot into the center of his back. But he deserved it, even if he had the paperwork to legally carry a concealed firearm.

"It's good to see you, too," I whispered against King's lips.

Not only could Walker have gotten himself killed, but he put us all in danger because he was packing heat. I was still mad at him but refused to let it ruin my night. The smells of dinner were tempting my empty belly to step inside the house. If King kept holding me like he was now, I'd rather starve than be let go.

"You promised I wouldn't be a third wheel, Alex." Carol King called out to us from the living room couch.

Alex reached behind his back and shut the door.

"Hey." I took my bottom lip between my teeth and slapped my hand over his heart. "That's no way to treat your mother."

King's eyes hooded. "Just one more kiss."

King's kiss was better than his last and it had my toes curling deep into my flats when we both pulled back and laughed. I nuzzled my nose in the crook of his neck and as soon as we stepped inside, I asked if he'd heard from Avery.

King moved to the kitchen, glancing at the clock on his way. "Still a little early, but I told her to stop by whenever she was finished with her shift."

He made no indication he knew what happened and I debated whether or not I should tell him. I didn't want tonight to be awkward, but all I kept hearing were the vile threats Walker spat into Avery's ear.

"How was your day?" King asked.

I hemmed and hawed my way toward the inevitable, deciding how best to describe my day. It ranked up there with one of my worst, never truly recovering from walking in on him and Angelina.

I said, "I don't want to discuss work."

King lifted a bottle of red wine and I nodded.

I sat on the stool, mulling over how Avery was beyond apologetic—nearly embarrassed—when she realized her partner was frisking me. But I understood. She was just doing her job—and so were we—but I still needed to know who called the police on us. If Boyd was hiding out inside, watching it all go down. We never did find out, but maybe King knew.

King slid my half-full glass across the counter and I joined Carol in the living room who was busy polishing off her own drink.

"How is your new home?" I asked.

Carol gave me a sideways glance. "It's worse than prison. Same smells. Same crazy people yelling out in the middle of the night. I can't stand the place."

Alex was chopping vegetables for a salad when he reminded his mother, "You've never been inside a prison."

Carol turned her head just enough so Alex could hear what she had to say. "No. But I've heard stories. Your father was a very descriptive storyteller and I believed what he said."

We chatted about my job, and I asked if she was still painting. We talked about Mason and what I was going to do when the *Times* went out of business. Then a look of concern fell over her face when she asked King, "Alex, it's not like Avery to be late; shouldn't you call?"

I glanced at the time. Carol was right. Moving to the kitchen, I finally thought I had the courage to tell King what happened today.

"She's probably just getting worked hard by that old dog, Smith," Alex said to his mother, wiggling his eyebrows as he watched me come back into the kitchen. When I stood next to him, he lowered his voice to a whisper and said, "Smith is probably reviewing what happened at Boyd's house earlier today."

The look I gave him was an admission of guilt.

"You really shouldn't have been there," he said. So he did know.

"Why? Is there something I should know?" I asked after telling him my side of the story.

King set down the knife and sighed. "We're looking for him too, you know?"

I told him everything I knew. How Boyd seemed to have been hiding in plain sight, the dog that nearly bit off my fingers, and the mysterious window shatter. It was all in the report, but what wasn't was how I still didn't know if Walker was behind the broken window or not. Walker said he was innocent and I wanted to believe his story. His concealed weapon that he kept secret until the worst possible moment made me skeptical of everything he said.

"What are you doing with a guy like Walker, anyway?" King was back to chopping vegetables for the salad. "He sounds like trouble." I couldn't disagree with that.

Carol shuffled her way past the kitchen on her way to the bathroom. "Who's trouble?"

Alex swept his gaze to his mother. "No one, Mom." King's focus was back on me. "Listen, going after a guy like Boyd is dangerous enough. When you add Walker's inexperience, you never know what might happen."

He didn't have to tell me. I sighed before saying, "He wants to invest in the blog and podcast."

The thin line of Alex's lips lightened as he kept his mouth shut.

"He wants to blow us up," I continued, hoping he'd say something. He just kept chopping vegetables. "I'm not sold. Erin, on the other hand, is ready to dive right in. But there are too many red flags. I don't know his motivation or intention. He is obsessed with cold cases."

That finally got King's attention. "Cold cases? Walk away, Sam. Walk away. Let the police do their job, and you'll get

Real Crime News where you want it in your own time. But walk away."

I appreciated King's concern, but I could sense there was more to his story than what he was telling me. After asking, King mentioned how he stopped in Boyd's old place of employment. "And?"

King pushed his wine glass to the side and palmed the countertop. He held my eyes inside of his for a moment before saying, "The owner said Boyd showed his face just last week, ranting about making sure the cops paid for what they did to him."

I thought about the note King received and wondered if it was Boyd who had given it to him.

"Alex, honey, who are you talking about?"

King was still looking me in the eye when he said, "No one, Mom."

"Did I hear you say Orville Boyd's name?" Carol shuffled her way into the kitchen. "Well, did you or didn't you?"

King's eyes were reluctant to leave mine but, once they did, I felt my lungs expand. "Yes, Mom. You heard correct."

"And you failed to mention this to me because...?"

"It's just work, Mom."

"Like hell it is. I'm the perfect target."

It was impossible not to look at Carol and know she was right.

"Ah, Avery is here," Carol said at the sound of the door-bell, seeming to forget what they were discussing.

"I'll get it," King said, hustling to the door.

I was anxious to speak with Avery myself but I wasn't prepared to face what came next. As soon as King opened the door, everything inside of me went still and my eyes locked with hers.

CHAPTER THIRTY-FOUR

THE SHADOW STALKER MOVED THROUGH THE GLOOM OF the night like a coyote on the prowl. Without drawing attention to himself, he stopped near a tree, bracing himself when tipping his head back and looking toward the sky.

The sky was without the soft glow of the moon and a sea of stars flickered in its place. It was exactly the way he liked it. Dark, mysterious, calm—an unassuming abyss with incredible powers. But what he appreciated most about a moonless night was that it provided the cover he needed to stalk his next victim.

Calmly inhaling, he studied his surroundings while feeling the coarse bark from the tree scrape against the tips of his fingers. Tonight was one of the darkest he'd seen in a while but that didn't keep people from moving about the neighborhood. It was mostly adults at this late hour—the small children tucked safely inside their beds, reading their bedtime stories—fearing people like him would later appear in their nightmares.

Two houses up and on the opposite side of the street, a front porch light flicked on.

The Shadow Stalker turned his head slowly and watched as a middle-aged woman stepped out, collected her mail from the box, and slipped back inside her house without ever realizing she was being watched.

"And that is what makes my job so easy," he whispered to himself as he grinned.

In the night, he was free. No one knew who he was, what he was up to, or what his plans were. Not even the great Inspector King could have anticipated what he'd planned to do tonight. That brought him great delight.

He turned his attention back to the house across the street and thought about how sweet old Peggy Hill didn't quite get King's attention like he had hoped. Not to worry, the Shadow Stalker had a plan—reeling the inspector in closer until they were standing side-by-side.

But he couldn't move too fast. It had to be a natural evolution. Perhaps even spell it out for him. There was a riddle behind each of his clues, but the Shadow Stalker didn't want to make it too obvious for Inspector King, either. He liked playing games, but he liked winning even more. And, so far, he *was* winning.

"One to zero, against the great detective." He smirked.

A car turned onto the street. The Shadow Stalker leaned into the tree, pressing his weight against the trunk until he became one with the bark. The car passed without slowing and as soon as it was gone, the Shadow Stalker opened his wallet to double check the address he'd written on the back of a punch card.

"A perfect match," he said, confirming he was looking at his next target's house.

Tucking the card behind the same worn twenty-dollar bill as was before, he continued to wait. The minutes passed, but time wasn't any concern to him. He had the entire night ahead of him. He'd been waiting his whole life for this moment and wasn't in a rush to finish.

Suddenly, the woman appeared in the window.

A flutter of excitement rolled up his spine.

Standing still, he watched as she floated between front rooms, finishing her hair, applying the last touches of makeup. She was incredibly beautiful. Young and vibrant. He wanted to touch her flat belly and firm breasts, get lost between her thick thighs.

Soon, he would, because the world was his oyster.

Without her uniform, she looked like a new woman. As the Shadow Stalker stared with wide eyes—fantasizing about what he wanted to do to her—he couldn't help but think how tonight would put the inspector's skills to the test.

The woman stopped in front of the mirror one last time, fluffed her hair and took her purse into her hand. She was nothing like his last victim but would most definitely mean something to Alex King. And that was the point the Shadow Stalker was trying to make. Because this wasn't about her. It was about him. It was about bringing the two of them together for a long overdue reunion.

The lights in the house went off and the front porch light turned on.

A second later, the woman stepped out and locked the house behind her. Trotting up the block, she moved with purpose. The Shadow Stalker paused for a moment before following. Staying hidden in the shadows, he kept his head down but his nose up.

"You smell that, Momma, it smells like flowers at a funeral," he joked as a warmth bloomed across his chest.

Zeroing in on his target, he felt his pupils dilate when seduced with the thought of killing her.

The woman turned up the next block and headed for the bright floodlights in the park.

"Yes. That's it." His words passed over his lips in tiny raspy breaths. "That is where we will meet."

He'd played this exact scene over inside his mind so many times before, he could recite it perfectly. The way it had to happen. The marks on her body he needed to leave behind. Where the attack needed to take place and exactly where the body needed to be left.

The clues.

The riddle.

Every detail planned accordingly in order to paint the familiar picture.

Calculation was key to delivering the perfect message to the inspector. It had to be presented in perfect fashion.

Skirting the chain link fence, he watched as the woman quickened her steps once inside the boundaries of the park. The last of the night's games of kickball and softball were winding down and the Shadow Stalker could hear the teams planning which bar to continue the party at as they congregated and moved in swarms toward the parking lot.

Then, as if a miracle occurred, the lights turned off at the exact time the woman neared the ravine of overgrown bushes and tall trees. He watched her stop and swivel her head on her shoulders, looking for light with her phone in hand.

Even from a distance, he could see the fear flashing over her vibrant eyes. In her brief moment of distraction, the Shadow Stalker saw his opportunity and went for it.

Without bringing attention to himself, he swiftly flanked his target from the side and swallowed her up into his arms. It happened so fast, she didn't know what hit her. Muffling her cries with his gloved hand, they disappeared into the grassy ravine without ever being seen.

"You should know better than to walk through the park alone at night," he whispered into her ear as she fought to free herself from his anaconda strength grip. "Didn't Inspector King tell you that it was dangerous?"

The Shadow Stalker laughed his way further into the bushes. Heading toward the black hole where no light reached, the young woman kicked her legs through the air as if swimming to her death.

CHAPTER THIRTY-FIVE

JAMAAL MARTIN WAS RUNNING DOWN THE COURT LOOKING over his shoulder when he suddenly saw the basketball heading straight toward his face. At the last second before impact, he put his hands up in the air to catch the ball but the timing was off and it slipped through his fingers. It bounced off the court and into the darkness.

"That's the last pass you'll be getting from me, butter fingers," Jamaal's friend Paul said.

"It's impossible to see," Jamaal argued.

The floodlights in the park had been out for nearly an hour but the boys kept playing ball, using the streetlights as their guide. Basketball was there life. Rain, snow, or shine, they played—even on a night as dark as tonight, the game went on.

"You hear that, boys?" Paul strode down the court, talking his head off like always. "Jamaal is having trouble seeing in the dark."

Mason Bell and the other boys laughed—too afraid to admit they were having trouble seeing as well.

"Here's an idea," Paul said. "Why not have Jamaal join you

two and I'll destroy each and every one of you all by my lone-
some self?"

Jamaal stood with his hand planted into his hips, rolling
his eyes at Paul. The other boys were too afraid to speak out,
but Jamaal knew they, too, wanted to call it quits.

"No takers?" Paul looked to each of them.

"I'll play," someone said from the shadows.

Paul's head lifted as he turned to see who had accepted his
challenge. Squinting his eyes, he watched a dark silhouette
step up to the court. "Who said that?"

The stranger showed his face, tossing their ball back to
Paul. "I did."

Paul caught the ball which was passed with incredible
strength. He looked the man up and down, assessing his
worth. Though a teenager, Paul stood taller than most men
twice his age—including the big muscled stranger who looked
more like a linebacker than a basketball player.

"You want to play me?" Paul laughed. "Sorry, but I don't
want to humiliate you."

The boys kept their chuckles to a minimum, smart
enough to know when to keep their smart remarks to themselves. But this was their court, their turf, and Paul proved
day after day that he was the best who played on it. If they
were in the park, they had rights to the game first, and
anyone who challenged them faced an uphill battle. They
were the best at what they did and they were arrogant
because of it.

The stranger dropped his duffel to the ground and
stepped onto the court, challenging Paul. "Let's see what
you got."

"It's two on two, old man," Paul said, holding the ball
under one arm. "Take a seat on the bleachers and maybe
you'll earn your turn after I clean up what I started with these
other fools."

"Forget it. I'm outta here," Jamaal said, turning to Mason. "Yeah, me too," Mason said.

Paul looked to his friends, already walking away from the court. "Fine, old man. One on one. You and me. But as soon as I beat you, I'm gone." He tossed the ball into the stranger's chest—who caught it with a thud—and the stranger immediately took off, sprinting toward the hoop.

Jamaal heard a swish and the stranger made sure Paul knew that he was first to score.

"Dumbass," Jamaal said, getting Mason to laugh.

Heading home, Jamaal talked about getting something to eat when a whimpering from the bushes near the ravine caught his attention.

Jamaal turned to look at Mason. "Did you hear that?"

Mason had heard it, too, but didn't want to admit it sounded human. "Probably just a coyote or somethin'."

Then they heard it again and Jamaal's heart raced faster.

Toggling the flashlight app on his cell phone, Jamaal shined the light into the tall grass. It was difficult to see, but then he spotted something that looked like the bottom of the shoe. Moving beneath the thick canopy of trees, he pushed his way deeper into the bush.

"Holy shit," he yelled back to Mason. "It's a body."

Mason turned and looked behind him. They were alone. "Are they alive?"

Jamaal took another step closer, thinking it wasn't a he but a she. "She looks dead."

Mason shook his head and trudged through the tall grass. Peering over Jamaal's left shoulder, he asked, "What should we do?"

Jamaal's palms were sweating as he stared wide-eyed and scared at the bloody woman he wasn't sure was alive or dead.

Mason nudged Jamaal's shoulder. "We have to call 911."

"No way, man." Jamaal flipped around and grabbed Mason by the shirt. "This is the time we run."

Mason slapped Jamaal's hand away and growled. "Fucking call 911. She's going to die if we don't help."

"She's already dead. Look at her." Jamaal pointed to the woman.

Mason swiped Jamaal's phone out of his hand, turned, and made the call. Then Jamaal kneeled closer to see if the woman was still breathing when suddenly the woman's eyes opened.

"Help me," she said. "Please. I'm a cop."

CHAPTER THIRTY-SIX

"THAT WAS DELICIOUS," ANGELINA SAID AS SHE DABBED AT her mouth with her napkin. "You don't know how good it feels to be surrounded by people I consider family."

She had joined us for dinner, not Avery. And I knew she wasn't referring to me when talking about her family. We'd only met this morning, and though I was certain we both knew much more about each other than we were willing to admit, I couldn't believe this was how it appeared I'd end my night.

"You'll always have a place at the table," Carol said with bright eyes.

Angelina kept stealing glances at King and completely avoided my gaze from across the table. I got the sense that she didn't have anyone else now that her mother was gone, but that didn't give her the right to try to take what was mine.

While I could only think about Avery and where she might be, no one mentioned her, seeming to have forgotten her with Angelina's arrival. My concerns for her were growing and I kept glancing at the time, wondering when King would start to worry himself.

"Thank you," Angelina said, making sure King looked her in the eye.

Perhaps King was too wrapped up in consoling Angelina's wounded heart that he didn't remember who he'd invited to dinner in the first place. Either way, I couldn't sit on it any longer.

"Sorry to interrupt, Alex, but shouldn't we check on Avery?"

"Oh, she's fine." Carol pushed her plate forward and turned her friendly gaze to me. Beneath the table, she gently patted me on the knee as if reminding me to stay in my place.

"This meal was fantastic, Alex," Angelina said, inching her arm closer to his.

I sipped my lemon water, wishing the night to be over, when Angelina once again took King down memory lane.

"This reminds me a little of the summer we got engaged," she said without any regard to his current relationship status.

I might as well not have been at the table as Angelina kept reliving their past. It was hard to listen to. My imagination was starting to fool me into thinking I was witnessing the rebirth of their relationship.

King was sitting next to her and they looked great as a couple. Her banter was playful and he laughed at just the right moments. It was clear they were an easy fit—but was she better than me? Doubtful.

I fought to find an excuse to leave, but didn't want to be that woman who created drama out of nothing. Tonight would pass as any other and tomorrow would be a new sunrise. I remained quietly at the table until the conversation moved into Angelina talking about having to sell her mother's house.

"The house is filled with too many memories, I'm not sure

I'll be able to pack them up myself." Angelina bowed her head and everyone cast their eyes to the table. The room went quiet as I listened to the refrigerator hum in the kitchen, waiting for someone to say something. When no one did, Angelina continued, "And, of course, I'll have to start thinking about planning Mom's funeral, too."

I felt bad for her, I did. But her approach to drum up sympathy was just odd. Angelina dabbed at the corners of her eyes. There were tears pooling but she held it together considering the lump I imagined closing her throat.

"Alex will help you with all that, sweetheart." Carol turned her eyes to her son and raised her painted eyebrows as if not giving him a choice in the matter. "Won't you, son?"

Alex flicked his gaze to me and we locked eyes briefly before he rolled them back to his mother. "Of course." He turned to Angelina. "We're here for you. Anything you need, just ask."

Angelina squeezed his hand and, when she did, I couldn't stop myself from immediately looking to see what rings were on her fingers. There was a silver and gold one that matched her bangles sliding up and down her arm, but her ring finger was absent of any kind of metal. I hated to think her leaving the engagement ring behind was done on purpose—but the thought hung there like an elephant in the room.

Carol said, "Alex has a suspect in your mother's case."

"Already?" Angelina sounded surprised.

"Mom," King gave his mother a stern look, "I really shouldn't talk about work."

"Why not? Everyone knows Orville Boyd's name." Carol leaned forward and stared into Angelina's ghost white face. "Don't worry, honey. Alex will catch the son of a bitch who did this. We all loved your mother. Including Marshall, who I know is already showing her around Heaven."

Suddenly, I didn't know where to cast my gaze. I felt

awkward and uncomfortable as I sat across from Angelina, not knowing what to say. But I could imagine how she felt—broken and battered with nothing to look forward to—until now, as she learned the name of the person who might have killed her mother.

"I hope so," Angelina murmured.

Carol had shared too much, too soon, and I could see that Angelina was feeling overwhelmed.

"It's getting late," Alex said after a moment of silence. He stood and began collecting empty plates. Putting them into a pile, I began to help.

Angelina tipped her head back and looked up to King. "The reason you called—"

"Right." King stopped what he was doing. "The ring."

Angelina nodded and King said he'd be back with it. As soon as Alex disappeared into the kitchen, Angelina set her focus on me. I smiled awkwardly just before she asked, "Have you two been dating long?"

"Nine months." I smiled.

"He's amazing, isn't he?"

Angelina's long lashes batted over dreamy eyes that held a knowing glimmer of what she'd given up and what I now held dear to my heart. I didn't know what kind of response she was looking for, but before I could answer she had already jumped into her next thought.

"Your blog has become quite popular, has it not?"

I fingered my water glass. "I suppose it has."

"Well, I find it rather entertaining." Angelina tipped forward in her chair. "If I would have known that you were dating Alex, perhaps I would have taken your information a little more seriously."

My mouth opened but nothing came out. She was digging into me hard. Carol didn't seem to notice Angelina's catty remarks, but I did. Her attack was subtle but sharp. Was she jealous that I was dating her ex? Or was it because of some other reason I didn't yet understand? Whatever it was, I only felt more uncomfortable with her being here and I couldn't wait for one of us to leave.

As soon as Angelina heard King step back into the room, she brushed her bangs off her eyes and turned to smile at him. I watched her lips curl with the same look of satisfaction one experienced after squishing a pesky mosquito. King held out the ring and I watched Angelina pinch it between two fingers. Her head angled to the side as she stared at it.

"Is that your engagement ring?" Carol blurted out. "What's it doing here?" she asked King, sounding equally surprised.

I said under my breath, "Left at the bathroom sink."

Angelina was still staring at the expensive diamond glittering beneath the light. "I must have left it here by accidence, but honestly, my memory has been splotchy since... well, last night."

"Funny to still be wearing it," I said.

King gave me a look of disappointment. It was a rude comment, but Angelina had already crossed a line. I was tired, ready to call it quits on the night.

"I don't remember wearing it." She looked up to King. "Not since we broke up."

"It was your mother's, wasn't it?" Carol asked.

Angelina confirmed it was. She thought she could have picked it up last night when she learned that her mother's house was broken into. "I can't believe this wasn't taken. If they knew how much it was worth..."

Carol launched into another story about Angelina and Alex dating, then asked, "Did your mother still have those engagement photos? I loved those pictures of you two. So did Marshall. They were absolutely perfect."

"I believe she did," Angelina said. "You know how she was. Mom never got rid of anything."

Carol's face beamed. "I'd really love to see those sometime."

I finished my water and watched Angelina slide the ring onto her empty ring finger. Shaking my head, I excused myself from the table and went into the kitchen to make a pot of coffee when I heard Angelina say to King, "Mom never let go of hope that one day we'd get back together."

Gripping the counter's edge, I leaned over the kitchen sink. Closing my eyes, I was just about willing to do anything but sit through more of their stories that were making me doubt what I had with King.

I busied myself with cleaning the kitchen and, after several minutes, King snuck up behind me at the sink. My thoughts were on how Angelina mysteriously replaced Avery for dinner and changed the entire course of our night, making it all about her.

When King's arms constricted around my torso, I turned to face him.

"Are we okay?" I asked.

His brows pinched. "Yeah. We're good."

"I'm worried about Avery," I said, not wanting to let my insecurities drive my emotions.

King had left a voicemail on Avery's cell just before we sat down to eat, but she still hadn't called back.

"She was excited to be coming here for dinner. She told me that," I reminded him. "Will you please call her training officer just to know she's okay?"

King's forehead rested against mine as he held me in his arms. Our noses brushed when he nodded and agreed to call just as his home line started to ring. Taking the phone from the cradle, King answered.

I turned back to the kitchen sink and listened to him talk.

I stopped washing dishes when I heard King's tone change. His voice went deeper, darker, until he'd hit stone. When I twisted around to look over my shoulder, I watched his expression grow serious. When he ended the call, I knew something bad had happened.

CHAPTER THIRTY-SEVEN

WE DROVE SEPARATELY. I HATED FEELING LIKE WE WERE worlds apart. King rushed out of the house without an explanation to Angelina or his mother. It was just work, always work, an ugly reality to the world we lived—something we had to accept if we wanted King in our lives.

My heart was in my throat as I drove. I kept having to dry my sweaty palms on my thighs to keep a tight grip on the steering wheel. I couldn't afford to spin out of control as I fought to keep up with King barreling forward.

King had his sirens blazing, lights flashing. I tailed him, following as close behind him as I could without risking a crash. We drove fast, speeding through red lights and squealing around turns. The spike of adrenalin had reawakened my senses and anything I might have been cursing Angelina about only minutes ago were now gone with the wind.

No one knew what had happened but it was Avery who had been found badly injured in nearby Commons Park. The details were anybody's guess, but I kept saying my prayers, hoping she would pull through her injuries.

I dove my hand inside my tote and reached for my cell phone. Thumbing the screen, I dialed Erin's number. She picked up after the second ring.

"Have you spoken to Walter Walker?" I asked.

"Not since we dropped him off. Why? What's going on?"

I told her about Avery, starting with missing dinner, and then filled Erin in on the initial reports coming in. Avery had been found in the park barely hanging on to life.

"Lord." Erin gasped. "I hope she's okay."

Erin's response nearly killed me. Since Walker pushed his way into our lives, Erin and I hadn't been on the same page. I wished she would have caught on to why I was asking her to call Walker ASAP, but I didn't have time to explain.

Erin didn't mention anything about the threats I heard Walker spitting off like bullets to Avery earlier, but it was the only thing I could hear now.

"Call him," I said into the phone. "Learn his location, but don't mention anything I just shared. Give me a call as soon as you know where he's at."

Two minutes later, I curbed my car behind King's. There was another dozen cop cars already on the scene and an ambulance was sitting idle, waiting on standby. That was never a good sign, but I refused to let go of the little bit of hope I was still clinging to until we knew for sure Avery was okay.

King stepped out and I met him at his door. He wasn't focused and looked worried about what he would find. It was so dark—the crimson and blue lights flashing overhead nearly blinding me—and I swore I watched a part of King leave his body as he looked around, taking in his location as if debating his own safety.

"Go," I said, knowing I didn't need to waste time fighting my way past the police line I'd never get through. He had work to do. We both did.

Detective John Alvarez was waiting for his partner and King dragged me along with him, telling me to stay close behind. As we approached, I knew I wasn't welcome but King tightened his grip and I followed.

"Stay back, Sam," Alvarez said to me. "We're still working the scene. Give us time and maybe we'll get you in here tonight."

King turned his sights on Alvarez. "Where is she?"

Ignoring my presence, Alvarez asked King, "Does this park mean anything to you?"

The look on King's face when we arrived flashed behind my eyelids. Now my mind was churning, wondering what it was he was piecing together but not telling me.

"Where is she?" King grew agitated.

Alvarez's face paled. His eyelids hooded over, his pupils the size of black holes. He flicked his dull gaze to me, then back to King. I knew the look well. It was a look I'd seen hundreds of times before, yet somehow this one was different. When Alvarez shook his head, we both knew Avery was dead.

My entire body went numb and my hand started trembling the moment King let go of it.

King's face went purple just before he wound his hand back behind his head and swung a mighty punch into his opposite hand, sending a quake loud enough to shake the earth below.

I flinched and stood there in absolute shock.

King crumbled to the ground and I fell with him, draping my arms over the backs of his shoulders. His muscles bounced and cried as he grappled with the sudden news of Avery's demise. I couldn't believe it. I'd known something wasn't right—but this? How could this be?

My phone buzzed in my back pocket. I stood and

answered the call from Erin. "Tell me you found him," I said through clenched teeth.

"Sam, Walker's not answering. What should I do?"

Keeping one hand on King's heaving body, I said, "We need to know where he was tonight. It's important we find him ASAP."

"This doesn't have to do with Avery, does it?"

I couldn't tell Erin that Avery was dead, not over the phone. But I was glad Erin was finally hearing what Walker said earlier when snooping around Orville Boyd's house. Instead, I kept my response short. "Just keep trying to track him down."

I ended my call and King had caught his breath and regained his focus. Standing, Alvarez leaned closer and explained more about what they'd found. "There was a message with her body on a twenty."

"From the killer?" I asked.

Alvarez stared, debating whether or not he should say. Then he said, "We're assuming so." He swung his heavy gaze to King. "But it was directly addressed to you."

King stared at his partner, wide-eyed and confused. "To me?"

Alvarez nodded and I pushed my hands through my hair.

"What did it say?" King asked.

Alvarez knew he shouldn't be talking with me there, but he also knew that King's life was being threatened. That made this investigation different "You played one hell of a game, Inspector Alex King."

I turned to King. "Mean anything to you?"

King lifted his gaze and looked to the baseball fields shrouded in darkness. "Who found her?"

I put my hand between his shoulders. "King, what game is this wacko talking about?"

They both ignored me and Alvarez pointed to the teenage

boy still being questioned near a squad car. His head was turned, impossible to see his face. Then Alvarez said, "Your high school team won the championship twenty years ago on this very field, didn't they?"

King stood with a gaze as distant as that memory.

We stood holding our breaths as we waited to hear King's response. My thoughts were grinding hard and I was already piecing together the clues. Whoever attacked Avery was making this a game. It seemed to be the killer versus King. But were they also tallying points? Was this their first kill? Something told me they were, and it wasn't.

King finally snapped out of his thoughts, nodded, and said, "We won that game over there twenty-two years ago this spring."

Alvarez scrubbed a hand over his face and King said he needed to see the body.

"No. Not this time." Alvarez pressed his palm into King's chest, stopping him in his tracks.

King's eyes widened a fraction and I watched his muscles flex. "Get out of my way."

"You remember that case four years back?" Alvarez was still hanging onto King's coat. "The woman brutally beaten and raped in City Park?"

King's jaw ticked as recognition flashed over his eyes. "The one we couldn't solve."

Alvarez nodded. "It's nearly identical."

My mind floated away as I glanced behind me and peered into the growing crowd. I knew the case Alvarez was referring to. It was a brutal, ugly murder. I couldn't stop myself from thinking how this made for the second murder this week to be taken directly from King's cold case files.

"Don't fuck with me," King growled.

"It's true," Alvarez said.

A shiver rocked my core. News vans were arriving. Dozens

of eyes peered through the lights, wanting to know what happened. I still couldn't believe it. My heart was heavy, but my mind was on fire.

Was this about Orville Boyd wanting to get payback, or was there a scarier killer out there who was torturing King, reminding him of his inability to solve big cases? I didn't know. The only sure thing was that King was in more danger than I originally thought.

Suddenly, I locked eyes with the man I had been looking for—the same man I knew for certain had a peculiar fascination with cold cases. Walter Walker stood behind the crowd, staring directly at me. We locked eyes and I watched a smirk curl his lips toward his ears just before he turned and disappeared into the darkness as if his job here was done.

CHAPTER THIRTY-EIGHT

A THIN BEAM OF LIGHT SHOT THROUGH THE DRAPES LIKE the long blade of a glowing yellow sword. The tip of it was flirting dangerously close to the jugular of Gemma Love as she stirred awake in the light.

Turning onto her side, she rolled directly into a wall of muscle.

The man didn't move and she barely opened her eyes as she nuzzled up next to him, his familiar scent as relaxing as wine. Draping her right leg across his muscular thigh, she spooned his naked body as she nibbled his ear and asked, "When did you get in?"

Without opening his eyes, the man spoke in a deep baritone. "Sometime after midnight."

Gemma kissed his neck, slid the balls of her hands down his washboard abs, pushing the tip of her fingers beneath the elastic band of his boxer briefs. "Anything to report?"

He squirmed his way onto his back, pressed a hot hand to her cheek. Her eyes swayed inside of his and instead of answering her question, he fisted her hair and brought her lips down to his for a hard, satisfying kiss.

Gemma mewed, her soft body melting deeper into his chest. By the way he kissed her, she knew his night didn't go as well as he'd hoped. His silence spoke for itself but it was the wave of fear traveling down her spine that had her wondering just how bad it really was.

There were risks involved, the stakes were high. They both understood that nothing came for free. When she asked him again, she hoped he'd relieve her concerns by telling her it was nothing to worry about. Instead, he wiggled out from under her, leaving her cold and alone.

He flipped his feet over the side of the bed and hung his head as he sighed.

Gemma followed her man to the edge, rubbed her hand in small circles across his back. They were in this together, through thick and thin, no matter what.

Then he said in a raspy whisper, "Samantha was there."

Gemma perked up with sudden interest. Her hand stopped moving, the tips of her fingers pressing deeper into his flesh. Suddenly wide awake, a flood of questions rushed to her lips but only one came out. "Did she see you?"

He rolled his neck, looked over his shoulder, and gave a single nod of his head.

"Christ, Walter." Gemma pulled her hand away. "How could you let this happen?"

Walter Walker answered again with silence.

Gemma knew that this was a bad idea. They were out of their league, walking a path where they didn't belong. She knew Samantha was already the broken link to securing their investment, but how were they going to convince her to sign on to their deal after this?

Gemma fell back on her heels and let her gaze fall between the window drapes.

She debated backing out while they were still ahead, but they couldn't just let this go, either. They needed Samantha more than they needed anybody else. She held the keys to the vault of secrets, knew things that no one else knew. And Walker might have blown their chances at obtaining any of that.

"Samantha will want to know why you were there," Gemma said calmly, debating what the implications were of Walker's mistake.

"You think I haven't already thought of that?" His words were harsh, full of personal guilt.

"I'm just saying." Gemma knew Walker was already thinking of his response when the question came. "There's still hope," Gemma said.

Walker turned his head and met her gaze.

"I spoke with Allison Doyle," she said.

Hope flashed over his eyes. "And what did she tell you?"

The corners of Gemma's eyes crinkled with a smile. "Her relationship with King goes further back than we previously thought, but it's unclear if Samantha is aware of just how deep it went."

Walker asked, "Are we wasting our time focusing all our efforts on Samantha?"

"You're not having doubts, are you?"

Walker reached behind Gemma, gripped her hip, and pressed his lips to hers. "I told you they were our best option. And I still believe that."

Pressing her breasts into his skin, she mewed, "But you might have blown our shot."

Walker looked forward, ironing his hands down his thighs. "What's done is done. Maybe it's good that she saw me there."

Gemma's lips parted, wondering how they could spin this into a positive. "She's not stupid, Walter. If anyone will figure this out, it will be her."

"Then this will be the test to prove how great of a detective she is."

Gemma shook her head. "By making the game easy?"

"What is the game, anyway?"

"You know what I want," Gemma said, pulling the sheet further up her chest. "It's what I've always wanted."

Walker spun around and reached for Gemma. "Then if what Mrs. Doyle says is true, this is perfect. Better than we could have imagined." His eyes glimmered as they bounced around her face with sudden excitement. "Christ, how did we not know this before?"

Gemma's eyebrows pinched. "Because we didn't think we had to know it."

Launching to his feet, Walker quickly put on clothes choosing to forgo a shower, and prepared to head out the door.

Gemma was still sitting in bed when she said, "Then let us make sure we don't lose her."

Walker hooked his finger beneath Gemma's chin and stared into her glimmering eyes. He could see that she already had an idea and asked, "What do you have in mind?"

"You leave it to me. Samantha will come around," Gemma said. "I'll make sure of it."

CHAPTER THIRTY-NINE

My eyes were dry and my body felt numb.

Reporting on Avery's death was the hardest story I'd written in quite some time. I kept hearing Avery's voice echo between my ears as I jabbed at the keys. The few times I blinked, I could still see the glimmer of excitement shining in her beautiful eyes that came from the pride of wearing a badge. Now she was gone. We'd never get her back.

I kept asking myself if this could have turned out differently if King had called her earlier. What if we had dinner another night? Would it have changed anything? I wasn't convinced it would have, and it tore me up inside knowing that we couldn't turn the hands of time back and ask for a redo.

My fingers kept tapping the keys as the hours passed. By the time I completed my final sentence and sent it off to Dawson for edits, I fell back into my chair and stared at my screen as Avery's death reached a new level of reality.

I glanced to a photo of Avery and King, the pressure in my chest building. The master and his protégé smiling in each other's arms, a perfect moment captured for eternity.

The tears finally came. My vision blurred as I darted my gaze around the tiny room I had locked myself inside of to hide from the outside world.

I wanted to disappear. Escape from the truth. Avoid the potential dangers that seemed to be blazing a trail straight to King.

As I swiveled around in my chair, my throat closed up and I pressed my hand over my mouth in an attempt to lock everything inside.

But it was useless. The pain was too raw to keep from pouring out. My spine curled and I caught face in my hands. Tears continued to fall like thick rain drops above quivering lips. I buried my face deeper into my hands, not wanting to wake Mason who was sleeping peacefully on the other side of the wall.

Shrouded beneath a dark cloud of depression, I questioned everything. Including the relationship I had with King.

Since Angelina had come back into his life, even the security I found in his presence seemed suddenly fragile. I didn't want to blame him, but it was too easy not to.

What happened to Avery was heartbreaking. A young vibrant life with a promising future stripped away in such an ugly manner. I'd seen the worst mankind had to offer before, but this was different. As I wiped the tears away from my face, I kept thinking about the note tacked on Erin's door telling King to burn in hell.

It was the message that started this all. Set the blaze that now seemed uncontrollable. Now a third message had been left for King. There was little doubt in my mind that these murders were related. I didn't have the proof, and couldn't say how exactly, but it was clear someone was coming after King. That scared the hell out of me.

Who was it and what did they want? I didn't know. How

the hell did Avery get caught in the crossfire? That was the mystery I needed to figure out before the next victim was me.

I scooted forward—the wheels of my chair gliding me to my desk—and flipped through pages of notes I had taken, both past and present. I had little to work with but Orville Boyd was the obvious suspect. With his whereabouts still unknown, I was left with only anxiety.

It felt like I was losing my touch—that maybe I wasn't making the same kind of impact I was used to. I was too close to this last murder to think clearly when suddenly I heard a thumping on my office door.

Wiping the tears away, I prepared to face my son. Hiding all evidence of Avery's death, another thump magnified across the small room.

"Just one second," I said, scrambling to contain the mess. Then I rolled across the floor and reached for the knob.

Cooper nudged the door open with his long snout and made me smile. I rubbed behind his ears as he wagged his tail with his long tongue hanging out of his mouth.

"Hey buddy. You worried I left without giving you breakfast?"

Cooper's ears perked up at the idea of food. I laughed and hugged him, thankful to have my confidant always there for me when I needed him most.

Somewhat relieved it was my dog and not my son, I picked up my cell to see who had just messaged me. It was King asking me to stop by ASAP.

I didn't know if it was Cooper's presence or the weight of last night, but the idea of stepping away from the paper seemed like a good one.

I could take a rest, take a sabbatical and give myself a chance to pursue other interests without constantly being reminded of how dark this world really was. Perhaps even focus on stories of my choosing. But everything I was considering was exactly what Walker was offering. Any other day, it wouldn't be a problem. But I still had my doubts when it came to working with him.

I stared into Cooper's big dark eyes, asking myself what Walker was doing there last night at the park. It unnerved me when remembering his promise to give Avery what she deserved. Could he have been the one to kill her? His presence could have been purely coincidence, but my gut told me it wasn't.

Cooper danced on his toes at the door, antsy to be fed. Before I did that, I reached for the folders Walker presented to Erin and me.

I shuffled my way through the stack of cold cases, hoping to find the article from four years ago that resembled Avery's attack, the same story Walker had linked to another brutal crime. It had to be here, but it wasn't. He kept it only for himself and I asked myself why.

Was I trying to make Walker into the villain? Or did I have him all wrong? Could Erin be right? Was this our opportunity of a lifetime? Was I pushing him away because I was afraid of success?

My head was pounding with pressure. Then my cellphone rang.

"I heard about last night," Dawson said as soon as I answered. "I'm sorry."

"No one knows Avery is dead," I told him, adding how I promised King I would hold off on publishing the fact until Avery's family had been notified first.

Dawson didn't have any objections and made me feel slightly better by saying, "It's a beautiful piece. Avery would be proud."

CHAPTER FORTY

"I'M TELLING YOU HE WAS THERE." AS SOON AS I GOT OFF the phone with Dawson, I called Erin. I didn't have to worry about her being awake. She slept about as well as I did—which meant, hardly at all.

"That doesn't make Walker a suspect," Erin countered.

"Maybe not, but it does make him suspicious."

I needed her to agree with me. Avery deserved justice just as much as Peggy Hill did, but I knew we couldn't continue diving into our next story so long as Walker was around. Our work needed to remain confidential and as long as he remained suspicious, I'd treat him the same as our missing Orville Boyd.

There was a pause on the line before one of us said something we would regret.

I could still hear Erin breathing as I asked myself again if Walker could have attacked and murdered Avery. It certainly seemed plausible. But that would mean that he had also been involved in Peggy Hill's murder.

"You heard what he said to Avery yesterday."

Erin inhaled a deep, controlled breath. "Before we get ahead of ourselves, why not just ask him?"

"And scare him away?" I said, hearing Erin's doorbell ring. "I want nothing to do with this guy."

"Hang on." A rustle through the line had me imagining Erin's bare feet shuffling across her floor. "There's someone at my door."

I had just parked in front of King's house and told Erin we'd finish this conversation later. She didn't object as it gave us both time to decide how we were going to proceed with Walker.

Opening my car door, I stepped out and locked my vehicle before climbing up the stairs leading to King's front door. I wasn't at all surprised to find it locked. Apparently King was feeling as paranoid as I was. That gave me even more reason to feel reserved around the man I loved.

I jabbed the button and listened to the doorbell ring.

Wrapping my arms around my body, I turned to face the street. It was a pleasant morning, on its way to heating up to unseasonably high temperatures. Yesterday's storms never materialized but we desperately needed the rain. A minute later I heard the lock click over. King cracked the door open.

I spun around, anxious to hold him, but his dark eyes and deep wrinkles had me hesitating to jump into his arms. Tucking my insecurities away, I forced a weak smile. "Hey."

His distant gaze traveled over my head and I took a step back.

His hesitation had me retreating into those same insecure thoughts I was trying so hard to avoid. He'd had one hell of a night and it showed in the heavy bags beneath his eyes that were as dark as the drape-drawn room that he stood in front of.

"Can I come in?" I asked.

Our eyes met and I could breathe again.

King's pupils opened a fraction wider. "I wasn't sure you got my message."

I gave him an arched look. "I said I would."

King seemed distracted, not fully present, and was slow to respond. After a brief pause, he nodded his head and stepped to the side. "Yeah. Come inside."

I touched his arm as I passed. He didn't seem to notice. His concern kept him searching the quiet suburban street as if expecting to find someone else.

I didn't want to ask because sometimes not knowing was better than having all the answers.

The door clicked behind me and I turned on a heel and faced him. His swollen, sad eyes avoided mine at nearly every turn. Needing him to be present, I stepped forward and hooked my hands around his neck, clinging onto him as tightly as I could.

It took a minute, but his big hands finally gripped me hard as I watched his eyes close. Pressing his forehead against mine, I nearly broke.

"I'm here," I whispered, knowing he felt personally responsible for Avery's death.

It was important I stayed strong for him. He had the biggest heart of anybody I knew and he deserved to know he wasn't alone during this time of mourning.

"I'm here," I said again, getting King to fist my clothes even tighter.

He didn't have anybody but his mother and I doubted he'd broken the news to her yet. It was just too much, too quick. But I asked him anyway if he had.

He opened his sad tear-glossed eyes and shook his head no.

I could feel his pain as I squeezed my eyes shut, trying my hardest to be his rock. My own feelings of sadness bubbled up inside of me but I remained strong for him.

I held on to him for what felt like hours. I loved how this big strong man felt confident enough to cry in front of me. We went a long time without saying a word. I'd never seen King as shaken up as he was today. Only hours ago, an awkward dinner was our biggest worry. Now we were drifting into uncharted territory. We'd both take last night back if we could—even if it meant me having to sit through more of Angelina's jabs.

"Sam, I don't know what to do."

I met his gaze, my fingers kneading the nape of his neck, unsure of what to tell him or what he needed to hear.

His eyes swayed with mine. "How can I tell Mom that two of her friends have been murdered this week because of me?"

I took his face into my hands and said, "None of this is your fault."

"It is."

"No. You're wrong. It isn't."

He turned his attention to the kitchen table. I followed his gaze and found my core go cold. He'd been looking for answers and it appeared that he might have found what he was after. The problem was, it looked like my worst nightmare.

CHAPTER FORTY-ONE

His service Glock lay on the table for a quick draw. Its muzzle was pointing directly at me. I suspected there was a bullet in the chamber, but that wasn't what had stolen my attention or made me hesitate. Instead, it was what King was attempting to piece together that had me inching my way closer to the kitchen table.

The floor creaked as I traveled over it. Dozens of photographs were spread across the table and, though I didn't know what they were about, I recognized a couple of faces without having to look too deeply.

I looked over my shoulder and glanced back to King.

He was staring at the table, his head hanging lower than normal. He had one hand buried inside his pocket while the other rubbed the back of his neck. A look of uncertainty had me questioning whether or not I should go any further.

Taking my eyes off his crinkled brow, I reached for the photograph nearest me and turned it upright with my fingers. My heart started beating faster. I couldn't believe what I was looking at, but should have known he'd resort to this.

"What is this, Alex?" I asked when referring to his engagement photos with Angelina.

They were beautifully done, just as Carol had said. I hated to admit it, but I could see the happiness in both their faces —the love they once shared, long before King and I became an item.

Why was he looking at these when mourning Avery's death? This certainly couldn't be part of his ongoing investigation. Could it?

King's eyes widened below a tightening brow. He rubbed his face, desperately searching for the words to explain what I was looking at. He couldn't seem to string a sentence together.

As I waited for him to speak, I circled the table like a hawk, looking for potential vulnerability. I took it all in as I reminded myself to breathe. I knew the moment I found Angelina's engagement ring in King's bathroom, she would cause trouble. But I never expected it to get this deep so fast.

My mind was pushing for me to make assumptions, let the accusations fly. Instead, I could only look at King with disbelief hollowing out my chest.

He was still standing with legs wide, feet firmly planted into the floor. He couldn't look at me despite my silent pleas for him to tell me what this was about.

I'm here, I wanted to tell him. *Look at me.* But even as I stared, he never did.

I turned back to the images and asked, "What's this about?"

King sighed before saying, "It's about my dad."

I lowered my brow and cut my eyes to the source of our strife. King licked his lips, visibly swallowed, and moved to the table. He lowered himself into a chair and plucked a photograph of Marshall King out of the pile.

Marshall was sharing a laugh with Angelina. As I watched

King get lost in of the memory captured in time, I needed to know what it was he was thinking.

I said, "Can you please explain this to me, because I don't get it."

"Dad was so angry when he learned we called off our engagement." King's tone was soft as he slowly came out of his shell. It was the hardest thing I had ever done, but I kept my mouth shut and strained to open my ears further, with hopes of understanding him. "He blamed me, of course, for letting her go."

"Why are you telling me this?" My voice was a soft murmur in the quiet room.

King swung his head up to me, locked his eyes on mine. "Because if my father ever had a chance to meet you, he'd realize he was wrong about Angelina."

I struggled to maintain my balance as the air was suddenly knocked out of my lungs. King had completely swept me off my feet with his answer. I was thankful and confused. Without making too much of his professed love for me, I could hear the clock ticking.

"How does Avery fit inside all this?"

I wasn't convinced she did, but she must have if I knew King like I thought I did.

King stood and quickly got to work. His arms fanned out from his sides as his hands swiped from left to right, reorganizing the thoughts shuffling inside of his mind and spread out in front of him.

"My father trained Officer Smith to be the cop he is today."

"And you assigned Smith to be Avery's training officer?" The pieces started to click.

King gave a somber nod and went on to mention the personalized messages he was receiving on twenty-dollar bills —clues left for him at both crime scenes. The included details about his father that not many knew. "Avery just got caught up in whatever this asshole is trying to prove to me."

My thoughts immediately jumped to Orville Boyd—the mysterious Pillow Strangler who we thought might be responsible for her death. He was still missing. When I asked King, he told me how Boyd's house had been under constant surveillance since last night.

"You were right." King looked me in the eye. "I should have called Avery the moment she was late to dinner."

"No. Don't do that to yourself," I said.

He was still blaming himself for what happened. I did my best to keep him on track, hoping he could provide clarity to how Avery's murder was made to look like the case laid out in the article I wrote four years ago—the same headline I saw on Walker's corkboard attached to an older, unrelated case.

"Why was Alvarez so concerned about your high school championship last night?" I asked.

King picked up a photograph and flicked the corner with his finger. "Because that game has everything to do with why Avery's killer chose to murder her there."

I leaned in and took a closer look at the youth championship baseball team King was part of. At the end of his seventeenth year, I could just make out the man he was becoming.

He said, "My dad missed the game that night."

"And that's how this is all connected?" I pinched the skin of my neck, trying to keep up.

"It was the best night of my childhood and Dad missed it." King stared at the image, a memory of mixed emotions still as raw as they were nearly twenty years ago. King picked up his head and looked me in the eye. "Irony is, it was also the best night of his life, too."

I asked what he meant, and he told me about a horrific killer his father had been chasing by the name of Frank Lowe.

I didn't recognize the name, but the case details were vaguely familiar—though I couldn't put a finger on how I knew it.

"Dad made the arrest that night and, because of it, was recognized by the mayor for his efforts."

Complete irony, I thought as my mind traveled back to the boxes of his father's awards we'd rifled through the other morning. "Was he given an award?"

King nodded. "The Merit Award for Excellent Arrest. It solidified my father's legacy as being one of the best DPD detectives to ever work for the city of Denver."

Suddenly, it was beginning to make sense to me. This was the reason King lived in his father's shadow, working tirelessly to live up to the reputation Marshall carved out for his son.

"So, what are you suggesting?" I asked. "We should be looking for Frank Lowe instead of Orville Boyd?"

King shook his head. "Frank Lowe is still in prison."

My thoughts were scrambling, trying to read between the blurry lines.

Since that note on Erin's door, I'd known someone was coming after King, but now it seemed we had the evidence to prove it. But who was it? It had to be someone who knew the specifics to King's past and there was only one person who came to mind—

Angelina Hill.

That didn't explain why Angelina's mother was a victim. Or how each victim was made to reflect a crime from King's past. I had another person's name for that. I had to ask myself if Angelina and Walker knew each other.

There was a light knock on the front door before John Alvarez stepped inside.

King didn't give any indication he heard, so I quietly stepped away from the table and traveled across the room to speak with John in private.

He greeted me with a hug. It was a clear reminder that a cop had been killed and nothing could be taken for granted.

Alvarez asked, "How's he holding up?"

I glanced back to King who was still working the table like a puzzle. He was so deep inside his head he barely noticed we were there. Turning back to Alvarez, I whispered in his ear, "He might be onto something."

Alvarez quirked an eyebrow.

"This is personal. Someone wants to kill him softly."

Alvarez inhaled a deep breath and sighed.

After what King revealed, I was more determined than ever to help him find the suspect he sought. "Keep an eye on him, will you?"

Alvarez closed his hand on my arm and squeezed. "You know I will."

Staring at King, I murmured, "I can't lose him like I lost Gavin."

Then I was out the door to see if my suspicions were right.

CHAPTER FORTY-TWO

ALLISON WAS THINKING ABOUT GIVING MARTY A QUICK education in technology when the knife slipped off the apple and sliced her finger.

"Yeow," she growled through the sharp pain.

Plunging her finger into her mouth, she sucked on the tip to help stop the bleeding and stopped to stare at her breakfast with mild disdain. With the tip of her finger throbbing in her mouth, Allison knew this was the breakfast that would keep her healthy, but what she really wanted was a plate of pancakes, bacon, and eggs to sustain her throughout the long day ahead.

Allison winced as she turned to the faucet and rinsed her finger beneath the cold water. The cut wasn't as deep as she initially suspected, but stung like high heaven. Wrapping it in a paper towel, she turned off the water, grabbed her bowl of food, and sat on the stool at the island counter, trying to remember what she was thinking before she nearly amputated her finger.

Her eyes peered down into her food. "Maybe after the marathon tomorrow I'll trade you in for something heartier."

She took her first bite and looked at her food again with a spurned look on her face. Her breakfast was missing something and she knew exactly what that something was.

"You'd be a lot better with maple syrup," she said to her bowl when suddenly the phone rang.

Her eyes sprang open and she lunged toward her spinning mobile hoping to silence the vibrations before waking her cousin, who she assumed was fast asleep in the back of the house. In the process, she accidentally knocked over a full glass of orange juice with her elbow, sending it crashing to the floor. Allison cringed and answered the call from Susan.

"And I thought my day was starting bad," Susan Young said into the phone after hearing Allison's clipped tone. "What's tightening your bra?"

Allison stared at the orange pool spreading across the floor, then flicked her gaze to her unappetizing bowl of oatmeal. "Breakfast," she grumbled, planting her behind back onto the stool. "And you?"

Susan didn't waste any time launching into a full-scale moment of panic. Allison bent her elbow and propped her head up as she prepared to settle into whatever was bunching up Susan's shorts.

"The marathon is tomorrow," Susan was saying, "and I wake up to find an email stating how the course is being forced to reroute."

Allison arched a single brow and put off cleaning up her mess. "I guess our lunch date is off?"

"Are you even listening to me?"

Allison pushed her bowl to the side and reached for a towel, still thinking about the eggs and bacon she craved. Beginning to wipe down the kitchen counter, she said, "I'm listening. An email about the course being forced to reroute."

Susan's tension could be felt through the line. "Then

maybe you can tell me what I'm going to do now that the marathon can't go through the park."

Allison stopped everything and felt her expression pinch. "The park?"

"Yes. Haven't you looked at the course map? You are still running, aren't you?"

Allison hadn't looked at the race map but Susan didn't need to know that. "Walking, actually."

"Whatever. You aren't listening." Sounding annoyed, Susan reminded Allison of the marathon route and the impossible task of having to look for an alternative route with less than twenty-four hours to go. "I don't know who Hazel Beck thinks I am, but I'll tell you what I'm not: a miracle worker."

"Isn't that your job description?"

"Trust me, I'm praying for a miracle to happen but I'm not sure this can be done. Hazel is asking me to do the impossible. I don't know how we're expected to zone off an entire mile that hasn't gone through the security checks."

Allison was still standing and staring speechlessly as she was afraid to confirm what park Susan was referring to. Casting her gaze to the floor, she stared at the chipped glass and asked, "Why is this happening now?"

"You haven't heard?" Susan didn't give Allison time to answer before launching into a long-winded frantic explanation. "A woman was found in Commons Park last night." The name of the park made the blood in Allison's face drain. "Apparently it was a bad sexual assault and the woman who was attacked was left for dead. Now the park is closed until the police wrap up their investigation."

Allison wiped up her spill and bunched up the juice-soaked towel inside her hand, feeling a distant gaze fall over her eyes. Marty said he was going to play basketball at the park. Even without saying the name, Allison had known which park he'd meant. Commons Park. The one he used to play at as a kid. It didn't take long for her mind to come up with a dozen questions she didn't have the courage to ask. "Assaulted?" *Left for dead?*

"Yeah. But I'm just going off of what the news is saying. I haven't spoken with Samantha and am still waiting to hear back from the chief of police about having to secure a new route. Either way, the park is closed until further notice and tomorrow's race is jeopardized if I can't solve this problem today."

Allison glanced over her shoulder and stared into the back of her house, thinking about Marty. He couldn't possibly be responsible, could he?

"I'd never known that park to be dangerous," Allison said in all seriousness.

"I guess it just proves you never can be too sure." Susan sighed. "Anyway, I just called to say I won't be making it to lunch."

Lunch was the furthest thing from Allison's mind. She wished her friend good luck, offered to help in any way she could, and got off the phone. Then Allison tiptoed her way toward the guestroom, wondering if Marty was even home.

She never heard him come in last night and, with her pulse ticking, Allison tossed the juice-soaked towel into the hamper along the way when something else caught her eye.

Paused, Allison looked to Marty's closed door, then dipped into the laundry room where she found Marty's shirt inside a clothes hamper. She plucked the dirty, sweat-stained shirt out of the bin and held it up in front of her face when suddenly she gasped and dropped it to the floor.

Hovering over the wrinkled cloth, she couldn't believe her eyes. The small dark spots she noticed weren't dirt, but dribbles of blood.

Sounds coming from Marty's room sent Allison down the

hall where she pressed an ear to his door. She wasn't sure what it was she was hoping to find, but hoped that her cousin had nothing to do with what Susan said happened last night.

Holding her breath, Allison strained her ear and listened.

"Marty, no. Please tell me this wasn't you," she whispered out a prayer.

But there was blood on his shirt and, with it, questions that needed to be asked.

CHAPTER FORTY-THREE

IT FELT LIKE EVERYTHING WAS MOVING IN SLOW MOTION AS I sat staring at King's front door from behind the steering wheel of my car. I hated leaving him when he appeared to be so vulnerable. But he had work to do and so did I.

Once my vision cleared, I turned the key in the ignition and pulled away from the curb.

I was reminded of the day my husband died. I hated that I kept getting sucked deeper into thinking I was one day closer to losing King, too. The thought was crippling, but I couldn't deny the truth he seemed to be uncovering. King was the common denominator in both the murders and that made him the next likely target in my book.

I drove in silence, reminding myself what I had seen spread on King's kitchen table.

I couldn't stop thinking about Walker, or how Marshall King missed out on the best night of Alex's youth. I could see the pain in King's eyes when telling me the story—reliving the memory of celebrating the victory without him. It was the first flaw I'd ever heard anyone speak of Marshall, and that was telling. But so was the name Frank Lowe. Who was he? Did his story have anything to do with what was happening now? King made me believe it did.

My tires bumped along as I drove instinctively while allowing my thoughts to continue to ramble.

Soon I was back inside the cold case files Walker first presented to Erin and me. I tried to place them with Peggy Hill and Avery; tried to understand who else might know as much about King's past as Angelina must. I thought about visiting Carol King but didn't want to be the one to tell her about Avery. That was King's responsibility and, besides, she'd learn of it once my article went to print and triggered a tsunami across media outlets.

Before I knew it, I was parking behind Erin's red Bronco and I entered her house without knocking. The windows were open and there as a garden-fresh smell to the air that uplifted my spirit.

I heard her clunking around her office and, when I stuck my head inside, I found her surrounded by a castle of unopened boxes that were stacked five feet high.

"What's all this?" I asked.

Erin grinned, posted her hands into her sides, and let her gaze fall to the boxes. "New equipment."

Surprised at her investment, I thought about the inheritance she received after her father had died. I would have normally assumed that was all this was until I looked once more to the boxes' labels and found a card on top. I took it without asking and opened it up. After reading it, I flicked my gaze up to Erin.

She sheepishly shrugged.

"Really?" I held up the card from Walker. "You can't accept this gift."

"Why not? You read the card. There is more waiting for us at his office. Aren't you at least a little curious to know what else he has for us?"

I closed my eyes and rubbed my face inside my hands.

Why hadn't she told me about this on the phone? Didn't she remember anything I said last night? We couldn't have been further apart in our assessment of Walker. By accepting a gift of this magnitude, we'd be forever tethered to the man I wasn't sure I could fully trust.

"Sam, I didn't ask for this."

No, I knew she didn't. I didn't know if changing the subject was the smartest move, but that was exactly what I did when I told her I was coming from King's.

Her brow creased and I knew what she was thinking. "Is Walker a suspect?"

"He's on my list of suspects," I said, but Erin already knew as much. "But we didn't get that far in our conversation."

When she asked what I talked about with King, I told her. Murders made to look like cold cases from King's career, the locations of those lookalike murders to be a link to King's past—not to forget the headline on Walker's corkboard.

"Whoa," Erin raised both her eyebrows, "that's heavy."

Visions of King's dark eyes flashed behind my eyelids. "I'm worried about him."

"What about Orville Boyd? Is he dead in the water now, or should we keep looking?"

Erin was anxious to pick up where we had left off yesterday. But first, I needed to do a quick internet search on Frank Lowe to see if he would get me closer to confirming my suspicions of Walker. Or Angelina.

I skirted around the boxes and got behind Erin's computer, pecking away at the keys. Erin asked who Frank Lowe was and if he had anything to do with Walker. I told her I didn't know, then we both got sucked into what I pulled up.

It was all how King said it was. Marshall King's investigation into Frank Lowe was a long and arduous process that stretched into months of grueling work that seemed to go nowhere.

The murders Lowe was accused of committing were both intense and horrendous, resulting in a city-wide manhunt. Denver was on edge throughout it all. By the end, Marshall King emerged as a savior who ended the reign of terror.

"Did you know King's dad was a hero?" Erin asked.

"I'm just learning of it now," I said. Then I clicked on the next article detailing the murders Lowe had committed. Neither of us could believe what we were seeing.

"You recognize that?" I asked.

Erin tucked her chin and said, "I wished I didn't."

Scrolling, I knew I had recognized Frank Lowe's name but never expected it to come back full circle like this. We both stared at the screen, pointing out specifics, and I wasn't surprised to see it was a case also of interest to Walker. Except this one was different than all the others. Erin noticed it, too. It wasn't a cold case. This one was solved. And not by King.

Erin asked, "But if King's father caught the killer, then why would Walker have it on his corkboard?"

I was asking myself the same question. Did Walker consider this to be a cold case? Why was he interested in Frank Lowe? Or was this exactly what I feared and it wasn't about Frank Lowe at all, but rather Alex King? The tips of my fingers went cold as more evidence was pointing toward Walker being our killer. It certainly was a possibility. But then the call from Allison changed everything.

CHAPTER FORTY-FOUR

THE SHADOW STALKER PACED IN TINY FIGURE EIGHTS AS his socked feet trampled the carpet with each step. A muted twenty-inch flat screen TV flickered and cast dark shadows across the eggshell white walls, lighting up the room.

All night he couldn't sleep. First it was adrenaline keeping him awake. The high that came after the kill. Now, a buzz of energy like that of a swarming hive played constantly in his ears. It was fear that had ensnared him with anxiety, keeping him a prisoner inside his own room. The fear of getting caught.

The Shadow Stalker had made a mistake, and he knew it. But it was the persistent nagging being whispered into his ear that was grating on his nerves now.

His chest heaved as he listened to the words telling him he wasn't good enough to be recognized as the best. Soon, he couldn't take it anymore. Clenching his meaty fists, he spat into the dark corner of the room, "I am the best."

There was no response, nor was he looking for one. He kept pacing.

Silence draped over him like a heavy blanket of doubt,

slowly draining him of his self-worth. He walked the same path as before, asking if it was figure eights he was making, or the symbol of infinity. He preferred the infinity analogy—infinity ensured a lasting legacy—and he kept tramping down the same trail, allowing his thoughts to churn.

Pushing his hands through his hair, he flexed his muscles and shook his head back and forth as his agitation grew. The voices grew louder as the minutes passed and the attacks on his shortcomings sharpened and became more personal.

"I'm not making it too easy on him," he muttered in a tone above a whisper, not wanting his voice to be heard through the walls. "You don't know what you're talking about, old lady."

The Shadow Stalker knew he might have moved too quickly in his grand scheme to draw Inspector King in. It wasn't the victim he chose, or the location that made him question his strategy. It was the fact that he was nearly spotted by those boys surprising him with their lights as he hovered over the frail and dying Avery Morgan, working her into a piece of art. Now he worried that, because of them, he might have left his victim alive.

He raced around his track, his feet scuffing over the carpet faster and faster until they burned with heat. The whispers swirled around him like a stiff winter's breeze that only the Shadow Stalker could hear. The pressure inside his head increased as the voice behind him grew louder.

His nostrils flared and he felt trapped, like his heart was about to burst. Suddenly, he snapped. "I know I almost got caught!"

With balled fists, he breathed the fire out of his chest.

As soon as he admitted his failure, he knew he'd lost. It was difficult to admit, but sometimes the truth hurt. Willing to do anything to win, it had felt like forever since he lost at anything.

He turned his back, covered his ears, and shook his head violently. No matter what he did to try to escape the constant banter of failure, he couldn't stop himself from hearing her disappointment.

"You might have won this one, Inspector, but not again."

Then it all stopped and he caught his reflection in the mirror.

His grey eyes grew with surprise as he inched his way closer. He couldn't believe what he was seeing. Bringing his hand to his neck, he tipped his chin back and swiveled his head from left to right, inspecting the scratch he hadn't noticed until now.

"No. This can't be," he said to himself. "You're better than this."

His heart pounded in his ears as he went over each of his actions since running from the park. He'd followed the bike path exiting the park, stuck to the dark edges of the sidewalks, slowly making his way home without being spotted. As much as he wanted to believe a tree branch caught his neck somewhere along the way, he knew that it was Avery who'd done this to him. Once home he'd stripped his clothes to get rid of any potential evidence to link him to the crime, but a scratch was trouble.

You're a loser. You will get caught...He's beating you.

With nerves on high, the Shadow Stalker caught sight of the news in the mirror. He reached for the TV remote and unmuted the volume. Turning on a heel, he watched as the news anchor told the story of his crime. He'd been waiting for this moment, hoping for glory. Turning up the volume, he moved closer to the TV.

The voice behind him was back, telling him to turn it down.

"Shut up." He spat over his right shoulder. "It's not too

loud." He pointed the clicker at the TV and increased the volume.

"Last night, members of the Denver Police Department responded to a distress call inside Commons Park. There, first responders found a woman in her twenties, badly injured but alive—"

The Shadow Stalker's eyes widened. His worst fears were now a reality. The voice was there once again, laughing behind him for being so stupid.

"Quiet." He snapped his fingers and pointed to the armchair in the corner. "This is important." He inched closer to the TV.

"It's unclear at this time as details are still emerging, but no suspects in the case are being named. The park will remain closed until the investigation is complete. Now, if you're planning to run in tomorrow's marathon, this does affect the original course but we're being told that everything will go on as planned."

The Shadow Stalker stood there quietly, staring at the TV, when suddenly he heard someone at his door.

CHAPTER FORTY-FIVE

Allison was speaking in a hushed tone that made it difficult to hear. I asked, "Are you sure?"

"I'm sure, Sam."

She was clearer this time, probably having closed herself away in a private room to make sure there wasn't any mistaking what she wanted me to hear.

"He was at the park where the news is saying a woman was attacked." Allison's words were clipped, shooting off her tongue in rapid bursts of fire. "Do you know anything about this?"

With my elbow planted on Erin's desk, I pinched the bridge of my nose and closed my eyes. I thought about Marty Ray and Allison's determination to help him readjust to life after incarceration. It was a noble effort—and a difficult one at that—but I wasn't as convinced as she was when thinking he might have been the one to have attacked Avery.

"There were a lot of people at the park last night," I said, masking my skepticism as best I could.

"Then how do you explain the blood on his shirt?"

I lifted my head and glanced over my shoulder to find

Erin staring. I clicked over to speakerphone and announced Erin's arrival.

"This is too big of a coincidence for me to ignore," Allison said to us. "I'm worried that he might have done something. You know what he just got out of prison for?"

We did, though none of us wanted to say it out loud as if somehow hearing it would confirm Marty's guilt. Besides, there was other evidence I knew about that I couldn't discuss with Allison that had me doubting Marty had anything to do with this at all. Instead, I asked where Marty was now.

"He's in my guestroom talking to himself."

"What's he saying?" Erin asked.

"I don't know. Mumbling about something. Look, I was listening through the door and didn't stay long enough to have him find me eavesdropping. It's important I don't lose his trust."

"It sounds like you already have," I said, instantly regretting my brutal assessment.

Allison mostly ignored my comment when she said, "If he's responsible for what happened, then yes, you're right, I have. Why do you think I called you? Don't you know something that can help ease my worries?"

Erin and I shared a look. She shook her head no and I knew what she was thinking. We couldn't divulge anything until King gave me the go-ahead, even if the information was already being leaked to the press.

"We're still working the story," I said. "There are some things that can't be shared."

"So it's possible?" Allison sounded pessimistic.

I said, "Don't give up on him just yet."

"How can I not when you're making me believe that I'm right?"

I asked again about last night, this time asking Allison to

break down the last time she saw Marty and what his behavior was like.

"We were leaving the office," Allison gave a time and I jotted it down, "when I was approached by a client. Marty and I were on our way to dinner so, not knowing how long my visit would take, I gave him a twenty so he could buy himself some food. That's when we both promised to see each other back at the house."

Erin asked, "And he didn't say who he might have been meeting up with at the park?"

"If he did, I didn't hear him."

"What time did he get in?" I asked.

"That's just it. I don't know. I fell asleep before he got home and then, this morning, I find his clothes in the hamper with blood on them. I'm freaking out right now and think that maybe I should call his parole officer."

I thought about what I heard Alvarez tell King last night. "You said you gave Marty a twenty-dollar bill. Can you tell me more about that?"

Allison paused for a moment. "Yes. A regular old Andrew Jackson. Why? What does that matter? I promised him dinner and knew he didn't have any money to buy something himself."

Erin was holding my eyes inside her curious gaze as I thought about the message left for King on the twenty-dollar bill last night. Could it be our killer's signature? Maybe. Another message had been scribbled on a twenty Peggy Hill's house. But I didn't have a way to trace the bill back to Marty. Even if I did, it would only take me back to its original owner, Allison. We had nothing.

"Samantha, tell me. What should I do?" Allison's thin voice floated through the phone line like helium. "Am I now an accomplice in a crime I had nothing to do with?"

"Relax," Erin said. "You did the right thing by calling us first."

"Who was this woman anyway? And why do I get the feeling you know more than what you're saying?"

I stood and knew I needed to talk with King in person. "If Marty leaves, message me."

"Sam, who was this woman?" Allison raised her voice and I heard her desperation coming through the line. "Marty is innocent, right? He couldn't have done what I'm thinking he did, could he?"

I didn't have the strength to tell my friend her cousin's criminal record suggested he did have it in him to be the monster I knew we were looking for. Instead, I said, "Just call me if he leaves the house."

CHAPTER FORTY-SIX

As soon as Detective Alex King was within sight of the police station parking lot, he knew they were in trouble. He felt Alvarez tense in the seat next to him as he spun the steering wheel to the right and headed straight for the small crowd of people.

The sadness in his heart had since hardened and turned into anger. His Glock was ready to fire, his muscles pumping for a fight. As he prepared to leave the house, he had made a personal pact to both Avery and Peggy, promising to bring their assailants to justice—God willing, by his own hands. Not only had a cop been murdered, but they were his friends first, and that was something that couldn't be replaced.

"Christ," Alvarez muttered into his hand as they approached the half-dozen reporters. "Did I miss something? I thought we were keeping this under wraps."

King eased his foot onto the brake pedal and nudged the nose of his vehicle past several TV reporters already shouting into their window. "There must have been a leak."

Alvarez turned away from the cameras and gave King a stern look. "Just what we fucking need."

King tried his best to avoid his face being captured inside the frame of a long lens, but a reporter's thirst to be the first to reveal new details was impossible to avoid. They were like mosquitoes swarming, nipping and biting until it drove a man mad.

Alvarez was still giving King a look, and King knew what his partner was thinking—Samantha was the one who'd dropped the bomb. "Samantha has the exclusive once I've been given the green light, but this wasn't her."

Alvarez raised his skeptical brows and rolled his gaze out the window.

Once King parked, they both stepped out and met the hungry members of the media with stoic faces that revealed nothing. Their lips were sealed, their ears open to learn what secrets the media already knew. The questions started flying like arrows across the field and the two detectives dodged each and every one of them like seasoned warriors.

"Why is the police department not revealing the name of last night's victim?" A reporter shoved a microphone into King's face. "What have you got to hide?"

The detectives kept walking. King resisted the urge to smile. This wasn't about the murder of a cop, but rather the lack of information being shared with the press.

"Hospital have no records of a woman coming in. Is it safe to assume the victim died?"

"You'll get your questions answered at the press conference." Alvarez stopped and tugged on his sports coat, enjoying his minute of fame. "Until then, enjoy the sunshine." He smiled and joined King at the door before stepping into the station together.

The air was cool but frantic inside and it was clear Avery's death had the entire station hungry for revenge. As soon as the other officers saw King, everything went quiet. King ignored the stares and brushed past the nods as he felt his colleagues circle behind him like sharks smelling blood in the water.

Suddenly, an officer across the room shouted, "We'll get the bastard who did this. Avery was a damn good cop even if she was only a rookie."

King stopped, turned, and stared into the officer's eyes, feeling a sense of unity he'd only experienced a few times throughout his career.

"Blue lives matter," someone else shouted and the entire department erupted into a roar that shook the floor.

King's chest buzzed with a surge of adrenaline as he made his way to Lieutenant Kent Baker's office. Baker's door was open and King found him hunched behind his computer reviewing surveillance tape. King double tapped the door with his knuckles and LT waved for them to come inside.

"Close the door," Baker said.

Alvarez shut the door and the outside noise was immediately muffled as the men took seats across from their lieutenant.

LT leaned back in his chair and met King's gaze. "We have the entire department looking for Orville Boyd."

King's jaw clenched as he felt his muscles tense. Alvarez glanced at him sideways and King knew he was thinking about the theory he had assembled overnight.

"We've had eyes on his house since last night and will continue that way until we catch this bastard." LT paused before standing. He turned to the window and continued, "The entire department has their fingers on their triggers, ready to send Avery's killer straight to hell." He looked over his shoulder. "Chief Watts will be meeting with the press," he glanced at his silver wrist watch, "in one hour. After that, the city will learn a cop has been killed."

"They're outside now," Alvarez said, "close to guessing the truth of what happened last night."

"They'll hear it all soon enough." LT lowered himself back into his desk chair, opened a drawer, and retrieved an evidence bag he slid across his desk for King to take. "Forensics wasn't able to pull any prints off the note you gave them."

King tipped forward in his chair and took the bag into his possession. "I didn't think they would." King thanked LT for checking anyway, pocketing the *burn in hell, pig* note found on Erin's front door before this nightmare started.

"Where are we at?" Alvarez asked, sounding frustrated. "Has anyone checked the recycling plant where Mike Kern said Boyd was now working?"

LT nodded. "According to records, Boyd hasn't held a job for nearly eighteen months now."

"Christ, so we're just chasing a ghost."

"Unfortunately, CSI hasn't been able to lift any prints—let alone anything beneficial—at either crime scene." LT locked his eyes on King. "Alex, I can put added security detail on your house until this is finished."

"Waste of resources," King said. "Besides, whoever is sending me a message isn't interested in killing me. If they were, I'd already be dead."

LT leaned back and glanced to Alvarez. "As you know, the park is still closed off and I've been sealed inside here watching tape. We have the boy, Jamaal, who called it in—and that led us to a couple more names who Jamaal says he was playing basketball with nearby right before he discovered the body."

"What do we know about these other boys?" Alvarez asked.

"Just that they stayed playing ball even after the lights went off." LT flicked his gaze over to King. "We're working on bringing them in for questioning now."

"So we have nothing." King rubbed at his forehead.

"Not exactly." LT shifted his weight. "Jamaal mentioned a

man they didn't know approach them on the courts about the time we believe Avery was attacked."

"Was it Boyd?"

"Unfortunately, there weren't any cameras where she was found but we did pick up this image."

LT clicked his mouse, zoomed in on a blurry image, and turned the computer screen toward the detectives.

"So who is this guy?"

"John Doe."

King asked, "Is that as clear as you can get it?"

LT nodded and locked his gaze on King. "There's another problem." King's expression pinched. "Mason Bell was in the park last night."

"So?" King shrugged. "And probably a dozen others, too. You can't possibly think he's a suspect?"

"We're not ruling anything out, but watch this and tell me what you think."

King watched LT's hand fall to the computer mouse. Time slowed and he noticed he stopped breathing as he waited for the video to play. A couple of clicks and LT turned the monitor to face King. The monitor was paused on surveillance video of the park. King was afraid of what he was about to see but told LT to play it anyway.

"Here, you can see our John Doe." Lieutenant Baker pointed to the screen with the tip of his pen.

King noted his profile. Black male. About six foot and two hundred pounds of muscle. The time stamp was only minutes before the 911 call came in from Jamaal.

"And here is Mason running away about the same time Avery's call came in."

Alvarez shifted his weight and flashed King a sideways glance.

King said, "I'll speak to him."

LT nodded, leaned back in his chair. "Does Samantha still want the exclusive on this?"

King knitted his brows. "You know she does."

LT tipped his head back. "Give her the good news first—she'll get her exclusive. Then tell her about us needing to pick up her son for questioning." LT's expression hardened. "I don't want this to be a surprise, so fair warning, the DA's office expects us to deliver a confession by the end of today."

King's muscles flexed against his undershirt. "What's the rush?"

LT's brow furrowed. "Mayor Goldberg needs it to disappear ASAP from the minds of his constituents."

King pushed his heels into the floor and stood. "At the cost of potentially getting it wrong?"

LT threaded his fingers and stared up into King's eyes. "Politics isn't my forte. Just do your job and let's make sure we get it right."

CHAPTER FORTY-SEVEN

"Sam, we can't just leave Allison in the house with a monster like that," Erin argued, as I closed up the browser and hurdled over the boxes of new equipment, preparing to leave.

"No, maybe not," I said, checking my phone. "But at least we know where she's at if new evidence emerges and suggests Marty was behind Avery's murder."

Erin gave me a resolute look as I began reminding myself of the facts, needing to convince myself that Allison wasn't in any immediate danger. Yes, there was blood on his shirt and she'd given him a twenty-dollar bill, but that wasn't enough to convict the man. Was it?

"Nothing suggests Marty knows anything about King's past or King's failure to solve specific crimes," I said.

"But he does have a history of sexual assault."

I shook my head, felt my bangs swish over my eyes. "Marty has been locked away for the last five years and is only on his second day out. The last thing a man like him would want is to be put back behind bars."

Erin folded her arms and took a confrontational stance.

"Or maybe that's exactly what he wants." Erin followed up by telling me about men who become institutionalized and know only how to survive in the prison system.

"Okay. Fine. But then how do you explain Peggy Hill's murder. And the note on your door. Someone was coming after King before Marty was out." Maybe I was only trying to convince myself that Allison was safe, but there was more evidence that Marty was innocent than guilty.

Erin rolled her eyes. "Working with someone. All kinds of alliances form on the inside. C'mon Sam, you're better than this."

The truth was, we didn't know Marty well enough to form an opinion and I wasn't going to work off of assumptions. "Allison will be fine," I said. "The person we're looking for is closer to King's life. That's what he thinks and that's what I believe, too."

"And what, you think that someone is Walker?"

I held her gaze for a moment, thinking about Frank Lowe. Then I said, "We have no choice but to confront him about why he's interested in the murders committed by Frank Lowe."

"Sam, let's not burn this bridge just yet."

My expression pinched and I refused to back down. "So we should just sit on our hands and not ask Mr. Million Dollar Man why he's interested in a case that's not even considered cold?"

Erin's glimmering eyes drifted over her new equipment. It was clear she wasn't willing to give it all up without first learning for certain we were right about Walker. "All I'm saying is that now might not be the right time to be slinging mud."

"I disagree," I said, exiting the office. Erin followed and I came to an abrupt stop, turning to face her. "Why was he at

Commons Park last night, and why do I have a feeling he wants to point out King's flaws to me?"

Erin couldn't give me a straight answer. The only thing I could hear was Walker's threats he spat at Avery only hours before she was killed. He needed to explain himself, especially since our reputation was now directly tied to his actions.

"Think about it," I said. "Walker enters our lives at the same time murders are made to look like cold cases, cold cases he's been investigating himself?" My cheeks were glowing hot, wondering why I felt the need to explain myself at all.

Erin knew what I was saying, knew we'd cracked cases in the past when dealing with less evidence than what we currently had. Yet she still hesitated to admit Walker was up so something fishy, but I could see it in her eyes. She was coming around and I needed to set the hook before I lost her again to Walker's bait.

"I need to see that corkboard," I said. "Ask him if his interest in Frank Lowe has anything to do with where Avery was found murdered."

Erin inhaled a deep breath through her nose and nodded. "Okay. Fine. We'll ask him what he knows. We've got nothing to lose, right?"

I reached for her hand and squeezed. "Right."

Erin looked me straight in the eye and said, "Walker will want to go after Boyd now that he's got a taste of what we do."

"I know." I sighed. "But I'm not about to let King work this investigation alone, and I also can't jeopardize losing our chance to bring justice to Avery because of the incompetence Walker has already shown."

CHAPTER FORTY-EIGHT

As soon as we arrived to Walker's office I received a call from King. I answered after unbuckling my seatbelt. King was quiet and slow to tell me why he was calling.

"Is everything all right?" I asked.

Erin turned her head and stared, feeling my sudden concern.

King's voice brought my attention back to him. "Have you seen Mason today?" he asked.

I felt my grip tighten on my phone. "Why are you asking?"

King sighed and I heard the line fill with static—the sounds of him scrubbing a hand over his face. Erin pressed her fingertips into my thigh and asked if everything was okay. I turned my gaze forward and asked King, "Alex, what did Mason do?"

"Did you know that he was in the park last night?"

I pressed my lips into a flat line and kept staring through the windshield. I hadn't known his exact whereabouts until just now. It was easy to tell myself King was wrong, that Mason was nowhere near where Avery was last night.

My heart beat in a steady rhythm. I'd tricked myself long ago into believing that my job never put my son into any kind of danger. But it had before and apparently may have again.

"I was with you, remember?" I said, not wanting to remind myself that Angelina was also at Alex's house for dinner. "Did he see something?"

King's voice was a deep whisper that made the hairs on my arm stand on end. "I've been tasked with bringing him in for questioning."

I froze before closing my eyes. I kept shaking my head no. What the heck was going on and why was my son a person of interest in a crime I knew he didn't commit?

"Is he home, Sam?"

"Mason didn't do this."

"Trust me, I know, but maybe he's a witness to something that could help us catch whoever did."

King was making his case. I knew he was only doing his job but, inside, I roared and swore to obey my vows as a mother to protect my young at any cost. "There must be others who you can question besides him."

I'd do anything to avoid having Mason go through the intense pressure of a police interrogation. I also knew King couldn't tell me exactly what they had on him, either, to want to bring him in. That was what really worried me. Mason—like any teenage boy—made mistakes. Sometimes mistakes with lasting consequences.

"You're right," King said. "It's not just him, Sam. We're rounding up everyone who was remotely close to the park last night. But Mason was caught on camera and LT has given me little choice in the matter."

I picked up my head and swept my gaze to Erin. "At least let me bring him to you."

Silence hung on the line and, after a moment's pause, King agreed but gave me a deadline I had to meet. "Thank you," I said, feeling his intense sense of urgency to get after tracking down Avery's killer. In return, I tossed him a bone. "In the meantime, you should question a man named Marty Ray."

"Marty Ray," King repeated as if writing his name down. "Who is he and why would I want to speak with him?"

I shared only what Allison told me. King asked for a description, where he might find him. That gave me hope that I still had time to ask Mason what the heck happened—and if I should be worried he'd done something he shouldn't have—before they put him under the microscope. As soon as I told King everything, I knew Marty was on King's list of suspects.

King asked, "You know this man?"

"He's Allison's cousin. Recently released from prison. And, according to her, Marty was in the park last night, too, about the time Avery was believed to have been attacked."

CHAPTER FORTY-NINE

ERIN WAS FIDGETING IN THE SEAT NEXT TO ME AS SHE waited silently for me to relay the message I just got from King. I gathered my thoughts and glanced to the clock. "We have two hours."

Erin swept her gaze up to me. "Two hours until what?"

We locked eyes. I was still feeling lightheaded as I thought about my teenage son being dragged down to the station for questioning. The timing couldn't have been worse. He needed a lawyer and I didn't have the money for one. But, beyond that, it was the emotional strain on his young shoulders that bothered me most.

"That was King," I said.

She gave me the look like she already knew. "Is he going to check out Marty?"

I nodded and caught her up to speed about Mason being in the park last night—including our two hour window before I had to deliver him up to King.

"Jesus." Erin glanced out the window and tucked a blonde lock behind her left ear. "Do you think he saw something?"

I hoped he hadn't. I still couldn't stomach what happened

to Avery, and that was with years of experience under my belt from working the crime beat. I'd seen a lot over the years and was somewhat hardened by it all, but I could only imagine the damage it would inflict on a young impressionable mind such as Mason. "He needs a lawyer."

Erin said, "I know someone I could call."

I turned my head and gave an arched look of doubt. "A criminal defense attorney?"

Erin raised both her eyebrows. "Want me to call her?"

I furrowed my brow. "Dare I ask how much?"

Erin's eyes softened. "Don't worry about it." She caught my hand and squeezed. "Let's just make sure Mason has the representation he needs to navigate those choppy waters."

My heart swelled with gratitude and I still couldn't believe this was happening. Mason was innocent—I was sure it was only a case of being in the wrong place at the wrong time— but that didn't get rid of the fact that he was going to be questioned. Questioned by detectives who often used aggressive and confusing tactics to get a confession.

Erin opened her door first and we exited the vehicle and made our way to the front doors of the building that housed Walker's office. The door suctioned to the rubber as I opened it and we made our way to the elevator.

My feet were heavy with uncertainty. As difficult as it was, I shifted my focus back to Walker and couldn't stop thinking about how both he and my son were near such a brutal crime about the same time. I didn't want to believe it was coincidence, but what else could it possibly be? Could Mason have been killed, too?

I stared at the digital display with arms crossed, counting off the floors we passed as we were whisked up.

The theory King presented to me this morning had me believing it was possible. In fact, I was now starting to believe that anybody who had ever meant anything to

him might one day find their name on a list of possible
targets. Why not it be my son? Or was Avery specifically
attacked for knowing King, a deeper reason beyond
something to do with his father we still hadn't figured
out?

As soon as we stepped off the elevator I heard heels
clacking their way toward us on the marble floor. A second
later, Gemma turned the corner and greeted us in the lobby
with a knowing smile.

"We're here to speak with Walker," I said, thinking how
strange it was she always seemed to know when we were
coming. There were security cameras everywhere, but did she
have access to those in the lobby, too? Or was she notified by
building staff?

"Of course you are." Gemma's lips curled without ever
revealing her pearly whites. "Unfortunately, Walker isn't in at
the moment."

"Do you know where we can find him?"

She arched a perfectly plucked brow. "I assume you're
here to thank him for the new equipment?"

The subtle undertone of her words was meant to make us
feel inferior. Why did Walker send the equipment in the first
place? Was it a bribe to get us to agree to their terms? Or was
this his way of apologizing for his brash behavior yesterday?
Every interaction with Walker and his staff was growing
stranger by the day.

I remained cordial when asking, "If you can't say where he
is, perhaps you know when he'll be back?"

Gemma hemmed and hawed her way nowhere fast. Her
lack of clarity did little to ease my suspicions about Walker's
true intentions, and I wondered if we were wasting our time
with him.

"I'm sorry, Samantha. I do apologize for my lack of
specifics." Gemma clasped her hands and made sure to keep

both Erin and me in her line of sight. "He was quite upset with what happened yesterday in the field."

My eyes narrowed. "So he rewards us with new equipment?"

Gemma's lips tightened as she gave me an arched look that reminded me vaguely of Angelina. They shared the same bitch qualities I wanted no part of. Being around Walker and his associates was like attending a circus.

"It's the DPD who are incompetent. Am I right?" Gemma let out a tiny cackle. "Anyway, we should all be packing heat in our line of work. And, besides, I heard the rookie officer took it too far." Gemma paused to stare me down, waiting for me to react. "Walter could have been killed." She gave a curt nod. "Actions do have consequences."

Our line of work? I felt my fingernails dig deep into my palms and Erin must have felt me fuming with anger because she stepped in before I flattened my hand and smacked that smirk right off Gemma's painted face.

Erin said, "Walker's note said he had something for us. Maybe we could get that and be on our way?"

Gemma blinked and peeled her gaze off me. "Oh, yes. Of course. Right this way."

We followed her into the fishbowl and I was anxious to see the corkboard, if the crimes of Frank Lowe were still on display as I'd seen them yesterday. I still didn't understand why Walker had my article linked to that particular case. As long as Erin could occupy Gemma, I could hopefully get some answers to the questions I couldn't stop asking myself.

Erin followed Gemma to the table and I turned to the corkboard only to find everything had been wiped clean. There was nothing about Frank Lowe—my article gone, too. In its place, a new photo was prominently tacked.

Was this the reason Walter Walker asked us to come here

in the first place? From my assessment of who he was, it seemed likely.

I glanced to Gemma. Erin had her distracted and, with their backs turned to me, I floated across the floor toward to the corkboard. I asked myself why I was now staring into the face of Angelina Hill.

CHAPTER FIFTY

"THE MAN LT COULDN'T IDENTIFY IN THE VIDEO," KING turned to his partner, "is Marty Ray."

Alvarez pushed back from his desk, the sounds of his chair rolling across the linoleum floor filling the air around them. "You sure?"

Suddenly, King's phone hummed in his palm. He glanced at the display and recognized the number. "I've got to take this."

Alvarez stretched his neck and followed King with his eyes, still waiting for his partner to confirm how he knew the name of their John Doe. "Was that Samantha you were just talking to?"

Without taking his eyes off his phone, King said, "Look up Marty Ray. His name should already be in the system. I'll be back in a minute."

"Whatever you say, boss." Alvarez mock-saluted King as he disappeared into the stairwell.

King's phone was still buzzing as the heavy door latched closed behind him. He took the call in private and recognized Tristan Knight's voice immediately.

"Sorry to bother you, Alex," Tristan's voice filled King's ear, "but you said to call if your mother started acting up again."

The pounding in King's temples intensified as he asked himself if his mother's move was worth it or not. His mother was becoming quite the handful—suddenly needing more attention than a toddler—and King was having doubts.

"Yes, of course. What's the problem, is she not playing nice with others again?" King hoped to lighten the mood by taking a playful jab at his mother's stubbornness.

Tristan chuckled a small laugh. "No, it's not that I'm afraid. Her behavior has improved since your last visit—"

King picked his head up and pulled his eyebrows together. "Than what's the problem?"

Tristan cleared his throat. "Your mother is refusing to be in her room."

King was still staring at the white wall ahead when he asked, "Did something happen to make her not want to be in there?"

"If something did, she hasn't told me. But she was found roaming the halls late last night and hasn't returned to her room since."

King's patience was thinning. He glanced at his watch, hoping Tristan got on with it before he regretted giving him his cellphone number. There was important police work he could be doing. The last thing he needed was to be helping the people he was paying a fortune to help babysit his mother. "Then what's she saying?"

"That she keeps seeing the Pillow Strangler."

King lifted his head and felt his veins open up. If Mr. Knight was trying to get his attention, he'd just found it.

"I don't even know what that means, but she's clearly frightened of it."

It? The Pillow Strangler was no it. He was a monster who may or may not be playing games with me, King thought as he reached behind his neck and wagged his head from side to side until he heard it crack. "I'll be right over."

"That's not necessary, Detective."

King disagreed. "Where is she now?"

"In the courtyard enjoying her coffee. Mr. King, I assure you we're doing everything we can to comfort your mother. I just thought you might have a message I could relay to her that might convince her that her room is in fact a safe place for her to live?"

King shifted his weight to the opposite foot and said, "No. That's quite all right. Knowing my mother, she won't listen to anybody but me."

"I really don't want to have you come here," Tristan solemnly said.

"Keep a close eye on her and I'll see you soon." King ended his call, not giving the nurse a choice in the matter, and pinched the bridge of his nose as he fought to contain the headache from spreading.

First Mason, and now his mother. Of all days for things to go wrong, he wished today wasn't it.

Blinking the stars out of his eyes, King asked what the chances of his mother actually seeing Orville Boyd were. Was it possible Boyd skirted past security to haunt his mother? Or was it a product of her imagination? King wasn't about to discredit either without first speaking to his mother, but he suspected this might be a result of the conversation she overheard him and Samantha having at last night's dinner.

The door opened behind him and Alvarez poked his head through. "Everything all right?"

King picked up his head, turned, and nodded. "Did you locate Marty Ray's record?"

Alvarez walked over and stood next to King. He tucked his chin and stared from behind a low brow. With hands buried in his pockets, he rocked on his heels. "Don't lie to me partner. I know when something's up. If you need to talk—"

King's lungs released as he continued to hold Alvarez's gaze. There was more he had to say, but not here. "We have work to do."

Alvarez didn't move. He continued to stare into King's eyes, blocking his pursuit. "You have something he need to say?"

King held his gaze and swallowed. "I do."

"Then go on," Alvarez's expression was stern, "say it."

"C'mon," King ducked his head and stepped around Alvarez, "I'll explain in the car."

CHAPTER FIFTY-ONE

KING WAITED FOR A RESPONSE FROM ALVAREZ WHO STILL had a blank look on his face. The red light flicked to green and King eased his foot off the brake and onto the accelerator.

He regretted telling Alvarez that his mother knew about Orville Boyd's possible return. He knew what Alvarez was thinking long before he said anything. Finally, after a long pause, Alvarez shook his head and flicked his gaze out the window. "Not the smartest dinner conversation to have, don't you think?"

"It's not like I planned her to hear what was being discussed." King kept one hand on the wheel as he drove steadily across town. Traffic was dense, the air hot and dry. "Mom overheard a conversation she shouldn't have. It happens."

Alvarez turned to look at King. "And who might have this conversation been with?"

King flicked his eyes to his partner, a knowing glimmer there.

"One of these days you're going to get yourself in

trouble."

King shrugged it off, knowing he needed Samantha as much as she needed him—both personally and professionally.

"You should really consider leaving work at work."

King knew a detective's life *was* work. Twenty-four-seven. Night and day. And dating Samantha wasn't anything new to Alvarez. King knew he walked a fine line when discussing cases with Samantha, but she was discreet and had a relationship with the department that was based on trust. It was a symbiotic relationship. One he hoped wasn't going to end anytime soon.

With one hand on the steering wheel, King flicked his eyes in Alvarez's direction. "You know she was approached by an investor?"

Alvarez turned and faced King. "Samantha?"

King nodded. "Walter Walker."

Alvarez's eyebrows raised. "The Million Dollar Man?"

"Wants to turn Samantha into a star."

"No shit." King nodded and Alvarez asked what the catch was. "There's always a catch. Am I wrong?"

King wagged his head. "Apparently he has a thing for cold cases."

"Just what we need." Alvarez looked ahead and curled his fingers over his kneecap. "More amateur sleuths following us around."

King put on his blinker and merged into the next lane over. "That's why they found themselves looking for Orville Boyd. Samantha was there when Officers Smith and Morgan responded to what was now Avery's last call of duty."

Alvarez's elbow was perched on the window sill, his hand over his mouth as he exhaled a heavy sigh. "I heard Lester isn't taking the news well."

"No, I imagine he's not," King said somberly, feeling his own heart ache.

The wheels hummed over the hot pavement as they drove in silence the rest of the way to the assisted living facility. After parking and setting the brake, Alvarez said, "You want to know what I can't stop thinking about?"

King cast his gaze to his lap and listened.

"Who the hell knows so much about you?"

King's heartrate spiked as he stared into the bushes ahead. He'd thought about the memories each of the crime scenes sparked, memories he'd thought he'd buried and forgotten. Peggy Hill was targeted because of him, and so was Avery. Alvarez knew it as well as King, but the question was *why*?

"I've been asking myself the same question," King muttered to a quiet cab.

Alvarez shifted in his seat. "And?"

In a low volume, King shared his theory about his father. "The night I won the baseball championship wasn't only the best night of my life. It was also the best night of his life as well."

After letting it sit for a moment, Alvarez asked, "Who would know that but you?"

King shook his head, unsure himself. "All I know is that Peggy and Avery weren't chosen at random."

Their eyes met and Alvarez said, "You know I like Samantha, but I'd be worried about her if I were you."

King's jaw clenched and he cracked his door open. A flood of dry heat came rushing inside the car. The truth was hard to swallow. King was worried about Sam too, but he was also concerned about his mother. If he was right about being the link to both murders, then either of the two women he loved most could be the killer's next target.

"C'mon." King's foot stamped down on the pavement. "Let's go see what's up with Mom. If anybody could pick Orville Boyd out from the crowd, it would be her."

CHAPTER FIFTY-TWO

KING STOPPED AT THE ENTRANCE TO THE FACILITY LONG enough to inspect the lock on the front door. He doubted Orville Boyd—or someone like him—would have the nerve to step inside a building like this with the amount of security that was in place.

As if reading King's thoughts, Alvarez said, "Boyd would be an idiot to walk in here and think you'd never know about it."

"Unless he wanted me to know," King said softly.

He brushed his thumb over the deadbolt, still hesitant to believe his mother had actually seen the Pillow Strangler. But the truth was, people close to him were being targeted. If they could get to a cop, they could certainly get to his mother.

"Detective King." Tristan Knight walked briskly to the door. "Thank you for coming. I'm so sorry to have to pull you away from your work."

King remained focused on the lock. Once Tristan was within earshot, he asked, "What time do these doors close for the night?"

"Nine p.m. we lock the facility." Tristan stepped forward and pointed to a chrome box on the outside wall. "After that, each resident and their guests must buzz themselves in."

Both King and Alvarez swept their gaze to the small speaker box attached to the outside wall. Alvarez asked, "Who answers that call?"

"Front desk." Tristan bounced his gaze between the men, reminding King of the security measures put in place. There were cameras and a login sheet that every visitor was required to sign, as well as a list of guests flagged whose visiting privileges had been restricted or revoked, often at the request of a resident. Then he added, "Night security escorts residents in and out after hours. No one comes and goes without us knowing about it. Which makes your mother's story all the more bizarre."

King reached his hand inside his sport jacket pocket and produced a photo of Orville Boyd. "Have you seen this guy before?"

Tristan pinched the corner of the image with his right hand. His eyes focused as he studied the photograph. "I have."

King tilted his ear toward Tristan, surprised by his answer. "You have?"

"Not here, of course." He swung his eyes to Alvarez. "After I called, I did some research on the internet and learned who he was. The way your mother couldn't stop talking about him, I needed to make sure that what she was saying was real."

King glanced over Tristan's shoulder toward reception and asked, "Where is she now?"

"We finally got your mother back inside her room." Tristan motioned for them to follow. "Please follow me."

King nodded and took the first step into the building.

Tristan was one step behind when he said, "She'll be happy to see you."

CHAPTER FIFTY-THREE

ALVAREZ CAUGHT KING BY THE ARM. "WE BETTER GET THE names of those working the nightshift."

King shared a quick glance with his partner before catching Tristan's attention. "Before we get to my mother, I'd like to see the visitor log from last night if you don't mind?"

Tristan shortened his step, looked unsure of himself, then nodded. "Not a problem."

The three men stepped up to the front desk and Alvarez smiled at the woman sitting behind the computer. Tristan made the request and soon King had the log sheet in front of him. He trailed his finger down the list of names, reading each one next to the date and time of when they arrived and departed.

"I don't see his name," Alvarez said.

King picked up his head. "It's not here."

"We had our fair share of traffic, but it was rather quiet for a Friday night," Tristan said. "It's not unusual for our staff to be quite busy most weekends."

Closing up the three-ringed binder, King said, "I'm sure it's nothing."

Heading to Carol King's room, they rounded a corner, passing other residents strolling the hallways. King caught glimpses into a couple rooms whose doors were left open. TVs were on and books were pulled up to noses—nothing unusual. No one looked panicked, no one seemed concerned by their presence.

The scent of lunch cooking grew stronger as they skirted the back edges of the cafeteria and, as soon they headed down the hallway where King's mother lived, they heard Carol's loud voice echoing off the walls.

King picked up the pace and hurried to her door where his mother was now calling for help.

"I don't want them," Carol King spat from inside her room. "Not until that man has been caught."

"Mrs. King, but what are you going to sleep with?" a woman's voice said from inside Carol's room.

Stopping at the threshold, King glanced to his feet. His mother's bed pillows lay in the hallway. King's expression hardened when his eyes met Tristan's.

"Mr. King," Tristan stepped forward, "I promise this was not like this a minute ago."

King gritted his teeth as he bent at the waist and scooped up one of the two pillows his mother had tossed into the hallway before he heard Tristan say, "Let me help."

King held up his hand and ripped the second pillow from Tristan's grip before asking for some privacy.

"Certainly." Tristan looked to Alvarez and stepped back.

King entered his mother's room—alone—holding both pillows. He wagged his head to the other nurse—whose eyes were wide and forgiving—to also leave the room. Her feet scampered across the floor just as Carol King cried, "Don't you bring those in here."

King ignored his mother's pleas and headed for the armchair near the floor lamp.

"I'm serious, Alex." Her saggy cheeks scolded her son. "I don't want those anywhere near me."

"Mom. Relax." King stacked the pillows on top of the chair and turned to face his mother.

"I'm not afraid to die," Carol kept shaking her small head at her son, "but I'm not going to be smothered to death in my sleep, either."

"That's not going to happen," King said calmly.

"What are you doing here, anyway?" she asked, raking her judgmental eyes over his front. "Aren't you supposed to be at work?"

King lowered his large frame and sat on the edge of the bed. He patted the mattress, motioning for his mother to sit. She obeyed and Carol climbed on top.

Looking into his mother's brown eyes, he asked himself how in the world he was going to break the news to her about Avery. He could see fear flashing over her eyes—hear the terror of her cries in his ears, her bones' subtle tremble. She would never admit any of it, of course, but it was all there.

Inside, he was shattered, but King knew he couldn't tell his mother now. Not with her already on edge and her mind convincing her that what happened to Peggy was also going to happen to her.

"Mom, tell me what's going on."

Carol hooked her hands behind her thigh and stretched her legs straight over her comforter. King watched as she lay on one side, tucking her arm beneath her head. He pressed his hand on her knee and felt his mother's electric pulse shoot up his arm. He'd never seen his mother appear so fragile and it concerned him.

"I can't sleep," she murmured.

King glanced to the television, fearing somehow his mother had heard about Avery. He turned back to his

exhausted looking mother and swore she'd aged overnight.
"The nurse said you saw someone."

Carol lifted her head and raised her eyebrows. "I did."

"Who, Mom? Who did you see?"

"It was him."

"Him who?" King wanted his mother to say the words.

"Orville Boyd."

King didn't react. His mother's eyes convinced him it was
true. "When, Mom? Last night?"

She shook her head. "This morning. He was inside my
room talking to me this morning."

"Here?" King jabbed his index finger to the floor.

"Yes." Carol didn't blink. "He was here. Right inside this
room. Just like I said."

Carol King had the best poker face of anyone King knew.
Her self-assurance was enough to erase any doubt King may
still have been having. Now King understood why Tristan had
made the call. This was serious.

"Mom. Are you sure? I was reminded of the security of
this place and Boyd's name was never registered in the visitor
log. I checked."

"I know what I saw." Carol pressed her lips together and
eased herself back down to the bed.

"Then why not call me?" King gripped the edge of the
mattress and glanced to the phone on the nightstand. "You
know I would have been here in a heartbeat."

Carol closed her eyes and said in a sleepy voice, "Every
time I close my eyes, I see him."

King flicked his gaze to the door. Alvarez was standing
guard. "Is he here now?"

"Are my eyes closed?"

King looked at his mother. Her eyes were certainly closed.
"Mom it's just in your head."

"It feels real to me." King could hear his mother drifting

off to sleep. "It's like I'm reliving the nights Marshall never came home." She yawned and snuggled deeper into the bed. "I was always stuck wondering if I would wake up to find that I had become a widow overnight."

King breathed in a deep breath of air as he pulled a blanket over his mother and stayed with her until she was fast asleep. Then he quietly exited the room and closed the door behind him.

Alvarez pushed off the wall he was leaning against and asked, "Well?"

King was staring toward the cafeteria when he said, "It's just in her head. She didn't see anyone."

Alvarez didn't want to push his partner into leaving, but he glanced to his watch, knowing they had important work waiting. "What do you want to do?"

King started walking. "There isn't anything we can do."

On their way out, King stopped at the front desk to talk with Tristan. He was busy packing his sports bag and also on his way out the door. "Let's walk and talk, Detective," Tristan said, "otherwise I'll be late for my appointment."

Tristan skirted around the desk and made for the exit.

"Apparently tomorrow's marathon course has been changed and I've been asked to approve the medical logistics with the organizers." Tristan held the door open with his hip and let the detectives pass. "Have you decided if you're going to run yet?"

King nodded and thought about Avery. "Yeah, I think I will."

"That's great." Tristan smiled. "Look, about your mother," he stepped closer and lowered his voice, "I want to make this transition seamless for both you and her. I don't like what happened last night and certainly don't need you coming down here to solve our problems for us. If there is anything I

can do to ensure I don't have to call you every time something like this happens, please let me know."

King heard what Tristan said, but was suddenly distracted
by the woman standing against his vehicle looking anxious to
speak with him. Asking himself what she was doing here now,
he pushed past Tristan as he turned and went his own way
and strode toward Angelina Hill.

CHAPTER FIFTY-FOUR

ALLISON DOYLE WAS AT HER COMPUTER WHEN SHE received a notification from Patty O'Neil to check her email. She immediately closed out her browser and opened a new one. Logging into her email, she clicked the link from Patty. A new page loaded and Allison stared with disbelief as she read the headline.

ROOKIE DENVER COP KILLED IN COLD BLOOD

Allison knew Samantha hadn't told her everything. But this? A cop? Really? Samantha should have at least mentioned this to her. This was big news, Allison thought as she flicked her gaze to the time stamp to when the article was published. It just went live. She kept scrolling.

Off-duty police officer, Avery Morgan, was on foot and believed to be on her way to a friend's house when investigators believe she was suddenly attacked by a suspect whose name isn't being released...

Allison couldn't stomach the details of the officer's injuries and skipped past them—too afraid that Marty might be the suspect whose name wasn't being released.

...She died on her way to the hospital. Officer Avery Morgan was only 24 years old.

Allison looked down at her arms. They were covered in goosebumps. Now she was really scared to ask her cousin what happened in Commons Park last night. She didn't want to believe Marty could be responsible, but the possibility was real.

She instinctively reached for her cellphone, wanting to call Sam and demand to know why she tell her an officer was killed last night when they'd spoken this morning. Instead, she pulled her hand back—delaying the truth for just a little while longer—and kept reading.

The police department is actively pursuing persons of interest. Witnesses are being asked to contact DPD. If you were in the park between seven p.m. and ten p.m. on Friday July 12th, 2019, the police would like to know if you saw this man.

Allison clicked the image to enlarge the photo. Though the image was blurry, it was clearly a photograph of a stocky black man that Allison believed could be mistaken for Marty —*if* it wasn't actually him—the police's primary suspect.

"Please, Lord, don't let this be him." Her words fluttered into the palm of her hand.

The guest bedroom door opened behind her. She heard Marty exit and step inside the bathroom. Allison heard the door latch and, a minute later, the shower turned on.

"This is my fault," she blamed herself, scrambling to figure out what to do.

Allison knew the risks that came with asking Marty to work for her, but she would have never imagined him doing something like this. *Why would he throw it all away when he had everything right here in front of him?*

She tipped forward and scooted to the edge of her chair as she took a closer look at the blurry image. There wasn't any doubt to what she was looking at. The longer she stared, the more she was convinced it *was* Marty in the photograph.

"Why, Marty? Why did you do it?" Her dry lips fluttered against the tips of her fingers.

Allison was afraid she pushed Marty too far, too fast. She should have made Gemma Love wait, schedule another meeting and left with Marty to dinner. But she hadn't. She wondered what would have happened if she had.

Her synapses were firing on all cylinders as she kept looking for a reason to explain what might have triggered Marty to relapse.

Was it the increasingly fast pace of life they were living, or the stress of having to learn a new job that triggered him into committing a crime? It could be anything.

Allison couldn't believe she was asking herself these questions, but she knew firsthand the culture shock new technologies presented. Today's world was so different from even a few years ago when Marty was first locked up. But what did she really have him do? Nothing. If he'd gone off the deep end, something else must have triggered his actions. But what was it?

Falling back into her chair, she reminded herself what Samantha told her on the phone earlier. *Just call her if he leaves.* And she planned to, but why didn't Samantha sound overwhelmingly concerned with Allison's worries? She must have known about this photograph. Allison swore it was doubt she heard in Samantha's voice, but maybe it was distraction?

She turned her head and stared at the closed bathroom door, thinking about Marty.

Allison could only imagine the anger and depression he must be experiencing. She knew nothing about his release, didn't have a way contact to his parole officer, and wasn't even sure she wanted to call if she did. It was just blood on his shirt, maybe even his own.

As soon as she heard the shower turn off, Allison closed out the article and pretended to be working on something else. A minute later, Marty was slipping a shirt over his head as he strode into the kitchen carrying a thick stack of files under one arm.

Allison tried not to stare but she couldn't stop speculating to what it might be he was carrying.

Marty opened the kitchen cabinet to the left of the refrigerator and reached for a coffee cup.

Allison watched his every move, unable to take her eyes off of what appeared to be a scratch running down the length of his neck. She had so much she wanted to say, to ask, but didn't know where to begin without prying. The best she could hope for now was that the color in her face hadn't completely drained when she finally had the stomach to ask, "What time did you get in?"

Marty poured himself a cup of coffee. "Things have changed," he said without ever looking up. "The neighborhood isn't what I remember."

"You were away for a long time."

Allison watched Marty stare deep into the cup as if looking at his own reflection on the surface of his drink. She wondered how she could ask about the scratch without upsetting him. An awkward silence filled the room and the minutes seemed to stall.

"Did you find people to ball with?"

"Ali, I know you're trying to help," Marty rubbed his nose and still wouldn't look Allison in the eye, "and I appreciate what you're doing for me, but I'm a convicted felon without a college degree."

Allison flicked her gaze across the kitchen table as she chose her next words carefully. "I can't imagine what you went through but you don't have to let it define you."

Marty's thick muscles bounced beneath his shirt and Allison watched his eyelids fall to half-mast. "They made me a criminal. Turned me into something I'm not." Marty turned his head and stared with intense, resentful eyes. Allison froze without blinking. "There is no getting back what they took from me."

Allison's eyes began to water and she hated how the system broke him down. He wasn't the same man she remembered—wasn't the same man she saw yesterday. As gutwrenching as it was, she was beginning to think Marty might have sabotaged his freedom by doing exactly what they expected him to do; mess up, so he could go back into the system and a life he understood.

"What happened in the park last night?"

Marty turned away and peered out the window for a long, silent pause.

"You were fine before it."

Marty shook his head, glanced at the clock on the stove. "I've got to go."

Allison stood and wanted to plead with him to stay—to talk it out—but the words never found their way out of her mouth. Sweeping the thick folder into his hand, Marty marched out of the house without saying another word.

Allison hoped her cousin could resist the negative influences she knew were out there, but feared that they had already gotten to him. As soon as the front door slammed on its hinges, Allison picked up her phone and messaged Sam.

CHAPTER FIFTY-FIVE

THE BUS'S BRAKES HISSED TO A STOP AND THE SHADOW Stalker leapt off the stairs, hitting the ground with a spring in his step. Gravel crunched beneath his feet as he walked. He kept his head down but couldn't stop glancing toward Commons Park across the street and thinking about Marshall King.

"Marshall, who could do no wrong in the eyes of the public." He shook his head, grumbled a few choice words, and kept walking. "Have you figured it out yet, Inspector? Do you see the message I'm sending you?"

Anger poured out of him in subtle bursts of built up energy. There was a lot to celebrate but it was what the old woman kept saying to him that shattered his self-confidence.

You shouldn't be here, the voice inside his head kept reminding him.

"But I have work to do," he would respond out loud, completely ignoring the sounds of the city around him.

Lost inside his head, the Shadow Stalker understood the job assigned to him and he was determined to get as close to the park as possible without anyone placing him at the scene of last night's crime. He was certain he'd done enough to disguise his presence last night, but there were never any guarantees in this crazy life.

"You taught me that, Mother," he said, stepping off the gravel and picking up his pace when his feet hit the sidewalk.

Visiting the park wasn't about a need to be recognized or to taunt the police who were still patrolling the area, working the scene, looking for clues. His presence didn't affect them. Though he'd have to be careful, the Shadow Stalker was here to drive another message home to the great inspector—a message that he hoped would finally open up his blind eyes to the truth no one had told him.

Moving at a quick clip, he thought about the initial news reports early this morning. He hadn't been happy to learn his victim had lived. But Samantha Bell's exclusive article—just released—was telling the world something different and he liked that message much more.

"I didn't make a mistake." He smiled, scanning the horizon in front of him. "It was all as it should be."

He was starting to really like Samantha Bell, but the Shadow Stalker still had to be cautious. It was true Avery Morgan was dead, but there were loose ends that needed to be tied up. Starting with the boys on the basketball court who he suspected were now being questioned by the cops.

He stopped at the crosswalk, waited for the light to change over, and tucked the binder he was carrying beneath one arm as he dove his free hand inside his front pocket. Inside, his fingers pulled out a crisp twenty-dollar bill.

Brushing his thumb over the president's face, he stared into Andrew Jackson's eyes thinking how this clue of all clues should have been the easiest to figure out. Yet, to his knowledge, the inspector hadn't. Why was that? Was he not making himself clear enough? Or was Marshall's protégé, Lester Smith, keeping his lips sealed on this?

A city bus passed, the air picking up as it did. As soon as there was a clearing in traffic, the Shadow Stalker jogged across the street holding his breath as he pushed through the black exhaust.

Once on the other side of the street, he looked over his shoulder as the feeling of being watched crept over him. Two officers on foot were approaching. The Shadow Stalker grinned with a sense of satisfaction that came from knowing he'd taken out one of their own and he was now the most wanted man in the city.

He knew the cops were looking at him as they hid their white eyes behind the darkly tinted lenses. That didn't stop him from silently taunting the boys in blue.

"Look, I'm right here you assholes." He lowered his brow. "Catch me if you can."

They didn't know just who they were looking at, but the old lady had him questioning if he was as good as he thought. To prove his mother wrong, the Shadow Stalker continued to stare the two officers down.

Suddenly, he heard the pitter patter of feet running toward him from behind. With his heartrate spiking, his mind envisioned the police performing a tactical maneuver to flank him while he wasn't paying attention to what was behind him. The moment he whipped around, his shoulder took a direct hit. Knocked off balance, the Shadow Stalker stumbled backward and watched a woman running her dog quickly apologize for not seeing him.

"I'm so sorry," the woman ran past, backpedaling she pointed at her Labrador retriever. "Sometimes I don't know who is running who."

The Shadow Stalker almost wanted to laugh. "My fault entirely," he responded. "I wasn't looking where I was going."

The woman smiled, turned around, and kept running without ever missing a beat. The cops took their eyes off him and put their gazes on her. Together, they stared, lost in her delicate, loose features when he noticed a green wrist band on her arm.

"Of course. Training for the marathon." His thoughts jumped back to the inspector.

"Hey buddy," one of the cops called out. "You lost?"

The Shadow Stalker rolled his eyes to the two officers and lifted his binder into the air. "Fine. Just needed to get some fresh air. Office work can be grueling on days like this."

Not once did they give him a second look. His confidence was back. With their attention moving on, so did he.

The Shadow Stalker continued his way up the path and was once again thinking about the boys playing ball on the court he was now eyeing. He wondered how he could learn their names, questioned if he even had to.

As he skirted past the park—still closed to the public—he caught sight of a father and son sharing a laugh. He cursed their happiness, blaming his mother for telling him his father had died when he now knew he hadn't.

"Don't you know someone was murdered here last night?" he muttered under his breath. "This is no place to bring your child."

The old woman might have been crazy but she was right about that. Children shouldn't be exposed to such sins. "Which is why it's now time to show the inspector that his father wasn't the angel the world remembers him as."

It was time to expose the truth and make the inspector see his father for who he truly was.

A liar.

A cheat.

A man only loyal to himself.

And as the Shadow Stalker rounded the path, he came within sight of the woman who would help him deliver the truth of his past.

CHAPTER FIFTY-SIX

I was still staring at the photo of Angelina Hill when Walker snuck up behind me. Together, we stared at the photo for a moment before Walker said, "Any new details about what happened last night?"

I turned to face him. He peered down, his eyes relaxed and calm. I was surprised to see he was holding a printout of the article I'd written about Avery—equally as surprised to learn Dawson had released it to the public without me first hearing from King.

"Detective King appeared to be extremely affected by what happened." Walker raised the printout and arched a single brow when referring to Avery's murder. "Unusual for a veteran inspector, but I didn't see *that* mentioned in your story."

I said, "Wasn't relevant." My blood boiled at the memory of seeing him at the park.

"No?" Walker locked eyes, searching past the colors of my irises. "I beg to differ. It's details like those that separate you from mediocre journalism."

I felt my pupils laser focus on his eyes like the lens of a

camera. "No, it's tabloid fodder like that and creating the potential for a defamation suit to follow that separates me." I paused for effect. "But if you knew anything about journalism, you'd understand that."

Walker chuckled as sparkles flashed in his eyes, reminding me of the stars he wanted to turn Erin and me into. "What do people want to really read? I'll tell you. Sensational news filled with drama. They're drawn to suffering that isn't their own and can't wait to see the next person fall."

I felt my eyes narrow when asking myself if this guy was serious. At first he made me believe he'd done his research into learning exactly who I was, but now I wondered if he knew me at all.

"Who is Frank Lowe?" I asked, still wondering what happened to the details that were tacked to the board only yesterday.

My question sucked the air out of the room. Both Erin and Gemma turned to stare. I kept my eyes locked on Walker's. His lips were sealed shut but the sparkle still twinkled in his eye.

Gemma swayed her hips across the room and whispered something I couldn't decipher into Walker's ear. My cell buzzed and I quickly read the message from Allison saying Marty had left the house. When my eyes swept back to Walker, there wasn't any visible reaction from him. Gemma's hand slipped off his shoulder and she eyed me before excusing herself.

"As much as I'd like to stay," Gemma smiled at me, "I really must be going."

As soon as she exited the room, Walker turned his attention back to me. "You're not curious to know why I tacked a picture of Angelina Hill to my corkboard?"

I had a dozen different theories as to why she might be there, but I decided to keep my thoughts to myself. Walker waited for me to answer and my crocodile stare did nothing to deter him from moving on.

Erin stood back, watching with an attentive ear.

"Let's get something straight," I said. "If you want to win me over, you can start by being a team player. Your behavior yesterday was unacceptable."

Walker lifted his eyebrows. "You don't conceal carry yourself?"

I clenched my teeth and stared at him from behind a curtain of lashes. "I'm talking about the way you threatened a cop after disobeying orders and leaving the car, and how you went against my wishes and shared information with Gemma." I shouldn't have to remind him that what happened in the field stayed between us. "Info you promised to keep secret until our investigation was over."

Walker tipped his chin back and flicked his eyes to Erin before landing them back on me. "Does this mean you're denying my offer?"

I could feel Erin stiffen—silently pleading with me to carefully think over my answer before responding. "I can't work with someone as irresponsible as what I witnessed yesterday."

"Sam—" Erin protested.

"I thought you might say something like that," Walker said, reaching to a table behind the corkboard. Reeling his hand back to his side, he dropped another cold case folder onto the table next to me.

One glance at the binder was all it took to see it was more of King's cases. "What do you have against Detective King?"

"Take a look." He prodded with his eyes for me to continue browsing his research.

I flicked my gaze to Erin before fingering the folder open. I turned the page, then another. It was the cold case from four years ago that was identical to how Avery was killed—

much of the same information I used to write the article he had tacked to Frank Lowe's case. "I don't understand. Why show this to me now when you already read what I wrote about the case back then?"

"Because, Mrs. Bell," Walker closed the gap between them, "repercussions are real, and every action has a consequence."

CHAPTER FIFTY-SEVEN

THIRTY MINUTES LATER, GEMMA LOVE EXITED HER UBER ride and paused to make sure she wasn't being followed. Deciding to meet at ground zero of where Officer Morgan had been attacked was her decision. The person she was meeting didn't like the idea, but Gemma knew hiding in plain sight was the best form of disguise. Though it took some persuasion, her contact finally agreed to go along with her plan.

A natural buzz of activity was expected in Lower Downtown, and today felt no different while going about their business. Jumping on and off buses, hurrying up the sidewalks with their noses in their phones. A cop was killed and a suspect was still on the loose, but no one seemed too concerned.

Gemma moved about freely. Once she was certain she hadn't been followed, she turned up Bassett Street and began making her way to the Railyard Dog Park.

With her cellphone in her right hand, she briskly walked while shaking off the feelings of paranoia sending waves of doubt down each of her arms.

Her and Walter's plan was quickly crumbling and she wasn't sure if she'd be able to save what they'd already established before it was too late. After hearing Samantha Bell ask about Frank Lowe, Gemma knew Samantha was onto them. What did she know, and who else knew it?

We can't keep this a secret for much longer, Gemma thought to herself when mulling over their current strategy. But they needed Samantha in order to get close to King. Without her, their plan would be foiled and they'd be back to square one.

If only Samantha hadn't seen Walter near Avery's crime scene, then maybe their situation wouldn't be so dire. But luck worked in mysterious ways and Gemma swore to do whatever it took to swing the pendulum in their favor—and she hoped that this meeting would do just that.

Once inside the dog park, Gemma found herself an empty bench and sat waiting to meet with her contact. Crossing her legs, her foot swung as she watched two dogs chase each other in loops. Ominous clouds billowed overhead and Gemma questioned what the weather might do when she caught sight of a man staring from behind the chain link fence. He was giving her a look that suggested he knew who she was, but she didn't recognize his face.

Pretending not to notice, Gemma opened her purse to make sure her handgun could easily be reached if she had to use it. Her heart beat in a steady drum as she discreetly snapped a photo of the person staring. Though she was certain no one knew what she and Walker were up to exactly, she also didn't want to make the assumption that their secret was safe.

A trained marksman, Gemma carried for both recreation and self-defense. Walker taught her, convinced her it was a necessity in today's world, and now she was glad to have a gun close by—if only to provide the false sense of confidence needed to get through today's meeting.

Gemma lifted her chin and swept her gaze across the horizon, pretending not to notice the man still staring with intense eyes. As her nerves sent waves of heat up her collar, she thought about how their plan depended entirely on Samantha's next move. Gemma hoped she'd make the right decision. In the end, Gemma was only after one thing —the truth.

A stocky man sat on the bench next to her. He was so quiet, Gemma didn't notice until he was already there. She turned her head before she was told to stop.

"Don't look at me," the man said in a low whisper. "Pretend like we don't know each other. There are too many cops around to take any chances."

Gemma turned her head to where the man she saw staring only a moment ago was standing. He was gone, and now she was second guessing her decision to come alone.

"It's possible we're being watched," she warned.

Continuing to pretend like they didn't know each other, the man asked, "Were you followed?"

Gemma looked in the opposite direction. "No."

Her contact slid a folder toward her thigh and Gemma retrieved it.

She asked, "Is everything here?"

"Everything you requested is inside."

Her eyebrows squished. "Feels a bit thin."

"Everything you need is there." A dog barked in front of them and took off running back to its owner. "Frank Lowe knows who's responsible."

"You're certain?"

Their eyes met for the first time. He nodded his head, then said, "You made a mistake stopping by last night."

Gemma didn't make mistakes. "Walter saw you in the park." The man never blinked. "You should have known not to go there after seeing me at your cousin's."

Marty Ray looked away—once again pretending not to know Gemma.

Gemma packed the folder away into her tote and stood. Looking down at Marty, she said, "If Walter knows, others know, too."

Marty gave an arched look. "I didn't kill that woman."

"No?" Gemma began stepping away. "Tell that to the cops after they arrest you."

CHAPTER FIFTY-EIGHT

As King approached Angelina, he noticed her hands clasped together in a white knuckle grip that suggested she had heard the news of what happened to Avery Morgan. His heart thumped hard in his chest, wishing this week would get easier. He knew it wouldn't—not until they captured whoever was behind these attacks. Once within earshot, he asked, "What are you doing here?"

Angelina's round eyes traveled over King's shoulder as she watched him and John Alvarez approach. "I came to see your mom." She looked down at her feet before meeting his eye again and saying, "I heard what happened last night." Her eyes held questions she didn't want to ask. "The news said it was a cop?"

King's core temperature spiked and his heart stopped. Nodding, he said, "It was Officer Morgan."

Angelina gasped and brought a shaky hand to her mouth. He watched her face crumble as she put the timeline of events together—Avery was killed while they were enjoying dinner. After taking a moment, she said in a soft voice, "I'm so sorry."

"Yeah. Me too," King said somberly.

Angelina turned her head and stared in Alvarez's direction. "Your mom must be devastated."

"She doesn't know." King relayed how his mother had a long night without ever name-dropping the Pillow Strangler or Orville Boyd and was now finally sleeping. "I couldn't tell her. Not after what happened to your mother."

Angelina reached for King's hand, prodding it for relief, comfort. A breeze swirled around them as the sun disappeared behind a thick cloud. The temperature dropped a degree but King's body still radiated heat.

Angelina said, "I've been doing a lot of thinking."

King wished he had time to do some thinking himself, but his last forty-eight hours had been nonstop. One punch after another. There was little time for reflection and, with each minute that passed, it only grew more difficult to catch the killer before he or she got away forever.

"I wish things worked out differently between us." Angelina forced a weak smile.

King felt Angelina's eyes on his, but he couldn't lift his gaze away from her hand holding his. He felt the throb of her heart pulse in the tips of her fingers and he couldn't stop wondering what his mother may have told Angelina after he left the dinner party early.

"I know it's silly to think about, but do you ever ask yourself what might have been?"

King still couldn't look her in her eye. He'd asked himself that same question hundreds of times before, and he always had an answer. But not today.

"I never told you this," Angelina's thumb brushed over King's knuckles, "and it still makes me cry every time I think about it—" King felt his throat begin to close. He didn't know what to say to get her to stop so he let her continue on. When their eyes met, Angelina continued, "—but even though I called off our engagement, your father still loved me the same."

King thought about how much his father liked Angelina—how he was so happy the day he learned she would join the family. "He was a great man," King said.

"The greatest." Angelina squeezed King's hand and smiled.

Alvarez called out, and when King turned to look, his partner tapped his watch with his index finger indicating it was time for them to go.

"I'm sorry," Angelina said. "I know you probably have lots of work to do."

King pulled his hand free from Angelina's grasp and told his partner to hang on just one moment longer. When he swept his eyes back to Angelina, he feared she might be confusing grief with jealousy after seeing him with Samantha but decided to let it go.

Angelina angled her head to the side and asked if the police had made an arrest for her mother's murder.

"No." King sighed. "Not yet."

"Any chance what happened last night is related to my mother's case?"

King's eyes squinted as he wondered what would make her think that. Was it that obvious he was the common denominator? He was once again wondering what his mother might have said on their drive back to her residence last night. Everyone was seeking answers, but King had none.

"I really need to be going," King said, extinguishing the glimmer in Angelina's eyes. His cellphone started buzzing in his pocket.

Angelina dropped her chin and cast her gaze to the tips of her toes as she nodded. "I understand."

"I hope you stay and visit with Mom." King's phone was still ringing as he gripped the device inside his hand.

She nodded and looked up at King from behind a curtain of dark eyelashes.

Her hair was blowing over her face and King couldn't deny how attractive she still was. "Break the news to her gently, will you?"

"Goes without saying." Angelina hooked her hands on King's shoulders, pulled her up to his cheek, and gave him a gentle kiss before heading inside to visit with Carol King.

CHAPTER FIFTY-NINE

"HE LEFT, ALEX. MARTY IS GONE."

King covered his opposite ear with his hand and asked Samantha, "Well do you know where he went?"

"You're not going to believe this, but Allison thinks he's headed to Commons Park."

King's eyebrows squished as he watched Alvarez open his car door. His partner caught King staring and he stopped to listen. If Marty was responsible for Avery's death, would he go back to the scene of the crime? Repeat offenders didn't change.

Samantha raised her voice. "Tell me you have eyes on him."

"Sam, I was just visiting my mother." He briefly explained Carol's nightmares, reassuring Samantha it was nothing more than his mother's imagination, then said, "We're sifting through a lot of leads, as you can imagine."

"So my advice means nothing to you?"

King rolled his shoulders back and wrinkled his brow. "Of course it does."

"Then tell me you've at least looked into him."

King shook his head to Alvarez, covered the mouth piece with his hand, and told him it was Samantha on the line. He turned his back and said, "Can't we talk about this when you bring me Mason?"

Sam's growl traveled through the line. "Was Allison right? Did her cousin kill Avery?"

"We don't know anything yet."

"Then why give my editor a picture of him to print next to my column?" Samantha barked through the phone.

King knew Sam was on edge—could hear it in her voice—but the situation wasn't as simple as she wanted it to be. "I haven't seen your story and I don't know anything about this picture you're referring to."

"Then let me tell you about it." Samantha's words were rapidly firing off the tip of her tongue. "It's a blurry image but it sure looks like it could be Marty, and now the entire city has their eyes out for this one man."

"You'll have to ask your editor about that," King said when thinking about what Lieutenant Baker showed him earlier. King also sensed Sam had new information. "I wish you would have said goodbye earlier."

Samantha apologized. "There is something I need to ask you."

The load on King's shoulder's lifted as soon as his gamble paid off. But if he wanted Samantha to open up further, he couldn't sound too urgent. "Can't this wait?"

"I'm afraid it can't." The wind kicked up and ruffled the connection. "I might know who left you that note on Erin's door."

King's eyebrows pinched as he recalled stomping out the fire on Erin's front porch. It was what might have begun this latest killing spree that reminded him of his imperfections. But, more importantly, it was the first real piece of evidence that could lead King to whoever might be behind these crimes. "Dare I ask how you discovered this piece of information?"

"Alex. Listen to me—"

King heard his name being called from behind him. He swung his head toward the building and caught his ex waving her fingers at him before disappearing inside.

"—it might have been Angelina."

CHAPTER SIXTY

SUSAN SWIPED HER THUMB ACROSS THE DISPLAY SCREEN OF her cellphone and checked the time. Hazel Beck saw her and said, "Relax. He'll show."

Susan sighed, deciding she didn't like it when someone was late without giving her a reason why. But what she disliked even more than that was being near Commons Park only hours after she knew someone had been murdered.

She lowered her phone to her side and continued scanning the area with her eyes. There were people everywhere—biking, driving, and briskly walking up and down the sidewalk. Oddly, they seemed to act like nothing happened here last night. Did they not know? Or did they just not care?

"That's not what I'm worried about." Susan's eyes locked on Hazel's.

Over the last thirty minutes, they had traveled up and down two different streets looking for an alternative route to tomorrow's marathon. She was confident the marathon safety director, Tristan Knight, would sign off on their new proposed plan, but doubted the city would be able to sign on, too. There were too many streets that would have to be closed off, too many businesses effected by the volume of foot traffic they estimated. Most of all, Susan feared her promises to little Katie Garcia would go unfulfilled. Combined, her stress levels were through the roof.

"This will work, Susan," Hazel said, reading Susan's anxieties. "Tristan has always been on board with my plans and there is no reason to suggest today will be any different."

"What about Chief Watts? Will he agree to it?"

Hazel sucked back a breath through her teeth. "He's a tough sell, but reasonable."

They were expecting both men to show at any moment. Though Tristan might be the easy link, getting Chief Watts on board was a different challenge—especially after they learned a Denver Police Officer had been murdered last night.

Hazel asked, "What other options do we have?"

Susan flicked the hair out of her face and thought of the two options they had already come up with. "You're right. We have to make this work," she said, feeling chills scurry over her arms. She hugged herself as her eyes stopped wandering the streets and locked on Commons Park once again. "There is a chill in my bones just thinking about what happened here last night."

Hazel followed Susan's gaze and frowned. They'd been reluctant to discuss the crime—too focused on their task at hand—but now that they were stuck waiting, the inevitable finally surfaced. "You saw the picture of who the police are looking for, didn't you?"

Susan had. "He looks like about a dozen people I know."

Hazel squinted her eyes, a distant gaze traveling to the ravine near the river. "He could be walking among us."

"Why would you say that?" Susan snapped.

"I hope you're not talking about me." Tristan arrived with a backpack slung over his shoulder.

The women turned and welcomed Tristan into their circle. "We were just discussing the murder that happened in the park last night," Hazel said.

"Tragic, isn't it?" Tristan shook his head as they all stared into the park. He turned his head and said, "You know, I met her?"

Susan said, "The woman who was killed?"

Tristan looked her in the eye and nodded. "You did too."

Susan stared with parted lips as Tristan reminded Susan about the young woman who signed up for the marathon yesterday. "I couldn't find her name in the system," she said, shocked it took her this long to make the connection to the image of Avery Morgan in Samantha's article, but yesterday's sign up had been hectic.

Tristan's eyes moved to Hazel. "She was running for the Denver Police Foundation."

As soon as Susan remembered the shirt Avery had been wearing, she rubbed her face inside her hands and murmured, "Oh my god, I had completely forgotten."

"Complete irony," Tristan said, staring at the police tape fluttering in the breeze.

Hazel angled her hips to Tristan. "So, would you like to hear our alternate route while we wait for Chief Watts to arrive?"

Tristan's eyes lit up. "That's why we're here, isn't it?"

Hazel led the way as they got to work. Over the next fifteen minutes, Hazel and Susan walked Tristan through their two proposed routes. Once they were finished, Susan asked Tristan, "Well?"

Tristan was staring down at his notepad, reading the notes he'd taken along the way. He shook his head and said, "I see potential problems in both options."

"No route is going to come without its risks," Hazel said, reminding Tristan that even the old route had his fair share of challenges. There had just been plenty of time to alleviate them.

"My top concern is the safety of race participants."

"As is ours," Susan said.

"I can already tell you that Chief Watts isn't going to like closing down these roads so close to Union Station."

"Where else can we go?" Hazel asked as soon as her cell-phone started ringing. "I've got to take this." She excused herself from the group and took the call.

With Hazel out of the way, Susan stepped forward. "We need this. It's not just for Katie Garcia, but also for Officer Morgan. The city needs you to step up to the plate and help us convince Chief Watts that this is the only option we have."

Tristan's eyes swayed inside of Susan's. He glanced down at his notes and said, "Option A has the best chance of approval."

Susan touched his arm and smiled. "Then that's the one we pitch."

"Hold up, people," Hazel said, walking at a fast clip back to the group. "That was Chief Watts who called. We may have a problem on our hands."

CHAPTER SIXTY-ONE

"DID HE BITE?"

After I got off the phone with King, I marched straight to my car and turned around to glance up at Walker's office window. Something told me he was watching us through the mirrored glass—checking if we'd actually leave after his bombshell allegation.

"You have to return the equipment," I said to Erin.

"Sam," Erin's shoulders sagged, "you're jumping to conclusions."

She gave me a look that said we should have stayed to hear Walker out. But he'd said enough. Blatantly accusing Angelina Hill of putting the note on Erin's door made me think the man was willing to do just about anything to throw my life into a downward spiral. I wasn't sure if he was trying to drive me away from King, or if this was a calculated maneuver to get me to agree to his deal. Either way, it was a good reminder to tread lightly.

"I don't think I am. You heard what he said." I reminded Erin what was inside the files. "Repercussions are real, and every action has a consequence. How else would he know if

Angelina put that note on your door? He might as well have admitted his own guilt."

Erin was pressing her palm to her cheek when she glanced back at Walker's building.

"He's blinded you with his offer," I said. "If he didn't murder Avery, then he at least had a hand in it."

I opened my car door but Erin didn't make a move. "Did you happen to hear what Gemma said just before she left?"

I hadn't. "What does that matter?"

Erin turned to me. "She left right after you asked Walker about Frank Lowe."

I remembered. It seemed like another obvious admission of guilt—not wanting to stay to hear why I was asking. Were they hiding something from us? I believed they were.

Frank Lowe was behind bars, convicted in a fair trial. Who was he and why did it seem like Walker and Gemma were transfixed on his crimes? I was confused by what they really wanted from us and why they couldn't let us go.

"They're hiding something," I said. "Whether it's murder or something else, they're not telling us the complete truth."

Erin didn't disagree as she dropped into the passenger seat. We both closed our doors just as my phone started ringing. I glanced at the display. It was Dawson.

Answering the call, he said, "Please tell me you're at the press conference happening right now?"

"Dawson I've already reported on Avery."

"Then you must know who killed her."

I closed my eyes and rubbed my brow, again thinking I'd made a mistake when telling King to go after Marty. It was a short-sighted move that backfired almost immediately. "You know the photo of the suspect you decided to print?"

"I do. I'm the one who okayed it."

"Where did you get it?"

"Why does that matter? I trust my source."

"You should have run it by me."

"We didn't have time with you running around town doing god knows what. And since when have you been promoted to editorial?"

I raised my voice and asked again. "Who was it, Dawson?"

He lowered his volume and said in a firm tone, "It came from the top."

"The mayor's office?"

"Sam, what's going on?" Dawson dodged my question completely.

I couldn't believe Mayor Noah Goldberg had found his way into this mess, but that was exactly what seemed to have happened. I rolled my gaze over to Erin and shook my head. Then I told Dawson, "I may have made a mistake."

CHAPTER SIXTY-TWO

WE HIT A RED LIGHT AND I TRIED CALLING MY SON. THE line rang but he still didn't pick up.

Mason was usually good about answering my calls and telling me what he was up to. Except last night he failed to mention anything about being at the park, even though I should have assumed he was heading there when I saw him leave the house with a basketball tucked under his arm to meet Jamaal.

My hopes spiked when the line clicked over. And they deflated equally as fast when realizing it was only his voice-mail answering. I didn't bother leaving him another message so I killed the call and tried the house line but got nothing.

Erin asked, "Could he be screening your calls?"

The light flicked to green and I punched the gas. The car lurched forward, but was slow to hit its stride. I asked Erin, "Why don't you try calling him from your cell."

"My pleasure," she said, taking my phone into her hand to get Mason's number.

My thoughts turned to worries when I began thinking about how I hadn't had time to ask my son about why he was in the park, if there were others besides him and Jamaal—or if Jamaal was even there to begin with. Could it be he wasn't answering my calls because of what he saw? Or was he afraid he'd get in trouble if he knew I had found out he was there?

Erin lowered her phone away from her ear and shook her head no. She glanced to my hands and I followed her gaze to see what she was looking at. My knuckles were ghost white as my fingers clamped hard to the steering wheel. I immediately released one hand and shook it out.

"He'll be fine, Sam. Chelsea Kennedy has agreed to meet us at the station. If anyone can work this out in a timely manner, it's her."

I nodded, thankful for Erin's friend to agree to sit in with my son at such short notice.

"Who knows, maybe Mason saw Marty at the park?" Erin pulled the visor mirror down and began touching her face.

When I mentioned Marty Ray's name to King, I was only thinking about myself. Now, there was a small part of me that regretted saying anything at all. Allison trusted me to do the right thing and I'd made the mistake of suddenly becoming the source of a published rumor that I wasn't convinced was actually true.

"We don't even know it's Marty who's in the photo," I said without conviction.

Erin pushed the visor mirror back into the ceiling. "If he's innocent, the police will pick him up, question him, and then let him go. Standard procedure."

I knew as much, but now that my son was facing the same standard procedure, suddenly it didn't seem fair. I just didn't like being the one to have started the manhunt. Marty's reputation was already fragile and I was still hoping Walker would be questioned about his whereabouts last night, too. Yet, to my knowledge, there'd never been any mention of him.

"Why did the mayor intervene?" My thoughts were still churning.

"A police officer was killed on his watch."

I was shaking my head as we turned onto my street. "I understand that, but Dawson suggested the image of Marty came directly from the mayor's office."

"Sam—" Erin's breath caught in her chest when pointing to the street ahead.

When my eyes traveled up the block, I couldn't believe it. Two cop cars were parked outside of *my* house and the front door appeared to be open.

CHAPTER SIXTY-THREE

HEATHER CAME RUNNING OUT OF THE HOUSE BEFORE I HAD the wheels stopped. My heart was racing with speculation as I pushed my car door open and asked my sister, "What's going on?"

Heather stopped a couple feet from my window. "Sam, they took Mason into custody."

The wind got knocked out of me as I twisted my neck around and found myself staring into the back of a squad car. Through the glare on the window I could see Mason in the back. His head hung low with shame—his spine curled over with fear. Either they were making a big mistake, or they had something solid on him to have made an arrest.

I heard boots traveling through my house. "You let the cops inside?"

Heather stuttered, giving a one shoulder shrug. "They said there was nothing to worry about."

Pushing my hand through my hair, I said, "And you believed them?"

"I did."

"Why?" I squealed.

"Sam, they said they were here on King's instruction."

My cheeks were iron hot. King was supposed to be at his mother's. What the hell was going on? "Is King here?"

Heather shook her head. "How was I supposed to know they would take Mason into custody?"

I swept my gaze to Erin and told her to head inside, make sure the police knew they weren't invited. I also needed to know that Cooper was behaving himself and not adding to the drama.

"They're going to want to hear that from you since you're the homeowner."

I told her to go regardless. Erin raced inside and I hurried to Mason with hopes of rescuing him. I banged on the window with my fists as I yelled, "I'm here. Mom is here. Don't say anything. Got it?"

Mason nodded—his round, scared eyes staring back at me.

"I'm going to get you out of here. There is a lawyer already waiting for you at the police station." Mason looked like he was about to cry. "Keep your mouth shut." Mason nodded again. "I mean it. Don't say anything without me present."

"I'm going to have to ask you to back away from the vehicle."

Footsteps sounded behind me. I spun around and faced the officer. He was an impressively tall and intimidating man. Looking up into his eyes, I said, "You arrested a boy?"

"Are you his mother?"

"I am." Every muscle in my body tensed. "Did you read him his rights?"

He gave me a look like it was the most ridiculous question he'd ever heard. "We're taking your son in for questioning."

"Let him out," I demanded. "I'll take him myself."

He shook his head no. "Too late for that."

"He's only sixteen years old." I was livid and hot and I felt like my hands were tied. Where was King and why hadn't he stopped this from happening? The two-hour window he gave me was barely half over, yet here we were.

"Miss, please." The officer held up one hand. "Step away from the vehicle before I forcibly remove you."

"And what the hell are you doing in my house?" I snapped, marching toward the front door. "You better have a warrant for that."

"We were given permission to step inside." The officer rolled his neck and glanced to Heather.

I hit my brakes and looked to my sister. Heather was sheepishly looking at me as I glared at her mistake. Running inside, I yelled, "Out now. Everyone, out of my house before I sue the department for misconduct."

"That's all right." Another officer stepped forward, exiting the house. "We're done here."

CHAPTER SIXTY-FOUR

GEMMA LOVE WALKED EASIER AFTER HER MEETING WITH Marty Ray. She left him there on the bench to think about who held the power. Though she saw doubt swirl in his dark eyes, she meant every word of what she said.

Her heels clacked over the concrete path as a grin stretched her lips thin. If what Marty said was true, and it matched what was inside the packet he gave to her, then she and Walker were one step closer to completing the mission they first set out on.

At the traffic light, she crossed the street and continued to head toward Union Station when an escalating commotion from the dog park behind her caught her attention. Turning on a heel, Gemma lowered her brow and smiled. She wasn't surprised to see Marty arguing with two cops as they restrained his hands behind his back.

"Don't worry honey, we all must make sacrifices for the greater good." Gemma smirked and shook her head at the sight of Marty's resistance. "This will all be over soon."

A car horn honked.

Gemma rolled her neck forward and saw a familiar black

SUV with tinted windows slow and pull to the curb. The back door opened and Gemma climbed inside. Walker greeted her with a kiss to her cheek.

She asked, "Did Samantha or Erin suspect anything after I left?"

Walker straightened out his shoulder strap and shook his head. The driver turned the wheel and merged into traffic. "I distracted her by telling them Angelina Hill left the note on Erin's door."

"Did she believe you?"

"Doubtful." Walker frowned when talking about how Samantha was still stuck on what he said to Officer Morgan. "Didn't even bother to ask how we knew."

Gemma opened her tote and retrieved the folder Marty gave to her. "I'm doubting we even need Samantha at this point."

Walker said evenly, "I'm not ready to release her back into the wild."

Gemma pulled out a single piece of paper from the folder and scanned the text with her eyes.

"Too much is happening for her to clearly see what we're showing her." Walker rolled his neck and flicked his eyes to the paper Gemma was reading. "I'm certain she'll come around. We just need her to see what's at stake."

"Holy shit." Gemma's voice was light with excitement. "He actually did it." She turned to look at Walker, tucking her hair behind her ear. "Marty confirmed who we thought it was."

Their eyes met and they shared a knowing look. Walker held her eyes, a slow smile curling his lips. "If this checks out," Walker tapped the folder, "then Samantha is the only one who has the power to free Frank Lowe."

Gemma's expression pinched.

"You don't agree?" Walker asked.

"I do."

"But?"

"There might be a problem."

Walker's eyes narrowed and his head floated back on his shoulders when Gemma showed him the photo of the man she saw watching her in the park.

Gemma asked, "Any idea who he is?"

Walker gave her a look that said, *should I?*

"He was watching me just before I met with Marty."

"It's probably nothing," Walker turned his attention forward, "but we better find out who he is and see what he wants before we go any further."

CHAPTER SIXTY-FIVE

I RUSHED INTO THE POLICE STATION AND CHECKED IN AT the front desk. The lady rolled her neck and arched her brow when staring at me.

"My son just arrived," I said, hoping I hadn't been lied to and Mason really was only here to be questioned—which meant he didn't need to go through the official booking process of an actual arrest. "His name is Mason Bell. He came in a patrol car just a few minutes ago."

The lady turned her eyes to her computer screen and began pecking at the keys.

"Chelsea's in the building." Erin's hand pressed between my shoulder blades. "She's going to meet us here."

Relief swept over me. Formalities were taking too long. I had told my sister to keep her phone close in case I needed some assistance, but I still couldn't believe the cops had been inside my house. I didn't see anything missing, but I didn't exactly take the time to check. More than anything, my frustrations were rooted in the principle of the fourth amendment and my desire to hold the department to a higher standard—even if they argued their visit was nothing more than a protective sweep to ensure everyone's safety.

My fingers drummed on the desk. The clerk was still on the phone. She covered the mic with her hand and asked me my name this time. Hesitant to give it because of my profession, I said, "My son's name is Mason Bell."

"Your name, ma'am. That's what I asked. That's what I need."

I tipped forward and lowered my voice. "Samantha Bell."

She nodded and went back to talking on the phone without any indication she knew who I was.

I heard footsteps hurrying toward me and, when I turned my head, I locked eyes with a long-legged brunette who had a lioness gaze filled with focus and determination. I knew who she was without ever having seen her before. She held out her hand and said, "Chelsea Kennedy."

"Samantha Bell. Mason's mother." I grasped her hand and thanked her for coming on such short notice.

"Erin has filled me in with what's happened so far. Anything else I should know before I go meet with your son?"

I couldn't think of anything, only adding that I wasn't exactly sure what they had on him to make an arrest.

"I'll figure it out," Mrs. Kennedy said, turning on a heel. She promised to have this sorted out as soon as possible. The desk clerk gave us access to head inside as well.

We broke through the gates and Erin followed close behind as I hurried through the maze of corridors and hallways, not sure where I was heading or what interrogation room they had put my son inside. Knowing eyes glared as if I was the enemy, but I brushed off the intense stares, my son bring the only thing that mattered.

Chelsea saw me rush by and stepped out of the room. She

called me over. "I'm still waiting to learn exactly why they have your son here, but he's doing fine."

"I'd like to talk to him."

Chelsea nodded and I felt a familiar hand touch the small of my back. "You shouldn't be here."

I twisted around to face King as Chelsea and Erin retreated back into the room to be with Mason. "How dare you not keep your word," I said in low growl.

King's eyes bounced between the walls as he said, "I didn't know."

I closed the gap between us. "You gave me two hours to bring him in myself."

"I'm sorry. This wasn't my call," he said in low volume. "But really, Sam, people won't like seeing you here."

"My son is here," I said through clenched teeth. "I have no choice but to be here."

King's fingers extended and reached for my waist, but I didn't want him to touch me. I was too tense to have the patience to hear him out. "I didn't even have a chance to speak to him." I looked up into King's eyes. "At least tell me why he's even here."

"We just need to get a statement from Mason about what he saw last night—if anything—then he'll be allowed to go."

"Are you sure? Because they came to my house to pick him up. They would only do that if they had evidence to believe he's been involved in a violent crime."

King sighed. "We can't talk about this here."

"Then where can we talk?"

"Come." King headed toward an open interrogation room. "Follow me."

CHAPTER SIXTY-SIX

Susan didn't like having to wait inside the police station. She kept twisting the rings around her fingers as her mind continued to play tricks on her, fooling her brain into believing the dull, white walls were closing in around her.

The unbearably bright overhead lights flickered their way into a sudden headache, and the constant glances in their direction made her feel like she was the one to have done something wrong. It was enough to make her want to leave. Instead, she asked the group, "What do you think it could be?"

Tristan was busy working through his notes when he lifted the pen off the pad. His eyes scanned the room and the people inside it. "I don't know, but it's never good when they make you wait."

"Keep the faith, people," Hazel said as she was answering emails on her phone.

The eerie feeling from the park followed them here. Susan didn't have a good feeling about this. Tension buzzed in the air, and suspicious eyes were looking for someone to blame. A cop had been murdered and an arrest hadn't been made. Everything about hosting tomorrow's marathon felt wrong.

"Now, which one of you is Hazel Beck?" an officer asked as he approached.

"That would be me." Hazel stood, extended her hand.

"I'm Officer Lester Smith." They shook hands. His tone was friendly but his shoulders were weighed down with obvious grief. "Police Chief Watts has asked me to fill in for him. I hope that's okay?"

"Is everything all right?" Hazel asked.

Susan was equally interested to know.

"Yes. Yes. Everything is just fine." Officer Smith kept glancing at Tristan like he knew him. "The chief apologizes for not being able to be here himself."

"Completely understand." Hazel introduced the team. Susan and Tristan stood, each offering a hand to Officer Smith.

"Tristan," Officer Smith said. "Yes, I remember you."

"I was hoping you wouldn't." Tristan smiled.

Hazel and Susan shared a look of confusion.

"You were one of the lucky few I pulled over who got away with only a warning."

"And I haven't forgotten." Tristan recalled being surprised by Smith yesterday during a traffic stop.

Smith smiled. "That's great to hear. And I hope you never will."

"So, about tomorrow's marathon," Hazel said. "We've come up with two proposals for an alternate route around Commons Park."

Smith listened but Susan could see something wasn't right. Then Smith broke the news to them. "I'm afraid that's why I'm here. Due to a reallocation of resources, we're going to have to cancel the event."

"What? No," Hazel protested.

"I'm sorry." Smith frowned. "Chief Watts will be in touch about how and when we might be able to reschedule the race."

"There must be something we can do?" Hazel glanced to Susan.

"I wish there was something I could do to help, but I'm afraid it's been decided."

"There must be something we can do to change the chief's mind?"

"I'm really sorry, but it's too late." Officer Smith frowned. "I'm afraid Chief Watts is relaying the message to the press as we speak."

CHAPTER SIXTY-SEVEN

AFTER A QUICK CHECK-IN WITH MY SON, KING LED ME into the open interrogation room next door. "What about Mason's friend, Jamaal? Is he here?"

King shut the heavy door behind him and said, "I'm not at liberty to discuss the investigation."

I saw that the camera in the corner was off, and I also assumed no one was listening. But I could never be too sure. "Yet you brought me in here to discuss my son."

King moved to the table in the center of the room. "Who told you about Angelina leaving that note?"

"Not until you tell me what this department has on my son."

King gave me an arched look that said he didn't have time for games and dropped several folders onto the table as he lowered himself down into an empty chair. "Mason was caught on camera running from the park about the time the call came in about Avery. Several witnesses have placed him there and we're curious to know what exactly he saw."

My pulse was ticking hard in my neck. "He probably ran because he was afraid."

"He made the call, Sam."

My eyebrows pinched. "Mason found Avery?"

King's half-mast eyes confirmed my worst fears in a single nod. "Mason called from his friend's phone."

I sat at the table across from King. "If that's all my son is accused of doing, why arrest him and make a show out of it? Mason could have told you that at home."

"Normally, I would agree with you. But, since Avery was a cop, everyone—including those at the top—are itching to place blame on whoever might be responsible."

"He didn't do this," I said.

"I believe you, but the truth is, Mason ran when he should have stayed."

"He's just a boy."

King sighed.

I lowered my gaze to the table and thought about how Dawson obtained Marty's photograph to be printed next to my column. I understood the urgency in wanting to make an arrest, but not if it meant having the police department make a mistake.

King asked, "Now, who told you about Angelina leaving the note behind?"

"It makes sense, right?"

"No, it doesn't make sense."

I was taken aback by his defense for his ex. Without asking, he mentioned how he'd just spoken with Angelina outside his mother's residence. *So, while Mason was getting rounded up, King was with Angelina?*

I asked, "Who else besides her knows so much about you and your father?"

King's eyes fell to the folder in front of him. "I'm still working on it."

"Then while you work on it, think about this," I said, telling him my theory about how Angelina and Walker working behind the scenes to point out his professional shortcomings.

King took a moment to shake the ideas around his head, then he asked, "You've seen these cases Walker is interested in?"

"First hand." I leaned forward. "And you heard what Walker said to Avery when we got caught snooping around Boyd's house."

"Officer Smith told me about it."

"Then why isn't Walter Walker here being questioned like my son?"

King continued to stare. "Walker hasn't done anything wrong."

I fell back into the chair and bit my lip. There had to be something I could use to get his attention. "Today, Walker showed me the cold case of yours that was made to resemble what happened to Avery."

"How did he know about that?" King brought his hands to the table as he leaned forward. "Sam, did you say something?"

I raised both of my eyebrows. "If that's not probable cause, then I don't know what more you need."

King fingered a folder as he stared at his hand. "We had a call come in." He picked up his eyes and locked his gaze with mine. "Boyd has been spotted."

My eyebrows knitted. "You're still thinking he could be responsible?"

"We've heard he may have threatened harm to officers no more than a week ago."

It could explain what happened to Avery, but not Peggy. "Then why hasn't he been arrested?" I asked.

"It's not concrete evidence. Only hearsay."

I thought about the window shattering when we were at Boyd's house, and the fact that his house has been under surveillance since Avery's death. Boyd had an elusive history with the police department, but did he know enough about King's past to be our guy? I was skeptical.

Staring at King's folder, I said, "I researched Frank Lowe."

King met my stare.

"When I first visited Walker's office, he had a very thorough map of one of Frank Lowe's murders and, next to it, an article I wrote."

King titled his head and asked, "What article?"

I told King which one. "Something about it doesn't feel right. But, get this, when I went back today, the mind map of Frank Lowe's crime was gone."

"Did he say where it went?"

I shook my head. "But it was replaced by a photo of Angelina Hill."

"And then he told you that she left the note?"

I nodded—feeling like we were close to zeroing in on our suspect but still couldn't put a finger on exactly who it was. Frustration built and I was afraid of what Walker might do before I learned what exactly he wanted to prove.

King asked, "Do you trust him?"

"No, not at all," I murmured when a couple taps on the door had both of us standing.

CHAPTER SIXTY-EIGHT

"No, it's too risky." Walker was pacing the room and shaking his head as Gemma looked on.

"We have to tell her. The evidence is all there." Gemma stood, leaned over her desk, and made the argument to contact Samantha Bell despite contradicting her earlier statement to move on without her. "Walter, what are we waiting for? If we don't do this now, we might miss our chance."

"What are we waiting for?" Walker abruptly stopped and snapped. "For her to sign the god damn papers."

"I don't care about the investment." Gemma squared her shoulders. "I just want the truth to get told, and now is the time."

"Not until we learn who was watching you." Walker shook his head.

They still hadn't been able to identify the man in the park who Gemma knew was watching her meet with Marty. It made her nervous, but mostly she was scared of potential blowback if their secret got out.

"We have a name," Gemma said. "Let's let Samantha take it from here and finally showcase her talent."

Walker's hands were firmly rooted on his hips. "She'll never go for it. Not as long as she's with Inspector King."

"This is your fault," Gemma blamed Walker. "First you ran your mouth then you were spotted in the park."

"Don't you blame me." Walker pointed at her.

"It's too easy when you refuse to do anything until you have full control over her career."

Walker ran a hand over his head and glanced at his watch. "It's getting late. We're both exhausted. Let's quit before one of us says something we'll regret."

"I'm sorry," Gemma said lightly, knowing she'd already crossed the line of no return. "But I can't leave until I have a concrete answer."

Walker's lips flattened. He stared into Gemma's narrowed eyes before finally giving up. There was no sense in fighting. She wouldn't be so foolish as to go behind his back but, if she did, he'd make sure there would be consequences.

Edging the desk, he kissed Gemma goodbye and left their office without another word.

CHAPTER SIXTY-NINE

With Walker gone and out of her hair, Gemma finally had time to think.

Working beneath the dim overhead light, she promised Walker she'd handle Samantha, get her to agree to their terms. Circumstances had changed. Now she saw no choice but to do this herself.

She uploaded the photo of the mysterious stranger in the park and zoomed in on his face. The bright screen lit up her face—his reflection shining bright in her eye.

As she stared into his dark eyes, it was clear he was studying her—looking at her like he knew who she was. But who was he? Was he there because of her? Or was he waiting for Marty? Her guess was as good as anybody's, but the look on his face had her insides rolling with uncertainty.

Pushing her chair back, she bent at the waist and opened a desk drawer to retrieve several files she had on Frank Lowe. Spreading them out across her desk, Gemma poured over her notes before glancing back at the man from the park.

"Do you know Frank Lowe?" she asked him. "Or did my secret get out?"

She'd scribbled dozens of names down in her notes and she wondered if this man was one of them. But without any photographs to go along with the names, it would be impossible to identify this stranger without outside help.

There was only one other person who might know if Marty's intel checked out, and Gemma knew she had no choice but to ask.

Reaching for the phone, Gemma paused when her eyes landed on the graphic images detailing the crimes Frank Lowe was convicted of committing. Whenever she thought about her reasons for doing what she was doing, she always stopped and used these as a reminder.

Bringing the phone to her ear, she made the call. "It's me," she said when the person answered. "Can we meet?"

CHAPTER SEVENTY

MASON SAT ANSWERING QUESTIONS FOR FOUR HOURS without interruption. Chelsea Kennedy and I were by his side throughout it all until the investigators were finished and he was finally free to leave.

Once the detectives exited the room, King stepped inside. Chelsea gave me a look and I shook my head. King remained professional—not congratulating Mason on a job well done or giving me any hints into what was to come. The only thing he said was, "If there is anything else you think of, give me a call."

Mason said he would, then King disappeared.

Chelsea stepped over to me. "If what Mason said is true, this should be the end of it."

I hoped she was right, because I wasn't sure how much more uncertainty I could take. "Thank you for everything," I said.

Chelsea touched my arm, said to give her a call if anything else popped up, and exited the room. I turned to Mason. One look at my son and I knew he was ready to eat a proper meal.

"Ready to go home?" I asked.

He was all out of words and could only nod his head.

I was happy to finally leave the interrogation box and breathe some fresh air, but as soon as we stepped into the hall, we were hit by a wave of shouts exploding around us like a surprise attack of mortar shells.

"What did you say to them?" a man shouted at my son. "Did you say it was me?"

I covered Mason's ears with my hands and stood in awe of what I was hearing.

The officers wrestled the man forward. When I heard Marty's name, I knew exactly what was happening. His image was just like what I saw printed in the paper.

"You're letting him go?" Marty kept glancing over his shoulders, arguing his defense. He was staring directly at Mason like he knew who he was. "He's as guilty as I am. There are others, too. I wasn't the only one who was there. Just ask him. I didn't do this."

Though handcuffed, the officers wrestled Marty into a room and shut the door. With my lungs gasping for breath, I grabbed Mason's hand and hurried to the exit.

I didn't stop at the sight of reporters crowding the entrance. They clicked their shutters and asked me for the inside scoop. None of them knew about Mason and I needed to keep it that way.

Once inside the car, I locked the doors and began to drive. My hands were still shaking from Marty Ray's attack and I promised to call Allison. But first I needed Mason to know something.

"You did the right thing in calling for help." I flicked my eyes to my son. "But why did you run?"

Mason was staring out the window looking completely broken. I wanted to heal him as quickly as possible, get him back to being a kid again. His next words broke my heart.

"I've never seen a dead body before," Mason whispered.

I hoped he never would again, I thought as Mason repeated how he found Avery.

"That guy shouting at us as we left—" I turned my head to look my son in the eye. "Do you know him?"

Mason turned to me and nodded. "He showed up at the courts, challenging Paul to a game of ball."

"And that's it? You've never seen him before last night?"

"That's it, Mom. I swear."

Remembering what Allison said, I asked, "What about blood on his shirt? Did you see blood on his shirt?"

Mason reminded me it was dark and the lights were out. "I didn't see any of that," he said.

Ten minutes later, we pulled onto my street and I curbed my vehicle in front of her house. "I'm going to need you to stay with Heather until I can catch some time off."

Mason unbuckled his seatbelt just as my cellphone started ringing. He didn't even protest to practically being babysat. He asked, "Mom, they're going to catch who killed that lady, right?"

The odds were looking slim but I said, "They'll try their best."

I kissed my son goodbye and watched my sister meet him at the door when I finally answered my phone.

Gemma said, "You want to know the truth about Frank Lowe?"

Everything went still. *Why was Gemma Love calling me about Frank Lowe?* "I do."

"Meet me in ten minutes." She gave me the address. "And come alone."

CHAPTER SEVENTY-ONE

GEMMA LOVE MADE ME BELIEVE SHE'D FOUND SOMETHING that I needed to see. I didn't know much beyond that, but the sound in her voice made me believe it was worth the risk.

Was it a break in the case to the murders haunting King? I hoped so, but it might just be another one of her and Walker's traps to test my skills.

I exited the highway and turned my wheels into a mostly empty Wal-Mart parking lot. The bright blue and white signs illuminated the entrance as I circled around to the northwest corner where Gemma was parked. Pulling up next to her, she powered down her window.

"I need to make this quick," Gemma said. "If Walter finds out I'm here—"

"What did you want to show me?" I asked, not feeling empathetic toward her.

"You were interested to know why Walter connected your article to Frank Lowe's murders?"

My suspicions were high but I played along. "I am."

"It's all in here." Gemma handed over a thick folder

bound by a thread. "It's not the first time Denver detectives got a case wrong."

There it was. The reason Walker had attached my article to Frank Lowe's murders. Hiding my excitement, I put my hand out my window and retrieved the heavy stack of papers. Flipping on the dome light, I opened it up and caught a few glimpses of what was inside before I asked, "How can I trust you?"

Gemma pursed her lips. "My word isn't good enough for you?"

I gave her an arched look. I wasn't amused. She'd given me about a dozen reasons not to trust her—Walker another dozen himself. One corner of her mouth lifted in a smirk before she handed me another damning piece of evidence.

"We're not playing games with you, Samantha."

Except they were. I took the flimsy postcard sized picture between my fingers and brought it into the light. Adrenaline pumped through me. It was a clear shot of Angelina lighting a small paper bag on fire on Erin's front porch.

"This doesn't mean anything," I said, looking Gemma in the eye. "For all I know, you could be working together."

"Trust me." Gemma's eyes glimmered. "I wish we were. It would have made this investigation a hell of a lot easier on me." Gemma put her car in gear and, just before she drove away, she said, "Go easy on Detective King. It won't be easy for him to learn his father was a fraud."

CHAPTER SEVENTY-TWO

ERIN HAD BARELY TOUCHED HER BEER SINCE I HANDED over the files Gemma gave to me not more than an hour ago. She left us with a heap of discovery to sift through and I still hadn't made sense of all. But I was beginning to see why she seemed nervous to share it with me. If this report proved to be true, it was enough to knock this town off its axis.

Erin fingered the photo of Angelina lighting a paper bag on her front porch and said, "I'm going to kill her myself." We locked eyes—the shared intensity buzzing in our ears. "She could have burned down my house."

I didn't disagree. "But why were they watching her? That's what I want to know."

Erin turned her palms to the ceiling. "If this is what Walker wanted us to investigate from the very beginning, why keep it a secret until now?"

I picked up a paper on Frank Lowe and held it out in front of me as I asked myself the same question I'd been mulling over since my ride here. My mind filed through the different cold cases Walker presented to us, and I reflected back on our first dinner meeting and how our involvement was about getting after some unspoken truth. Was this the truth they were after? It certainly seemed so.

"Something happened to make Gemma want to talk," I said.

Erin was looking down at the paper when she asked, "Did you know about any of this before now?"

I knew Frank Lowe was convicted of a brutal crime in the late 1990s, and despite his DNA not matching evidence found at the crime scene, he was still convicted based on a theory that multiple people were involved in the crime. That arrest sealed Marshall King's legacy. What I hadn't known, and what Gemma's report was suggesting, was that Frank Lowe was coerced and pressured by investigators, members of the Denver police department I assumed included Marshall King.

"This has to be why Walker is so interested," I said, holding up the paper on Frank Lowe.

Erin pointed to a black strip over the text. "You think it could be Marshall King whose name is redacted?"

"It has to be," I said. "Everything they've been showing us has been about Alex King. Why would this be any different?"

Erin read from the report. "Victims hands were swabbed for DNA but never tested?"

We locked eyes. "Strange, right?"

It was unclear why the evidence was never tested at the time, but then Erin said what we were both thinking. "I smell a cover-up of some sort."

I gripped the table's edge and pushed my shoulders back into the seat. "That is, if the report can be verified."

"But it might also explain our killer's motive."

Which had me thinking the killer was someone inside the department. Someone who knew both Marshall King and Alex King's past. Why hadn't I thought of this before? That could also explain why Dawson said the image of Marty was given by someone from the top. They were trying to throw us off the mark. But what would this person do if they found out we were on to them? I didn't want to know.

"The question then becomes," Erin asked, "can you trust Gemma Love?"

I wasn't sure I could, but what choice did I have? I caught sight of Susan making her way to the table when I said, "Only way to find out is to confront Angelina about why she left that note for King."

CHAPTER SEVENTY-THREE

AFTER SUSAN INTRODUCED HER FRIENDS, HAZEL AND Tristan, she asked, "Where's Allison?"

Now that Susan was here, our group didn't feel complete without her. I'd tried calling her, but wasn't surprised she hadn't answered—or messaged back—since we knew Marty was in custody. I just hoped Allison didn't blame me for what happened to him, but my article made it hard not to.

"You haven't heard?" Erin tipped forward. Susan shook her head no. "Her cousin was picked up by the cops for Avery's murder."

"That was him?" Susan flipped her gaze over to me. "Samantha, you got Allison's cousin arrested?"

"I didn't do anything," I said, hovering my hand over the folder Gemma gave me.

Tristan produced today's newspaper and everyone started looking at it. All I could think about was a possible cover-up and how the image everyone was now talking about was likely provided by someone at the top of our local government. If this really was about King's father, why remind Alex about his own shortcomings?

"Well, that's not exactly true." Erin gave me a sideways glance. "Allison did call to tell you her cousin was in the park last night."

Hazel asked, "Commons Park?"

I nodded, not liking where this conversation was heading.

Tristan arched a brow at Susan. "Maybe now that the police have made an arrest the marathon has a chance to go on as planned?"

"It's too late," she said, letting us know that they were coming from the police station and Chief Watts had cancelled the marathon. "They broke the news to us less than an hour ago."

"We were just there, too," Erin said.

"Really? Because of this?" Susan glanced to the newspaper.

I said, "Mason was in the park last night."

Susan gasped. "Was he arrested?"

I shook my head, sharing that he was with friends playing basketball. "Only questioned. But he found Avery."

"Oh my god," Hazel said. "Did he see who did it?"

Susan asked, "Was it Marty?"

"No," I said to Hazel. Then I rolled my eyes over to my friend. "Marty may have been in the park last night, but he didn't murder Avery."

Though my gut knew it to be true, it was still difficult to say. My ears were still burning from Marty's verbal attack against my son. I didn't understand what he was doing in the park or how he got blood on his shirt like Allison said. But he didn't seem to be connected to King. Nor was he a free man when Peggy was killed—which certainly seemed linked to Avery's murder.

"What are you saying, Sam? You know who did it?" Susan asked, telling everyone my special talent to solve high profile crimes.

I said, "We don't know who is doing it—"

"—just that it's someone who knows a lot about King," Erin interrupted.

"Jesus." Susan gaped as she tipped forward, lowering her voice. "Does King know this?"

I eyed Erin and gave her a look that said, *loose lips sink ships*. Then I told the group, "He was the first to connect these crimes to his past, but we really shouldn't be talking about this here."

I made the mistake of glancing to my hands. Next thing I knew, Susan managed to steal the folder out from under my fingers before I could stop it from happening.

"Frank Lowe? Who is he?" She fingered through the top sheets. "And why am I just learning about this now?"

Erin gave me a look before saying, "We'll tell you, but first we'll need your help."

CHAPTER SEVENTY-FOUR

AN HOUR LATER I WAS SITTING IN MY CAR BY MYSELF reading over more of Frank Lowe's report. I had been antsy to get out of the bar early and, now that I was parked outside of Angelina's apartment, I started second guessing my decision to come tonight.

I swept my gaze up to her apartment window. The light was on and every couple of minutes a dark shadow crossed behind the drapes. She was home and appeared to be alone.

I wasn't completely on board with Erin's impromptu invitation to invite Susan into assisting with our investigation, but we were running out of time. If anyone had the ability to pull off some fast research, it was her.

Digging deeper into more of Frank Lowe's case was going to be an uphill battle because, no matter who we contacted within in the department, no one was ever going to open up about a potential coverup that dated back to the 1990s.

The air was getting stuffy and I powered down my window to take the call from Heather.

"Is everything okay?" I asked.

"Mason's relaxed on the couch playing on my iPad."

I closed my eyes for a brief moment, counting my bless-
ings. "I'll be working late."

"It's okay. He can sleep here tonight."

The tension I was holding in my neck released and my
body deepened into its own relaxation as I thought how I
wouldn't be half the woman I was if it weren't for family and
friends.

"The news is saying tomorrow's marathon is canceled."

"Yeah, I heard."

"Sam, they made it official. Everyone knows a cop has
been murdered."

"I know."

"But there's more—" Heather paused, "—the police made
an arrest."

I opened my eyes.

"Someone captured it on their cellphone and posted the
video online. Now the news can't stop replaying it as if we
needed to see this man get arrested again and again." Heather
described the video to me and I knew immediately it was of
Marty Ray. "They're saying it's him. He may have murdered
Avery."

"Marty Ray."

"Yeah. How did you know? Did Mason help identify him?"

I pinched the bridge of my nose, shaking my head at the
way TV journalism was making assumptions before learning
the facts. Without asking, I knew it wasn't the police who
were saying this, but the evening news.

"They only got the story half right," I said.

"And that's why you're working late." Heather's voice was
light with revelation. "I get it now. You be careful, Sam. If
someone is willing to murder a cop, there's no reason to think
they won't want to kill you, too."

CHAPTER SEVENTY-FIVE

HEATHER HAD A WAY OF REMINDING ME OF MY MORTALITY. I could feel the danger quaking in my bones. She was right. Whoever I was chasing was getting dangerously close to me and the man I loved. But I couldn't stop until I knew King and my family were safe.

Was the person we were chasing part of Gemma's report? I liked to believe it was, and I also wanted to believe that Gemma was onto something herself. But, more than that, I needed to slow down and make sure I got this right before I really messed things up between King and me.

I closed the folder on my lap but kept it on my thigh.

The truth was, I was afraid of confronting Angelina. One false accusation against someone who shared a deep and intimate past with King and his family could be detrimental to my own relationship with him—a relationship I cherished more than anything. Then again, so could letting this sit if what Gemma was saying was true.

I picked up a quarter from between the seats and flipped the coin in the air as I continued watching Angelina's window.

I was indecisive. There was no easy approach. Angelina disliked me from the beginning, and it all started the night she took Avery's spot at King's dinner table. That night, Angelina made it clear she viewed me as a threat—a menace who needed to be put in my place.

The coin landed in my palm and I flipped it over. *Tails*.

Though my heart went out to her and her deceased mother, there was no denying how manipulative and cunning her message to King to burn in hell really was. That is, if it did in fact come from her.

I knew it had to be me to confront her on this. When I put the sequence of events together of how, and when, Angelina was brought into our lives, I couldn't deny how much of a coincidence it really was. She had to have been behind the note—just like the photo suggested. Just as I went to open my car door, her apartment door opened.

CHAPTER SEVENTY-SIX

MY HEART POUNDED IN MY EARS, MY EYES WIDENING AS I saw who stepped outside. With his hand still on the door handle, King glanced around as if not wanting to be caught.

I instinctively sank down further into my seat, my heartrate increasing with each passing second, wondering if maybe he had come for the same reason as I had.

Angelina reached for his hand and held on to it as King said something to her before walking away.

My palms pushed into the seat as I sat upright and I watched as he hustled down the steps and strode to his car. I was struggling to keep up with my racing thoughts when suddenly he stopped and glanced over his shoulder.

King's instinct was as impressive as his intellect and I wasn't surprised he turned to look in my direction.

With my cover blown, I exited my car and met him near the hood. "What are you doing here?" I asked.

Without saying a word, he closed his fingers around my arm and drew me close. He glanced back to Angelina's apartment and I did the same. Her curtains were halfway drawn, the light still on—everything the same as before.

"What am *I* doing here?" King's voice was a low growl. "What are *you* doing here?"

My eyes danced inside of his. I didn't want him to think that I didn't trust him or that I was following him so I quickly answered, "I came to ask her why she left that note on Erin's door."

King's jaw cocked as he ran a hand over his mouth. "Don't bother."

My neck craned as I inched my mouth closer to his ear. "Don't bother?"

"No." King's squeeze around my arm softened. "That's why I'm here, too."

"Did she admit it?"

A door opened behind us. We both turned to look, our hearts racing. It wasn't Angelina's door that opened but her neighbor's. King walked me to my car door. "We need to go somewhere to talk."

"I'll drive."

"No," King said. "I'll follow you."

CHAPTER SEVENTY-SEVEN

THE HOUSE WAS QUIET AND THE LIGHTS WERE OFF WHEN the Shadow Stalker arrived. He dropped his keys into the bowl near the front door and took today's newspaper into the living room where he flipped on a light.

His mother sat quietly in the dark room, perched neatly in her recliner with a fleece blanket over her lap. He moved to her, dropped the paper on the end table next to her chair, and took the TV remote from her fingertips. The news flicked on and, once again, the Shadow Stalker was all they could talk about.

"A cop killer on the loose?" The scent of beer was on his breath. "You don't say?" He smiled and looked to his mother. "But what is this new development? The police made an arrest?"

A clip of Marty Ray being taken into custody played on the screen. He looked over his shoulder to see if his mother had seen it too. A delighted chuckle rumbled deep in his gut.

"Gemma Love," he turned his attention back to the screen, "you sneaky little devil. Did you do that on purpose?" A deep belly laugh rolled up his body.

Though satisfied by today's events, he was feeling some-what conflicted.

On one hand, he thought Gemma made the mistake in sharing the truth about Frank Lowe and, because of it, she should pay. But on the other, she did just as he hoped she would. In telling Inspector King the truth about Marshall, it was only a matter of time before the dominoes fell and the truth of the past would finally be revealed. But could he count on her to finish the job?

He scratched at the itch gnawing under his skin. There was something uncomfortable about having others do his bidding for him. If his mother had taught him anything, it was to never trust others to do his job for him.

I told you, you're not as great as you think you are.

The Shadow Stalker turned to his mother. "Do you know who you're talking to, old woman?"

When his mother didn't respond, he moved across the carpet before kneeling in front of the old woman. Looking into her dull eyes, he extended his arm and touched the old woman's cold, pale face. Searching for secrets held within her wrinkles, his eyes traveled to Samantha's article neatly opened on the end table next to her.

The Shadow Stalker smiled when staring at Marty Ray's image. "Today was a good day, Mother."

His mother was still staring at the TV flickering between commercials behind him.

He smiled, remembering the look on Gemma's face after Marty revealed the secret identity to the man responsible for Frank Lowe's conviction. Their circles were growing increas-ingly closer by the day—but perhaps a little too close for comfort.

But isn't that what you always wanted? To get close to Inspector King?

"Mother, did you hear what I said? Today was a good day."

His mother looked ahead. The same deadpan expression on her face he'd become accustomed to. He kept talking regardless, knowing she was listening. "Marshall's legacy is slowly crumbling. King knows, Mother." He patted her cold hand. "And soon, because of it, we will have our family back."

CHAPTER SEVENTY-EIGHT

COOPER'S TAIL COULDN'T STOP WAGGING. HE WAS THRILLED I was home, nudging his big head against my leg, begging me to take him on a walk. I was grateful to finally be home, too, but more than anything else I wanted to know what Angelina said to King.

"Want a beer?" I asked King.

He nodded and I fetched a couple bottles from the fridge. It was impossible not to think about the police freely roaming my house earlier in the day, but I kept my focus on Angelina.

Making my way to the front of the house, I handed King his beer, As soon as his fingers wrapped around the bottle he said, "Angelina admitted to leaving the note."

I pulled the bottle away from my mouth, somewhat surprised to learn Gemma was actually telling the truth. Now I knew we were onto something—perhaps our biggest break in the case yet. Was Angelina also connected to the murders?

"Did she say why?"

I knew their story—knew the reason Angelina called off their engagement. She couldn't handle him being a detective

—the long hours, the dangers that come with the job—but was she having regrets after all these years? King made me believe she was.

King looked me in the eye and said, "You."

"That's insane," I said as my memory flashed back to the engagement ring she left behind at King's. "She could have burned down Erin's house."

King nodded and sighed, clearly at a loss of how to proceed. Then he went on to say that Angelina caught sight of us working the Loxley story and grew jealous of what it appeared we had. "She was right," King said. "I had forgotten about her."

"There is something I need to show you," I said, setting my bottle down on the dining room table and digging out the report on Frank Lowe. Angelina might be crazy, but maybe Gemma wasn't. I handed the folder over to King.

"What's this?" he asked.

"Just take a look and tell me what you think."

King moved to the couch and placed the file on the coffee table in front of him. Setting his beer off to the side, he kept stealing glances at me as he read over the documents. When he was finished, he asked, "Where did you get this?"

"Is it true?" I was on the floor giving Cooper a tummy-rub when I made sure King was looking me in the eye. "Alex, did your father put an innocent man behind bars?"

King stared at the papers as he frowned. I watched his posture go rigid and listened to his heel tap against the floor. He was quiet for a long pause and it was clear to me that he didn't want to believe what he'd just read. Then he stood and started pacing back and forth.

Cooper jumped to his feet and followed King around the room.

"My father was a good man." King breathed hard.

"I know." My voice floated through the air like a feather.

King stopped and pointed to the papers. "I didn't see his name in the report. Not once was his name mentioned."

I tucked my feet beneath me and sat on my heels. "But it could be his name that's redacted, right?"

"If my father is the reason Frank Lowe is serving a life sentence, then there is good reason for it." King's jaw tightened as she shook his head.

Was Marshall King the fraud Gemma suggested? I could only be sure about what the report said. But if it wasn't Marshall, then who?

I asked, "How is it possible the victim's hands were swabbed for DNA but never tested?"

"I don't know." King scrubbed a hand over his face. Then he went on the defense again. "My father isn't the man you're suggesting he is. He was a great detective and an even better father."

"But you said yourself he missed the best night of your life," I challenged.

King glanced at me sideways. "I can't fault him for protecting this city—the city we both love." King reminded me of his father's charity, Sunday church services, as well as his dedication to his wife and family. "No way could he live with himself knowing he put an innocent man behind bars."

I reminded King how someone from the mayor's office gave my editor the image of Marty Ray to print next to my story. Something told me King also knew Marty was innocent of Avery's death. But I didn't say anything. He caught on to my thinking himself.

King raised both his eyebrows. "If you're suggesting the department is corrupt, you're wrong."

"Maybe the department is clean now, but perhaps it wasn't twenty years ago?" I pushed myself to my feet and made my way to him. "King, a cover-up this big would give motive to target you, reminding you of your father's past. You must see it, too?"

"Except this isn't him." King pointed again at the report.

"Maybe it's not Marshall, but someone in the department? Is there anyone you can ask who can clarify this for us?"

King searched my eyes, a look of disdain on his face after realizing I wasn't going to just let this go.

"If I don't investigate this, an innocent man could die in prison. I can't let this happen," I said. "Especially since it seems his case was obviously mishandled."

King looked away and sighed. I didn't blame him for putting up resistance. If it were me, I wouldn't want to potentially destroy the image I held of my father, either. But someone obviously wanted King to know, and now I shared the same curiosity myself.

King's eyes locked on mine. "There is someone I can ask."

"Can we trust him to keep this a secret?" I asked, knowing that we were pushing ourselves further into the fire pit. As if this wasn't already dangerous enough, potentially exposing a corrupt police officer could be deadly.

"What choice do we have?"

King gave me a look that said we didn't. It was all or nothing and we were going all in.

CHAPTER SEVENTY-NINE

GEMMA LOVE PULLED TO THE SIDE OF THE ROAD AND waited for the headlights to pass.

Since her meeting with Samantha, she had been driving in circles thinking she was being tailed. One false alarm after another; this time it felt different.

Her eyes were glued to the rearview mirror and her nerves were high since having gone rogue. Walker would learn what she'd done soon enough, but her night wasn't quite finished yet. There were more questions that needed to be answered, and now that the ball was rolling it couldn't be stopped.

As the headlights got closer, Gemma pressed her shoulders into her seat cushion and continued to stare into the rearview mirror. Her heart beat wild in her chest, afraid to know what Walker might do to her once he learned of her actions.

Seconds froze in time and Gemma flicked her gaze to the side mirror when noticing the vehicle slow down as it passed by. Without turning her head, it didn't take more than a glimpse to realize the vehicle may very well have been Walker's.

"Shit." She sighed when looking to the license plate but it was too dark to read. Before she knew it, the vehicle was gone and she was left with only speculation and fear.

Though she wasn't certain it was him, of course Walker would want to be following her. He never trusted her to do this without him—even though this was her investigation.

She sat for another minute before putting the car into gear and continued on her drive east. Several minutes later—and with no other sightings of the black SUV—Gemma turned onto the quiet street in the Park Hill district.

Her GPS put her in front of the house and, as soon as she parked, Gemma checked her mirrors. There were no cars around, only a couple kids riding up and down the sidewalk on their bikes beneath the gentle glow of the street lights.

She reached across the seat and took the small envelope into her hand. Glancing through the passenger side window, she saw that the front porch light was on. The person she wanted to meet appeared to be home.

As soon as she exited her vehicle, she stopped with feelings of being watched creeping up her spine. A similar style SUV as to the one she saw earlier stopped on the corner two blocks up. She couldn't see who was inside—if it was Walker —but they kept their headlights on as if knowing they weren't going to stay long.

Then it eased off its brakes and drove away.

On edge, Gemma didn't waste another second. She hurried to the front door and lightly knocked. Soon thereafter, a short round black woman answered with a look of surprise on her face.

"I'm sorry to be coming unannounced," Gemma said.

Allison flicked her gaze to the right, then swept her eyes to the left. "I've said all I had to say about Samantha, probably more than I should have." Allison kept her body wedged between the door and the house, preventing Gemma from seeing the inside. Then her eyebrows squished. "How did you know where I lived?"

"I'm here to talk to you about your cousin."

"How do you know my cousin?" Allison squinted her eyes, her tone growing more defensive by the second. "Wait, is this about yesterday?" Allison lifted her chin and eyed Gemma with suspicion. "What's going on?"

"You cousin needs my help."

"Your help?" Allison stepped forward, closing the door behind her. "And how exactly do you think you can help him?"

Gemma didn't budge. She kept her feet planted when staring Allison in the eye. "I know something that can set him free."

"Set him free?" Allison planted her hands on her hips. "And what exactly do you know?"

"Not until you help me."

"Help *you*?" Allison inched closer, sarcastically laughing. "Haven't I already done that?"

Gemma handed Allison the small envelope and said, "Inside is a picture of a man."

Allison was slow to take the envelope. Her eyes studied the small package before locking in once again on Gemma. "And what do you want me to do with this picture?"

"Tell me who he is and I'll tell you how you can make sure Marty doesn't go down for the murder of Officer Morgan."

Allison glanced to the envelope and flipped it around. Though feeling blackmailed into helping, she would do anything to help Marty. "How do you expect me to know whoever is in this photo?"

"You're good with computers. Figure it out." Gemma headed down the steps. "And when you do, give me a call. My number's on the back."

CHAPTER EIGHTY

As soon as Gemma arrived home, she put both hands on the steering wheel and hung her head hoping her plan would shake loose. She'd done everything she could to make sure the truth about Frank Lowe would get out, but there was still a part of her that thought she could do more.

Gathering her things from the front seat of her car, she stepped out of her vehicle and walked past Walker's SUV. She stopped and looked around, wondering if it was him she believed had been following her. Placing her hand on the hood, she was surprised to find it cold.

"Huh?" She pulled her hand back and swiveled her head around. If it wasn't Walker following her, who was it? What kind of games was he playing?

Rounding the hedge, she stopped when glancing up to the front door. She knew immediately that something wasn't right. *Weren't the lights on when I pulled into the drive?* She couldn't recall. But now the lights were off and neither she nor Walker ever left the house dark—especially when one of them was yet to come home.

Digging her house keys from her purse, she stepped up to

the door and was surprised to find it unlocked. With her heart thumping in her ears, she nudged it open.

The house was completely dark and not a sound could be heard.

Now Gemma's pulse was thrashing hard in her neck as her mind let loose with wild imagination.

Where was Walter? And what was that smell?

Suddenly, her cellphone rang and made her insides jump. It was Allison.

"Did you figure it out?" Gemma answered the call, flipping the switch to an inside light that never came on.

Allison said, "Was that some kind of test?"

"If you know, who is it?" Gemma asked before her phone was knocked from her hand and a plastic bag was pushed over her head.

Gripping the man's hands around her neck, she heard her cellphone crash to the ground. Clawing at the overpowering arms, Gemma's screams were muted by a heavy hand, her body constricted by his brute force.

"I told you, love," a man said into her ear. "You should have left this inquiry to me."

CHAPTER EIGHTY-ONE

KING PUSHED HIS ARMS THROUGH THE SLEEVES OF HIS sports coat and I followed him to the door. Tugging on his hand, I pulled him in for a kiss. Our lips touched and I said, "Call me as soon as you learn anything."

"I will," he said as his cell buzzed with an incoming call.

I stepped back and King took the call on the front porch. Leaning against the door, I breathed in the summer night, feeling the humidity in the air. The clouds lit up with distant lightning and by the time King ended his phone call he turned and gave me that half-mast look that said his plans were being forced to change. I'd known it as soon as he took the call, but what I really wanted to know was why.

King said in a low voice, "Alvarez said Orville Boyd was picked up for drunk driving."

Surprised, I asked, "Will you talk to him?"

"That's why I was called."

I reminded King about his basement window being shattered and King said he'd ask him about it if the opportunity presented itself. But, more than anything, King needed to know if it was Boyd who was connecting him to his past.

King made a move toward his car when I said, "Hang on." I ran back into the house and closed Frank Lowe's file and handed it to King. "Take this," I said.

King cast his gaze to the report—the fear of potentially learning the truth about his father swirling in his dark eyes. "I can't promise anything this time of night."

"I know," I said, having my doubts Boyd was our guy.

When King turned away, the burden he held on his shoulders was clear. I stayed on the front porch until he drove away. When his taillights disappeared around the corner, I headed back into the house.

Cooper stared at me from his dog bed—knowing me well enough to know I wasn't going to be able to let this go tonight. He stood and clacked his way over to me. Rubbing his head, I said, "How could I possibly sleep with all I learned tonight?"

Cooper curled up next to me on the couch and I couldn't stop thinking about Angelina, Gemma, and Marshall. Everything was colliding and I was anxious to confirm Marshall King's role in Gemma Love's efforts. Without the files, I didn't know what I could do other than wait.

Then I got a call from Walker that changed everything.

I answered and Walker said, "Have you seen Gemma?"

My heart thumped in my chest as I didn't know what to say. He sounded genuinely worried, but could I trust him not to be playing games with me? I tipped forward and planted my feet flat on the floor. "Why, is everything all right?"

"Shit," Walker said in a voice that had me imagining him running a hand through his hair. "This can't be happening."

"Walker, what's going on?"

"I think she might have been kidnapped."

CHAPTER EIGHTY-TWO

Fifteen minutes later, Detective King arrived to the station and was barely a foot into the squad room when Alvarez caught sight of him. "We have Boyd in Interrogation 4 and everyone is waiting for you."

"Anyone question him yet?" King asked.

"He was a little buzzed when he got picked up. We're letting him sober up a bit before we get too deep, but LT specifically saved him for you."

They kept walking, making their way to the back of the precinct. King liked that Boyd had been made to wait—sweat over why he was here besides the DUI. He'd prepared his questions during his drive across town, but until he saw Boyd himself, how his interrogation would begin was still up in the air.

"He won't be happy to see you again." Alvarez gave a knowing look.

King smirked as he met Lieutenant Baker behind the glass. LT handed King Boyd's files. King took the papers into his hand and studied Boyd's slumped posture. Boyd looked miserable and tired, a thick beard and unkempt hair that told the story of his last few days.

King asked, "Where did he get picked up?"

"Pulled him over a block away from his house." LT rolled his gaze to King. The door opened behind him and Officer Lester Smith entered the room. King was surprised to see him here, but if Boyd did have something to do with Avery's murder, Smith would be the first to want to know. LT continued, "We've yet to charge anyone and the mayor is breathing down my neck. I expect you to put the pressure on and see what this asshole knows."

King turned and nodded at Officer Smith on his way out the door. He glanced at Boyd's files one more time before entering the interrogation box. Walking to the table, he thought about Mrs. Hill and Avery and how he'd like to have a hand in putting away whoever killed them. Taking a seat across from Boyd, the men stared into each other's eyes. There was no reaction by either of them when King opened the folder and showed Boyd a picture of Peggy Hill.

"Recognize this woman?" he asked.

Boyd kept staring—gave King the look that said, *should I?*

"She died two nights ago inside her house by asphyxiation." King lifted a single brow. "Care to guess how?"

"Not this again." Boyd shook his head and looked away.

"Care to tell me what you were doing two nights ago?"

Boyd rolled his neck back to King and quirked an eyebrow. "I was at home."

"You haven't been getting out much lately," King shuffled through the files, "it seems."

"Kind of hard when you're constantly being watched."

King flicked his gaze up to Boyd—assumed he was talking about the police surveillance parked in front of his house since Avery's murder. "We had a nice visit with your old boss, Mike Kern, yesterday. You know what he told us? That you paid him a visit." King stared, looking for any kind of reaction. "You made some very interesting comments, stuff that had Mike concerned for his own safety."

"Of course Mike would say that. He fired me for no reason."

"But then this happens." King flipped over an image of Avery's murder. "She was a cop, you know?"

"This is crazy," Boyd said. "I didn't kill that woman."

"But you killed this one?" King held up the picture of Peggy Hill.

Boyd's expression pinched.

"I'd believe you, except that Officer Morgan was murdered the same day she was called to *your* house." King paused to let that fact sink in. Boyd grew increasingly more uncomfortable and when King asked him about the shattered glass Sam told him about, Boyd lurched forward.

"You should ask that prick, Walter Walker."

"Did he break the glass?"

Boyd shook his head no. "I had to do something to push him away."

"Push him away?"

"He's been after me for weeks now."

King drew his eyebrows together. "What exactly does he want from you?"

Boyd was completely relaxed when he gave a strong headshake. "It's not what he wants from me, it's what he wants to know about *you*."

King tipped his head sideways. "Me?"

"Yeah." Boyd nodded. "He wants to know if you were trying to frame me for murder."

CHAPTER EIGHTY-THREE

"What the hell was that?" LT asked as soon as King exited the room with Boyd.

"A fucking nightmare," King grumbled as he leaned into Lester Smith's ear. "I need to talk to you."

Leaving LT and Alvarez to clean up the mess with Boyd, Officer Smith followed King out of the room. Once out of earshot, Smith said he heard what the lieutenant said about the mayor.

"This investigation is such a shit show," King said as they kept walking. Agitation stitched his side and now he was curious to know what the hell Walter Walker's intentions were really about with Samantha.

"Goldberg's approval rating is dropping and I hear he's about to escalate his tough on crime policy." Smith raised his eyebrows when he shared a look with King. "Should get exciting out on the streets when that happens."

King needed a win, but a legit victory and not one built on circumstantial evidence. He asked Smith, "How are you holding up?"

"I'm hanging in there." Smith inhaled a deep breath. "No

matter what pressure is being put on you to make an arrest, I want to get this right as much as you do. The last thing I want to see is Avery's death be the motivating factor in the next election." Smith flicked his gaze back to King. "Any idea who might have killed her?"

Behind them, the door opened. LT exited the room and gave the men a hard look. King lowered his voice and said, "Can we talk in private?" Smith's eyebrows squished. "There's something I need to ask you about my father."

As soon as they reached Smith's desk, King handed him the report from Samantha. Smith read it over and, when he was finished, King asked, "You know anything about this?"

"It was a long time ago." Smith leaned back in his chair, still holding a paper in his hand.

"You're the only person I can trust to discuss what happened."

"I was young, naïve, and certainly impressionable." A slight smile crossed Smith's lips. "But I'll never forget the hunt for Frank Lowe." Smith looked at King. "It consumed your father, but what does this have to do with Avery?"

"Is this my father in the report?" King pointed to the redacted name, his ears still ringing with Boyd's suggestive comment that Walker thought maybe King was the same as his father. "Did he get an innocent man convicted?"

Lester cast his gaze to the desk and sighed. Then he looked to King. "Why uncover the secrets of the past?"

"It wasn't my decision," King said, telling Smith about his theory that Peggy's death may have been motivated by his father's legacy.

Smith lowered the paper to the desk and asked, "If that's true, why murder Avery?"

"Because you were her training officer, just as my father was yours."

Smith's eyes watered with the realization that she may

have died because of him. "I hope you're wrong," he said, glancing to the paperwork, his eyes glimmering with memories of Marshall. "Your father," Smith cleared his throat, "was ambitious and rising through the ranks. He was extremely competitive and hated losing."

"Are you saying what I think you're saying?" King couldn't believe Lester wasn't denying Marshall's involvement.

"Marshall's focus was admirable. A quality I strive for myself." Smith locked eyes with King. "I learned a lot from your father but, like anybody, Marshall had his fair share of mistakes."

"Christ." King stood up and turned his head away. "How could he?"

"It's not as black and white as you want to believe." Smith closed the folder and handed it back to King. "But really, if you want to know the truth of your father and Frank Lowe, it's best you hear it from your mother."

CHAPTER EIGHTY-FOUR

THE SHADOW STALKER PUT HIS CELLPHONE ON THE TABLE and reached for Gemma's purse. Turning it upside down, he dumped the contents out. Papers fluttered and makeup clattered across the surface until the loud thud of a handgun silenced everything.

He stared at the silver glint of the pistol before grinning. "A gift to me?" The possibilities were endless now that he had a weapon with someone else's fingerprints on it. "You shouldn't have."

The wall next to him shook with several loud bangs. He cracked his neck and stood, leaving the gun on the table. Moving to the door, he opened it and felt the cool air hit his face. Flipping on a light he watched Gemma squirm on the floor, fighting her binds.

"Don't hurt yourself," he said to her blindfolded face.

As soon as Gemma heard his voice, she froze and started shaking.

Grinning, the Shadow Stalker stood in front of the table pushed against the wall. On it he had a fresh, just opened pack of Marlboro Reds and a never before used deer skinning knife along with a bundle of tie rope.

"You had a busy night driving around town." He turned to see how she'd react. "Did you find what you were looking for?"

Gemma breathed loudly through her nose but her body remained still.

"Tell me, that recruit of yours, did she help you find the answers to your questions?"

Gemma's legs kicked straight and flapped like a mermaid's flipper as she ripped a muffled scream through the duct tape covering her mouth.

The Shadow Stalker stepped away from the table and laughed. Kneeling next to her, he studied her tremors before placing a hand to her face. Gemma flinched and it only encouraged him to slide more of his thumb across her wet cheeks.

"Tell me, love," he rubbed her tears between his fingers, "which breast would you like me to cut off first?"

Gemma started crying—a pathetic sight in the eyes of the Shadow Stalker.

"I should have known you would be seeking to reveal the truth before me. You just couldn't help yourself, could you?" He reeled his hand back to his side, his gravel voice deepening by the second. "You know I can't let you do it first. When it comes to these types of games, I always win."

The Shadow Stalker turned his head to the wall. There, he had hung the detailed images of Frank Lowe's suspected murders to act as a playbook to draw inspiration from. Just like his other crimes, tonight had to be perfect.

"Though, to be honest, you surprised me with your tenacity. This wasn't how I imagined it coming to an end," he brought the deer knife to her breast, adding enough pressure to the tip for Gemma to feel it, "but you gave me little choice. Now I must teach both of you a lesson neither will forget."

CHAPTER EIGHTY-FIVE

THE RAIN BEAT DOWN ON MY WINDSHIELD AS MY WIPERS worked on overdrive. The explosive sound was all I could hear, but it didn't interrupt my thoughts of what I was on my way to do.

I was hesitant to meet with Walker at such a late hour. There were so many reasons I shouldn't be going. I kept asking myself if this was real or just a ploy Walker orchestrated to test more of my skills.

When it was hard to see, I gripped the steering wheel tighter and leaned my body forward.

It wasn't like we left on the best of terms the last time we saw each other. In fact, Walker scared me and made me believe he would do anything to get what he wanted. Not only was he manipulative and powerful with access to excessive amounts of cash, he also owned a gun.

I felt the tips of my fingers go cold on the wheel, and I took turns shaking blood back into my hands as I slowly made my way to Walker's house.

If what he said about Gemma was true, I had no choice but to see if she really was missing.

I drove and my mind swirled with possibilities. I didn't like working off of assumptions but I had little to go on. I kept asking if Walker had learned what Gemma handed me earlier. She'd made it clear she didn't want him to know. She seemed scared of what he might do if he learned the truth, and that kept me worried. A part of me kept thinking I was walking into a trap.

My heartrate kept me aware of my surroundings—driving on my sixth sense. No matter what might be waiting for me, I couldn't chance it. Gemma trusted me, and now I needed to trust them.

Nearing Walker's street, I got a call from Allison. With the driving conditions as variable as they were, I debated letting it go to voicemail. But when I reminded myself I may have put Marty in jail, I knew I had to answer.

"Ali, I'm so sorry," I said, thinking about her cousin. "I've been trying to call you."

When Allison didn't respond I wondered if I had been disconnected. I pulled my phone away from my ear and checked the display. The light was green—the time clock still ticking. I asked, "Have you talked to Marty?"

"Sam, do you know a woman by the name of Gemma Love?"

"I do." My vision tunneled as I pulled into Walker's driveway. "But how do you?"

Allison told me that Gemma approached her when doing a background check on whether or not I was a good investment for Walker. I was surprised to only be hearing of this now. As shocking as it was, it fit Walker's mold to operate in complete secrecy. Then Allison said something that had me pause.

"Gemma stopped by my house tonight."

"What in the world for?"

"Said if I could identify someone in a photo, she'd be able to get Marty out of jail."

"Who was in the photograph?" I asked, wondering what exactly Gemma knew to make such a confident claim.

"That's why I'm calling. Once I realized who it was, I called Gemma to tell her. But before I could say, the line crashed. I don't know what happened, but she's not answering her phone anymore."

I was staring at Walker's entrance door as the rain came down harder. *He wasn't lying, but did he take her?* "Allison, who was the person in the photograph?"

"I'll send it to you. His name is Tristan Knight."

CHAPTER EIGHTY-SIX

A FLASH OF LIGHTNING LIT UP THE DARK SKY, SENDING A crack of thunder shortly after. Susan flicked her gaze out the window, silently hoping her power would stay on long enough to continue her research into Frank Lowe.

A dozen tabs were open on her browser, each one of them open to a different article or specific fact she'd thought could be useful to Samantha's investigation. She took notes of it all, realizing that this search was only the beginning. Eventually, she would have to confront many of the names she'd written down, but that would have to wait until morning.

Navigating back to one of the first inquiries she'd opened, the graphic images of the murders Frank Lowe was found guilty of committing popped up on the screen. Goosebumps covered Susan's arms at the extraordinary sight of violence. Susan hoped to God Sam knew what she was talking about because she didn't want to assist in setting a guilty man free—especially the monster responsible for the atrocity she couldn't stop looking at.

Her cellphone rang just as another crack of thunder shook the house walls. "Hey."

"I'm surprised you answered," Tristan said.

Susan leaned back in her chair and looked out the window. "I can't sleep," she said, realizing those weren't exactly the words she should have used when talking to a much younger —and certainly very attractive—single man.

"Me neither."

An awkward silence followed and Susan asked herself what she thought she was doing when taking his late-night call at all.

Susan said, "Because of what we learned in the bar?"

"Yeah," Tristan murmured. Susan admitted to being on the computer now; Tristan too. "I can't stop thinking about Avery," he said.

"And to think her killer may still be out there."

"It's scary, right?"

Susan caught her own reflection in the window as the lights flickered overhead after the last lightning strike.

"Do you think the police really put an innocent man in prison like Samantha suggested?"

Susan said, "Impossible to say."

"What I can't understand is why there is very little mentioned about Frank Lowe's daughter. You would think if he was innocent, she would be the first person fighting hardest for his release."

Susan hadn't recalled ever reading about Frank Lowe having any family. "I didn't know he had family."

"Yeah." Tristan mentioned where he'd read it. "But apparently she changed her last name after he went to prison. Something about starting over."

"What's her name?"

"Gemma Love."

CHAPTER EIGHTY-SEVEN

A second after I ended my call with Allison, the photo came through.

I pinched my fingers on the screen and zoomed in on the man's face as the intensity of the rain grew into a shattering ensemble that drummed on the roof of my car.

There was no doubt the person I was looking at was the same Tristan Susan brought to the bar and I had drinks with tonight. It appeared to be taken in Commons Park, based on the buildings across the street in the background, but I didn't know when. Why did Gemma go to Allison with this after she met with me? Tristan was in the park today with Susan and Hazel to reroute the now-cancelled marathon, but why did she care who Tristan was? The photo came from Gemma, Allison told me, but did she take it? Was Tristan watching her when she snapped it? His expression in the photo showed extreme focus in the direction of the camera. But why? And why did Gemma care?

My mind scrambled back to the bar when I first met Tristan. He was tall, athletic, good looking—nothing suspicious about him. He even made me believe he cared for Avery.

A tap on the window had me startled. Through the rain lashing against the glass, Walker's eyes were staring at me with surprising intensity. He opened the door and said, "C'mon let's get inside."

I gathered my things from the front seat and stepped out into the downpour, running for cover. Chasing Walker into his house, my focus was back on Gemma's disappearance.

"Thanks for coming," he said. "I wasn't sure you would."

"Have you called the cops?" My eyes naturally went to places he might be packing. It was impossible to tell, but I assumed he was armed.

Walker shut the door to his house, swept a hand over his wet hair, and said he hadn't.

I didn't like how the rain forced us inside, and I was quickly reminded it was just us—alone inside his sprawling house. I had told no one where I was going. "You should really call the police," I said, feeling the rain seep through my clothes.

"I can't."

Walker had been testing me this entire time to see if I was worth his money and I didn't have any reason to think this was any different. "And why is that?"

Walker seemed anxious. He kept touching the back of his neck and giving me sideways glances. Did he know what Gemma gave me tonight? I assumed he did. I also assumed he knew I would have checked whether or not Angelina left the note for King like he said she had. But why did he seem to be on edge? I flicked my gaze around the room, looking for any signs of Gemma's belongings. I didn't see anything, but that didn't mean she wasn't here.

"Because," Walker's mouth tightened, "I'm afraid she may have been kidnapped by a cop."

CHAPTER EIGHTY-EIGHT

CAROL KING WOKE TO THE SOUND OF THUNDER. BLINKING the sleep out of her eyes, she turned to the door at the sound of the doorknob turning. Sitting up in bed, her heart beat faster as she wasn't expecting any visitors. The door opened and the hallway's light spilled inside.

"Hello," she called out, instinctively fisting her pillow.

When no one responded, a flash of Orville Boyd crossed her vision. Except the man entering her small room wasn't him at all, instead the nurse Tristan Knight.

"I wasn't sure you were awake," Tristan said.

"I wasn't until you woke me up." Carol's expression pinched with annoyance, unable to remember if she'd locked her door or not. "What's going on?"

"You have a visitor." Tristan stepped to the side.

"Tell them I'm sleeping."

"Mrs. King, do you really want me to tell your son to leave?"

Carol blinked and her body perked up. "Alex is here?"

King entered the room. "Hi, Mom."

"Boy, you have some explaining to do."

King nodded to Tristan as he closed the door on his way out. Turning on a lamp, the room lit in a soft glow that was easy on his mother's eyes. "I'm sorry. You're right. I should have been the one to tell you about Avery."

"Instead you let a woman who's already mourning do it? What kind of man are you?"

King knew it was useless to try to explain his way out of this one—knew his mother would never believe Angelina would leave a note like the one she had.

"Mom, what is this doing here?" King picked up a twenty-dollar bill left on top of her dresser. "Is it yours?"

"If you found it there, then I guess it's mine."

King looked to see if a message had been left behind. It was blank.

Carol glanced to the clock. "It's late. What on earth are you doing here that couldn't wait?"

King placed the money back where he found it and eased onto his mother's bed. "Mom, I'm trying to understand some things about Dad."

"Alex, I'm tired. Can't this wait?"

"It might have something to do with why Peggy and Avery were killed."

"That's absurd. Your father has been dead for nearly a decade."

"Someone is trying to show me something from his past." King explained his theory of how these murders were linked; that the murderer got his attention by copying King's past cold cases.

"That's crazy," Carol responded.

"Mom, did Dad ever talk about his investigation that led to the capture of Frank Lowe?"

"Everyone talked about it. It's what made him famous." Carol's eyes fell to her hands. "But why are you asking about it now?"

"There's been a recent discovery that suggests Frank Lowe may be innocent."

Carol's gaze retreated into her thoughts. King knew she was hiding something.

"What is it, Mom? Is it true? Did Dad say something to you at the time?"

"Go home, Alex."

"Mom?"

"I can't say." When she looked at her son, her eyes welled with tears. "It hurts too much."

"Mom, you need to tell me." King took her hand into his. "It's important."

Carol's gaze flicked between his face and their hands. "He didn't know it at the time. When he learned the truth, it was too late." Her gray eyes lifted and landed on King's. "It wasn't your father who coerced a confession from Frank Lowe, but another detective by the name of Andrew Jackson."

King's eyes landed on the dresser. He stared at the twenty-dollar bill, making the connection to the killer's calling card. "Why haven't I heard of him before?"

Carol's chin trembled. "Because if you had, you would have also learned that your father had an affair with another woman."

CHAPTER EIGHTY-NINE

I LET THE THOUGHT OF GEMMA GETTING KIDNAPPED BY A cop sink in before Walker told me again.

"Did you hear what I said?" he asked.

"A cop?" I shook my head. If he was right, it made sense why he didn't want to involve the police. But could I trust him? He gave me every reason not to. "What were you doing in the park last night?"

Walker's eyebrows knitted. "What?"

"I saw you there. What were you doing?"

"Gemma and I were securing our investment, doing our due diligence," he said, telling me that Gemma met with Allison, and he followed Marty Ray to the park.

It lined up with everything Allison shared with me on the phone, but I still wanted to know why he cared so much about Marty Ray. "Why follow Marty Ray? I don't know him."

"Marty didn't kill Avery," Walker said. "It was just a matter of being in the wrong place at the wrong time."

My head was spinning. Walker's behavior suggested time was running out, and I heard the seconds ticking, too. We were the only ones who knew Gemma was missing—the only ones who had the power to do something about it—but I needed to know I could trust him.

"Gemma was scheduled to meet Marty today. That's why I followed him last night. I knew very little about him and I didn't want her to meet with someone who might be dangerous."

Walker locked eyes and it hit me. He was Marty's alibi—the reason Gemma told Allison she knew how to get Marty out of police custody. But what did Marty know that they didn't? I was thinking about the photo of Tristan in the park when I asked, "What did Marty have that Gemma wanted?"

"The truth about Frank Lowe."

"Why do you two care so much?" My frustration was pumping through my heart as the room spun around me.

"Because my *wife* wants to see her father exonerated."

I blinked. Surprised again. "Gemma is your wife?"

"And Frank Lowe is her father."

"Jesus." I dug out my cell and showed him the photo of Tristan Knight.

Walker said, "Where did you get that?" I told him. His wild eyes locked on mine. "Is he a cop?"

"No," I said. "What does it matter?"

"Because this man," Walker took the phone from my hands and pointed to the screen, "has to be the one who took her."

CHAPTER NINETY

WHEN KING STOOD, HIS HEAD WAS DIZZY. HE COULDN'T believe what his mother just told him. How did he not know? After all these years, he'd been left in the dark about his father being a cheat.

Carol was still staring at him. King opened his mouth but nothing came out. A surge of anger and betrayal lit up his spine and heated his core. His father betrayed his mother, brought shame to the family. Even worse than that, Marshall guided King's entire existence. Even in death.

"He was your North Star," Carol said. "I couldn't tell you without you second guessing your entire career. You've done so many great things because of how you looked up to him."

King's chest was tight as he listened to his mother's words. "If Dad knew what Jackson did, why didn't he say anything?"

"Because I would have learned of your father's affair," Carol said with stern eyes. "You must understand that Jackson was a dirty cop who stopped at nothing to bolster his own career. He used your father's shortcoming against him."

King picked up the twenty-dollar bill on his mother's

dresser and stared into President Andrew Jackson's face. If his father hadn't had a secret to hide himself, would Detective Jackson ever have been able to get away with this? King thought not. Detective Jackson saw his opportunity to rise through the ranks and took it when coercing Frank Lowe into admitting to something he didn't do.

It was clear why the killer he was chasing was leaving messages on twenty-dollar bills. All this time, King was right. This was about him and his father's past. But who wanted to speak to him? Andrew Jackson? Or a person close to his father's affair?

King asked his mother, "You didn't know Dad had betrayed your trust?"

Carol shook her head, her face hardening with years of suppressed emotions.

"Then how did you learn of it?"

"The day Jackson died," Carol said, watching her son as she mentioned the date of his funeral.

King whispered, "Dad had already passed by then."

"That's right," Carol said. "Your father took his secret with him to the grave."

King cast his gaze to the twenty-dollar bill. With Jackson dead, there was only one other possibility to who could be behind the murders of Peggy and Avery. "Who was the affair with?"

"I never asked—and I don't care to know."

King clenched his jaw. "But who told you?"

"Jackson's wife found notes and photos her husband apparently kept to hold over your father's head. She gave them to me, not fully realizing what it was she had in her possession."

King sweated as he balled his hands into tight fists.

"He made a mistake, Alex. I forgave him, and I hope you can, too."

"It doesn't erase the fact that Frank Lowe has been in prison all these years."

"No, it doesn't. But now, maybe, this is your chance to do better than your father."

King's head floated back on his shoulders as he stared into his mother's loving eyes. He'd do anything for her—loved her more than the world. Stepping to his mother's bed, he took her by the shoulders and pressed his lips against her forehead and told her he loved her. "I'm sorry for waking you."

Carol apologized for not telling him about Marshall sooner. Then King left the room and put a call in to Officer Smith.

"Did you speak with your mother?" Smith answered.

"It was Andrew Jackson. He hid the truth—the reason the DNA was never tested on the victims." King nodded to security as he passed reception. The doors opened and he exited the building.

"The same thing will happen now if the mayor keeps up the pressure." Smith paused before asking, "What are you going to do?"

King didn't have a clear path forward. "Did Andrew Jackson have any children?" It was possible they wanted the truth to come out if they'd somehow learned it.

"Not that I know of."

King stomped over rain puddles from the storm that just passed. A light drizzle was still falling as he headed toward his unmarked police car. "Then what about the woman my father had an affair with—do you know who she is?"

Smith sighed. "Sorry, Alex. I don't."

"Can you meet me at my place?" Smith said he could. "I'm certain our killer is close to this affair. We just need to figure out who it is."

CHAPTER NINETY-ONE

WALKER SEEMED CERTAIN THAT TRISTAN WAS THE ONE who took Gemma, but I wasn't so sure.

"Tristan Knight?" I frowned as I took my phone out of Walker's hand. "Why him?"

"Because he was watching Gemma meet with Marty as Marty revealed the name of the dirty cop who coerced him into making a false confession."

The reason Allison said he was innocent of his crimes.

I peeled my eyes away from Tristan's image in the park, tried to keep up with what Walker was spitting at me in rapid-fire. I asked, "What was the name of the officer?"

"Detective Andrew Jackson."

I inhaled a deep breath and said, "Okay, say this is true, but Tristan was the safety director. Of course he was in the park today. They had to reroute it after last night's...event." Walker knew about the marathon so I continued, "My friend Susan was there with him."

"No." Walker adamantly shook his head. "This was differ-ent. Gemma would have never mentioned it to me if she didn't think he was someone interested in what they knew."

"Is he connected to this detective Marty said put him in prison?"

"He has to be someone connected to Andrew Jackson."

"But why?" I had to admit, their secret relationship to Frank Lowe was big, but I couldn't fit Tristan into the scheme of having taken Gemma. It seemed like if anybody was responsible, it would be a cop. Someone who would want to keep the past in the past. Perhaps this Andrew Jackson Walker couldn't stop talking about was responsible.

"I don't know, but we don't have time to debate this." Walker inched forward. "Your friend, does she know where we can find Tristan?"

"I could ask," I said, pulling my phone from my pocket and dialing Susan's number. "Thank God you're still awake," I said when Susan answered.

"Samantha, I found something that might be useful."

My eyebrows pinched.

"Did you know Frank Lowe had a daughter?"

"I just learned it." I locked my eyes on Walker. "Your friend Tristan, I need to know where he lives."

"I would hardly call him a friend. We just met. But— ironic you ask—because I was just on the phone with him."

"You were?" Walker quietly asked me what was going on.

"He's the one who told me about Gemma Love."

My heartrate spiked. I motioned for us to get into the car. Walker made a move and together we ran outside and I climbed into the passenger seat of his SUV. "How long ago?" I asked Susan.

"Maybe twenty minutes."

If Tristan did have Gemma, he already had her when he called Susan. "Susan, listen to me. I need you to figure out where he lives—or where he's at now—and do it quick."

"What's this about?"

"Tristan may have kidnapped Gemma."

CHAPTER NINETY-TWO

As soon as King dropped his cell phone into his pocket, he caught movement out of the corner of his eye. Tristan Knight approached with a glint in his eye. "Thanks again for getting me inside at such late notice," King said.

"Did your mother tell you *our* secret?"

King gave him a questioning look.

"I heard you two discussing our family's affairs." Tristan closed the gap between them. "Tell me, Inspector, do you not see yourself in me?"

King's eyes narrowed as she flicked his gaze across Tristan's physique. Then it hit him. "It was your mother my father had an affair with?"

Tristan grinned and pulled out a .38 Special revolver and told King to place his department issued Glock 17 on the ground. King lowered his hand to his side when Tristan reminded him, "Nice and slow now; I don't want any surprises."

King kept his eyes locked on Tristan and did as he was told. Once his gun was on the ground, Tristan told King to step away. Taking a step forward, Tristan scooped up King's

Glock in one swift motion. Then he tucked it into his belt and asked for King's phone.

King handed it over. "What are you doing?"

"Taking you on a field trip," Tristan said, telling King to drive.

"And where are we going?"

"Get inside and I'll tell you." King got behind the wheel and Tristan took a spot behind him in the backseat. "There's someone I'd like you to see."

King started the car and positioned the rearview mirror on Tristan's face. "What did you do?"

"We'll talk when you start driving."

King backed out of his space and turned south on Colorado Boulevard, feeling the barrel of Tristan's gun pointing at the center of his back.

"I just couldn't help myself," Tristan said. "I've been having an absolute blast enlightening you about your past. So, I thought, why stop now?"

King flicked his gaze to the mirror wondering what Tristan had done, and to whom. Knowing his mother was safe, his thoughts scrambled to both Samantha and Angelina. "If this is between you and me, we can work it out ourselves."

"Oh, it's more than just you and me, brother." Tristan flashed a wide grin. "Let's just say tonight we're honoring the great Marshall King and his extraordinary flaw."

"The affair he had with your mother," King guessed.

"Nice guess, Inspector, but no. If not for that, I would have never been born." Tristan flashed King a knowing smirk. "Our father's greatest flaw was arresting an innocent man and letting him go to prison for life."

Keeping one hand on the wheel, King was told to head east on Alameda Avenue. Then he said, "You're talking about Frank Lowe."

"You're quick," Tristan winked, "but not as clever as that girlfriend of yours."

King's grip tightened at the mere mention of Samantha. Keeping his mouth shut, he didn't want to spark Tristan into a rage that might get her killed—if that was who he had, and who he was taking King to see.

"But I'm afraid Samantha might be too smart for her own good. Lucky for me, I had a chance meeting with her tonight and I learned just how close she and everyone was to figuring out it was me behind the murders."

"If you wanted to make a point, why not just kill me?" King's temples throbbed with anger.

"What's the fun in that?" Tristan gripped the seat in front of him and peered over King's shoulder. "Besides, we're family and family is supposed to look out for each other."

"Yet, you're taking away mine."

The police band cracked and Tristan told King to turn up the radio's volume. They listened to the chatter before turning it back down. It wasn't anything Tristan had to worry about. No one knew he had kidnapped a cop.

"Yes, I suppose you're right," Tristan said. "It's quite selfish of me, now that I think about it, but can you guess who my latest victim might be?"

When King locked his eyes on Tristan, he felt his pupils shrink with built-up rage.

"No?" Tristan taunted. "Let me give you a hint. No. Better yet, let's talk about why I might have killed Peggy."

"Might have?"

"You're right. I killed her." Tristan cackled. "Any guesses as to why?"

"Because my father—"

"*Our* father," Tristan corrected King.

King's eyes were back on the road, "—wanted to see Angelina and me marry."

"That's correct, Inspector." Tristan clapped while still holding the gun in one hand. "And I hoped the engagement ring I left in your house would have sparked an affair like the one your father had with my mother."

Tristan's eyes glimmered with the clever manipulation that failed. Then he told King to turn south on Quebec Street. King put on his blinker and did as he was told, asking himself what else Tristan might have done to get Angelina to believe King would ever leave Samantha.

"Though I thought using a play from the Pillowcase Strangler file would have bought me more time."

"Time?" King said through clenched teeth. "You murdered Officer Morgan twenty-four hours after you killed Peggy."

Tristan tapped the barrel of the gun to his chin. "Yes, I suppose that was rather quick. But I was overcome with excitement in wanting to finally meet my brother."

"You could have just called," King said.

"That was certainly an option I explored."

"I would have learned about my father's mistake through you."

"There was just one problem with that scenario."

King quirked an eyebrow.

Tristan's face winced as if he'd made a mistake. "I had already killed my mother." They locked eyes. "She lied to me, brother. Told me my father died when I was just a baby. But then, your mother moves into the facility and, guess what? I saw the same man my mother had in her photos. Except he didn't die when she said, but many years later."

"So you killed her?"

"It was an accident," Tristan said sincerely. "I may have a temper that got out of control."

"You think?"

"It must be true with you, too?" Tristan didn't wait for a

response. "Our parents are flawed, Alex, and no matter what you do, you'll never live up to Marshall's name, nor should you want to."

"You reminded me of my own shortcomings at each of your crime scenes."

Tristan smiled. "Each specifically designed to get you one step closer to Frank Lowe and the deal Marshall made with the devil," Tristan pulled out a twenty-dollar bill from his pocket and waved it in the mirror, "Andrew Jackson."

King was told to take the next right when he heard his cell phone ring. In the mirror, he watched Tristan take the phone out of his pocket and glance to the display screen. King thought maybe it was Officer Smith calling to learn his whereabouts, but when Tristan silenced the call, he wondered if it was Samantha.

"You know where you're heading?" Tristan asked.

King turned into the cemetery without Tristan's direction. As soon as he saw it, he knew Tristan was taking him to his father's grave. King's heart beat wild in his chest as he rolled to a stop near the plot of Marshall's headstone.

"Have you guessed who my last victim is, Inspector?"

With both hands on the wheel and the engine running, King peered in the direction of his father's grave.

"It's not Marshall, because he's already dead." Tristan leaned forward and dropped his voice low as he pointed the gun's muzzle over the dash. "She's there, beneath the tree."

CHAPTER NINETY-THREE

The six-cylinder engine idled and Walker looked anxious to drive. Susan paused for a second to let the thought that Tristan might not be who she thought he was sink in. "Okay, Sam. I'll see if I can find him."

I thanked her and ended the call knowing we didn't have time to wait for her to track him down. If we were right about Tristan having Gemma, he called Susan because he wanted us to find him. This was a game to him. But where was he now? No one knew, and that bothered me.

I turned to Walker and asked, "Who framed Frank Lowe?"

"Huh?"

"Gemma gave me the report earlier tonight," I said. "Was it Andrew Jackson's name redacted in the report?" I'd thought it was Marshall King's name, but the signs were pointing elsewhere now.

"It had to have been," he said. "But I can't say for sure."

My mind flashed back to Walker's corkboard. This had to be what it was all about. With Gemma so close to Frank Lowe, was Tristan doing the unthinkable—repeating his accused crimes on her? That would also bring King into the mix, whose father had arrested Frank all those years ago. It was my best guess with what we currently knew.

"Do you have the cold case folder you first presented to me?"

Walker nodded. "Have a copy inside the house."

"Got get it," I said.

Walker ran inside the house and I called King. The line rang but he didn't answer. Was he still in interrogation with Boyd? I assumed he was, but I left him a message regardless.

"It's me," I said. "I may have got a break in the case. Call me ASAP. It's urgent. You're going to want to hear what I have to say."

A second later, Walker was back with the cold case file. I took it onto my lap and began flipping through each case.

"What are you looking for? Maybe I can help?" Walker said.

"A pattern to predict where Tristan might be taking Gemma," I said, instructing him to learn the location where Frank Lowe left his most famous victim—the woman whose breasts had been cut off.

Peggy Hill died at home and was made to look like King's cold case from six years ago. Avery was inside the park that held an important memory for King and was identical to a cold case four years ago. "If there is a pattern to his murders, logic would tell us his next victim would be taken from one of King's cold cases from two years ago."

Walker shook his head. "There isn't one." Walker licked his fingers and began flipping to the back.

My mind churned with doubt. The two murders so far were from King's past; were his flaws. But they pointed to great disappointment in the eyes of Marshall—he'd wanted to see his son marry Angelina and he missed King's big win. Which case would link both King and Marshall?

"This isn't right," I said, thinking about everything I learned since my meeting with Gemma. How did Frank Lowe play into this? "It's no longer about King's cold cases." I turned and looked Walker in the eye. "It has everything to do with Frank Lowe. Marshall's big mistake."

Walker's eyebrows knitted.

"Marshall King arrested Frank Lowe, but if it was Andrew Jackson's name in the redacted report, then it's Marshall's mistake for allowing Frank Lowe to go to prison," I said, explaining that the other cases pointed to Marshall as well, albeit through King. The cold cases were King's so far, but the history was all Marshall. "It's a long shot, I know, but what else do we have? There isn't a cold case from two years ago to follow."

"So, what are you suggesting? Tristan took Frank's daughter to the same place his victim was murdered?"

I shook my head. "No, I was wrong about this. She's either at Andrew Jackson or Marshall King's place. Somewhere that would hold great meaning to King."

We didn't know where to find Andrew Jackson, but I did know where we could find Marshall. I told Walker where to go and he put the car in gear. "Good enough for me."

CHAPTER NINETY-FOUR

KING KICKED HIS CAR DOOR OPEN AND RAN ACROSS THE green grass until finally skidding on his knees in front of the woman. He checked her pulse. There was nothing. The scent of burnt cigarette butts filled the air and the ground was soaked with blood. Shaking off his jacket, he covered the woman's torso and began administering CPR.

"You're not alone anymore. I'm here." King's arms pumped over the woman's chest. "Stay with me."

Tristan strode up behind King, laughing as he approached. "You know, brother, this is what I wanted all along. For us to be together."

King barely heard what he said. He kept applying pressure to each of the wounds, but it was impossible. The openings in the woman's chest were too large. Blood covered his hands and, though he refused to admit it, he knew her heart was dead in her chest.

"Christ, look at you." Tristan stood over their father's grave with his hands buried in his pants pockets. He was casually looking on, watching the show go on. "You are way better a person than Marshall was." Tristan's spine twisted when he looked over his shoulder toward Marshall's tomb-stone. "You hear that, Dad, way better." Tristan laughed and turned back to King. "If only your personal record reflected the effort I see you put into the job, you'd be winning awards, too."

King opened the woman's mouth and breathed into her lungs. "Who is she?" King asked, opening her eyelid to see her eyes rolled to the back of her head.

"It's too late." Tristan shook his head. "She's as dead as her father's victims—*alleged* victims."

King whipped his head around. "This is Frank Lowe's daughter?"

"Gemma Love is her name."

"You sick bastard, call for help!"

"And risk getting arrested?" Tristan raised his eyebrows. "I'm sorry, but I'm not willing to do that. She knows too much. And, besides, it's only appropriate I take the life from the man who gave our father his fraudulent award. That award defined Marshall's career, defined the man the public saw him as. But we know differently now, brother, don't we?" Tristan stomped his sharp heel into the grass over Marshall's grave. "Don't you see? I'm freeing you from having to live in our father's shadow. This is my gift to you. The least you can do is thank me."

King kept trying to resuscitate Gemma's heart until he heard the click of a hammer lock in place on Tristan's gun. "Stop. Just stop."

King fell back on his heels—breathing hard—he knew it was useless. Gemma Love was dead.

"Marshall only cared about you." Tristan approached King slowly. "I never even met my father."

King glanced over his shoulder and locked his eyes on Tristan. "And you never will."

Tristan's eyes grew wide as he stared down at King.

"That's where you're wrong, brother." A wild look flashed across Tristan's eyes when he raised the gun to King's head. "Together, we'll meet him in hell."

Fisting dirt into the palm of his hand, King threw it into Tristan's face. A shot was fired and the bullet grazed King's leg but missed. Tackling Tristan to the ground, King pounded two quick punches to Tristan's head before he wrestled the gun out of his hands.

Gripping King by the collar, Tristan used his massive weight to roll King onto his back. King wacked his forehead into Tristan's nose. There was a cracking sound, followed by a flood of blood pouring out of each nostril.

Tristan growled and kneed King in the thigh. Slamming his shoulders repeatedly into the ground, Tristan shook his blood over King's face. King pounded his fist into Tristan's gut and kicked him off.

Scrambling on all fours, King went for the gun. Tristan leapt through the air and dove on top of King's back. Pushing his face into the ground, Tristan crawled over King and closed his fingers around the handle of the gun. Flipping it around, he pointed it at King. "Haven't you learned? I *always* win."

King stared into the black hole of the gun's muzzle—making peace with the Lord—when he heard the sound of a large vehicle come barreling toward them, lights blazing.

CHAPTER NINETY-FIVE

As soon as we entered the cemetery, I spotted King's police sedan. "There!" I shouted, pointing toward where I wanted Walker to go.

Walker hit the gas and I said my prayers. The tires squealed over the pavement, but Walker never let up. "Do you see them?"

I was looking in the grass but I couldn't see a thing. It was too dark and a mist floated through the air. Then two heads popped up like daisies sprouting out of the ground. My heart beat faster. "It's Tristan and he has a gun on King," I said.

Walker punched the accelerator with his foot and the engine roared. Tristan saw us coming and I hoped to God he wouldn't shoot King before we could do something to stop it. We were almost there and I didn't know what our plan was once we arrived.

"Are you carrying?" I asked Walker.

"You bet I am," he said with both hands on the wheel.

Instead of shooting King, I watched Tristan load him into the back of the cruiser before he jumped behind the wheel and sped off.

"Shit," I said. "They're getting away."

Walker cut the corner and the tires hit the curb. My butt flew off my seat as Walker chased after them. I gripped the chicken handle on the ceiling and kept telling Walker to go faster.

Tristan cut in front of traffic and, once we were both on Alameda, our speeds got dangerously high. I didn't know how this could possibly end safely, so I called 911 to report the crime.

"I just witnessed an unmarked police cruiser get stolen," I said into my phone, giving King's plate number. "The officer has been taken hostage by the suspect and I'm certain I saw a gun."

Dispatch asked me where I was and I gave them the location but said we were in pursuit.

"Miss, I'm going to ask you to stop following—"

"I'm sorry, I'm losing you. What did—" I hung up and told Walker to stay on them.

"No question. Do you think Gemma's in there, too?" Walker weaved between traffic, honking his horn while my entire body flexed with each near collision. That's when it became clear Tristan knew it wasn't going to be easy to lose us. He exited off Colorado and accelerated at lightning speed onto I-25 southbound.

"I don't know," I told him as I kept glancing at Walker's speedometer until I stopped breathing when we crossed over 100mph. Then Tristan turned off his lights and slammed on his brakes as we watched him skid to a near stop.

"Christ, he wants us to hit him," I said, thinking we were going to get hit ourselves.

There were far too many motorists on the road to catch someone off guard. Without his lights, his car was difficult to see.

Tristan   sped   forward   again—approaching   100mph.

Walker was right on his tail and I was afraid of him slamming on his brakes again.

"He's going to do it again," I said.

"Then maybe we should hit him?" Walker suggested.

I didn't like the idea. Not at these speeds. Tristan zig zagged through traffic and kept changing up his speeds when I caught red and blue lights flashing in my mirror. Walker slowed to let the police car pass. They roared past us and quickly caught up to Tristan who once again completely surprised me when he spun his tires sideways, flipping the vehicle.

My heart stopped as I watched King's car roll a half-dozen times before finally coming to a stop. "Oh my god."

I'd never witnessed such an incredible accident before in my life, and my gut told me it was something no one could survive. The car crumbled and flattened into a pancake. I couldn't breathe.

Walker slowed as we approached and I couldn't stop looking at the debris from the crash. I felt like I had left my body when I opened my door and watched as the responding officer told me to stay back.

Backpedaling, I called out for King. "Alex! Alex!"

There was no response. Only a massive explosion that had me ducking for cover. The hood flew open and the entire car was engulfed in flames within seconds. The officer took off running and Walker caught me by the arm before I could follow.

"I have to go," I screamed.

"No. It's too dangerous," Walker said, though his eyes told another story. He still thought Gemma could be in there.

My fist landed on Walker's arm and he let go. I took off running toward the inferno. The heat grew more intense the closer I got, but the thought of losing King overrode every instinct that said to stay back.

By the time I reached the car, the officer was pulling King out of the backseat. King stumbled to his feet, caught sight of me, and ran to where I was standing. I slung his arm around of my shoulders and guided him to the nearby police cruiser.

Another minor explosion of air released somewhere in the burning car and the officer who was working to save Tristan stumbled back as an ear-stinging hiss filled the air. He shook his head and retreated back to his cruiser.

"How many were inside the car?" he asked King.

"Just me and one other."

"I can't get to him."

"He killed a cop," King said. "Let the bastard burn in hell."

The officer gave King a look, then turned back to watch the fire spread.

Walker seemed to be in a daze as he stumbled over to us. "Just you and Tristan were in there?" he asked King. King could barely nod. "Gemma—where's Gemma? I was sure he had her."

I gripped onto King's waist tighter and watched as a fire truck arrived on scene. King shook his head and looked to his feet when he told Walker that Gemma was dead. Indeed, at the hands of Tristan Knight.

A sea of white foam quickly drowned out the flames of the burning vehicle and we stayed until the fire was out. I never even noticed Walker leave, but his car was gone by the time I turned around to see if he was okay. I needed to know this was over, and King needed to see Tristan dead. Neither of us was interested in any more surprises.

Soon, an EMT pulled King away, sat him on a gurney, and began their evaluation to make sure there weren't any hidden injuries he hadn't yet felt. He looked beat up—maybe even experienced a concussion and some bruised ribs—but other than that, appeared to be okay.

King asked me, "How did you know where to find me?"

"I'll tell you all about it on our way to the hospital," I said as I climbed into the back of the ambulance with King.

"It doesn't matter." King brought my hand to his mouth and kissed my knuckles. "I'm just glad you did."

Just before the doors closed, we watched Tristan's charred corpse get pulled from the front seat by the coroner. A wave of relief swept over me and I felt King's entire body relax. He leaned his head back against the pillow and closed his eyes. "You know that vacation we talked about taking?" I said I did. "I think I'm ready for it."

CHAPTER NINETY-SIX

FIVE WEEKS LATER...

The press conference was packed to the brim with reporters—an intimidating sight for any public official who might have something to hide. A murmur of chatter filled the air as a wall of camera lenses and microphones perched behind me, all pointing toward the empty podium. We were all waiting for the mayor, chief of police, and the district attorney to show—and they were running late.

Walker glanced at his watch. "The longer they make us wait, the tougher it will get for them."

"Probably putting on more cologne to mask the bullshit they've been feeding us these last weeks," Erin said.

I chuckled and glanced to where King was standing. He was near the front of the room and kept looking at his phone as if expecting the call we'd both been waiting for.

The night Tristan died, King told me what happened—all the way back to his father's affair. I didn't believe Tristan could be his brother, and King had his doubts, too, but his mother had confirmed the affair. After considerable thought, I encouraged King to request a DNA test and put the matter to rest. He did, and we were still waiting on the results. Knowing an answer was coming soon put his mind at ease.

The door behind the podium opened and we all swept our attention forward.

Anticipation was high as journalists came in record numbers to hear the city admit their mistake. No one was sure they would, but the evidence suggesting Frank Lowe was innocent—or at least deserved a more thorough investigation—proved too overwhelming to ignore. Erin and I were crossing our fingers for good news, too. So was Walker. But, for the city, a mistake this big could open a floodgate to other cases they hadn't thought about in years, perhaps decades.

Since the death of Tristan Knight and the truth about the recent murders, local TV affiliates as well *Real Crime News,* couldn't stop covering Frank Lowe's questionable conviction. It was all anybody could talk about. It didn't take long for the story to catch on with local activists, and soon protests began as a snowball of public outrage grew in support of holding the city and the police department more accountable. Even more surprising was how Erin and I became the face of exoneration as we lobbied for Frank Lowe's release, starting with genetic genealogy to find the true killer once the victims' hands were tested for DNA evidence—that crucial step that was hidden away decades ago by Andrew Jackson.

"I think they're too afraid to show their face," I said when no one came out from behind the curtains.

"Maybe they are human after all," Erin said.

It had been a whirlwind month and my hopes were high despite the mayor's empty promises to get tough on crime. The truth was, his policy was failing and we were here to remind him of it with simple facts.

I watched King take a call and exit the room just as the district attorney, Chief Watts, and Mayor Goldberg took their spots at the podium.

The entire room went quiet and they didn't waste any time in addressing what we were all here to hear. The DA addressed the reporters and Mayor Goldberg couldn't stop staring at me.

I stared back and thought how they held Marty for nearly twenty-four hours after Tristan Knight had died. Eventually, Marty was released without charge, but the city never apologized for what they did to destroy his reputation. Instead, they left it up to me to apologize for them. Dawson signed on to my idea and gave me front page, above the fold.

Of course, I also apologized to Marty in person—who was more than forgiving. I also promised him I'd personally look into his own case—including the shady record of Andrew Jackson—with hopes of exonerating him of the crimes he was found guilty of committing.

The DA started speaking into the microphone and all I could think about was how this was the first public comment made about Frank Lowe since he'd been sentenced. My knee was bouncing and it didn't stop until I heard the DA say, "The Denver District Attorney's office has officially reopened the case file of Frank Lowe and we're actively reviewing the evidence—including DNA swabbed from each of the victims."

Erin turned her head and we shared a knowing smile. The DA fell short in admitting why the DNA was never tested, but it was a clear victory for Mr. Lowe.

Then the DA finished by stating, "We'll also be reviewing every case that led to a confession of guilt under the direct supervision of deceased Detective Andrew Jackson."

It was clearly good news for the city of Denver. Walker reached his arm over Erin and squeezed my hand. He smiled and said, "This was what Gemma wanted all along."

There was still plenty of work to do, but I understood his

message. Thanks to him and Gemma, mine and Erin's local stardom was heading to the next level. Just as he promised.

Once the conference was over, we stood and discussed how the city would be forced to prepare for the many lawsuits soon to follow—totaling in the millions of dollars.

"Speaking of money," Walker said, pulling out a white envelope from his sport coat, "this is for you two."

I knew what it was without looking and said, "We can't."

Walker uncurled my fingers and pressed the envelope into my palm. "Consider it an award from Gemma."

"But Frank Lowe's case is only being looked into. Her father isn't a free man."

"I have a feeling it will all shake out." Walker winked and promised his original offer still stood if, at any time in the future, we were in need of an angel investor.

I thanked him and asked, "What's next for you?"

"New York City."

I gave him a questioning look, as did Erin.

"Meeting with an organization who specializes in exonerations."

My lips curled at the corners. "Not one to miss an opportunity."

"A consulting detective never rests."

We hugged goodbye and promised to stay in touch. Erin walked him out just as I caught King heading in my direction. He was still walking with a limp but had otherwise healed well, considering the magnitude of the crash.

"So?" I asked. "I saw you take a call. Was it the results?"

"It's true. Tristan was my half-brother." King sighed.

I imagined the news was bittersweet. There was a lot King had to accept, but at least now he knew his past better than before.

Neither of us expected Tristan to be lying after the police raided his apartment and found his mother dead just like he said. Tristan killed her by asphyxiation and had left her there for nearly a week before anyone knew she was gone.

I had a feeling King just wanted to let this go—kind of like what he did with Angelina leaving that threatening note on Erin's door thanks to Tristan leading her to believe King wanted her back—because none of it really mattered in the scheme of life. The truth was, if we dug deep enough and long enough, we'd uncover flaws and secrets in everyone.

"I've got to get back to work," King said.

"Yeah. Me too."

He promised to call after his shift and I turned to the door with the intention of heading back to Erin's office to prepare this week's podcast. My colleagues called out to me as I passed, sent their congratulations, and told me to keep up the good work. I told them to do the same when I was approached by a familiar face.

The spokesperson for the mayor caught my arm and whispered into my ear, "You may have won today, but I suggest you stay in your lane, Mrs. Bell." He made sure to look me in the eye when he concluded, "Death is closer than you think."

Tap here to read the next gripping Samantha Bell mystery, MAD AS BELL. It's a riveting thrill ride you won't want to miss!

A WORD FROM JEREMY

Thank you for reading BURN IN BELL. If you enjoyed the book and would like to see more Samantha Bell crime thrillers, **please consider leaving a review on Amazon**. Even a few words would be appreciated and will help persuade what book I will write for you next.

AFTERWORD

One of the things I love best about writing these mystery thrillers is the opportunity to connect with my readers. It means the world to me that you read my book, but hearing from you is second to none. Your words inspire me to keep creating memorable stories you can't wait to tell your friends about. No matter how you choose to reach out - whether through email, on Facebook, or through an Amazon review - I thank you for taking the time to help spread the word about my books. I couldn't do this without YOU. So, please, keep sending me notes of encouragement and words of wisdom and, in return, I'll continue giving you the best stories I can tell. Thank you for giving me an opportunity of a lifetime.

Never miss a new release. Sign up for Jeremy Waldron's New Releases Newsletter at JeremyWaldron.com

ABOUT THE AUTHOR

Waldron lives in Vermont with his wife and two children.

Receive updates, exclusive content, and new book release announcements by signing up to his newsletter at: www.JeremyWaldron.com

Follow him @jeremywaldronauthor

facebook.com/jeremywaldronauthor

bookbub.com/profile/83284054

Made in the USA
Coppell, TX
13 July 2022